THE
ZIG ZAG GIRL

Center Point
Large Print

**This Large Print Book carries the
Seal of Approval of N.A.V.H.**

THE ZIG ZAG GIRL

ELLY GRIFFITHS

CENTER POINT LARGE PRINT
THORNDIKE, MAINE

This Center Point Large Print edition
is published in the year 2015 by arrangement with
Houghton Mifflin Harcourt Publishing Company.

First US Edition: Houghton Mifflin Harcourt, 2015.
Originally published in 2014 by
Quercus Editions Ltd., London.

The text of this Large Print edition is unabridged.
In other aspects, this book may vary
from the original edition.
Printed in the United States of America
on permanent paper.
Set in 16-point Times New Roman type.

ISBN: 978-1-62899-768-2

Library of Congress Cataloging-in-Publication Data

Griffiths, Elly.
  The zig zag girl / Elly Griffiths. — Center Point Large Print edition.
    pages cm
  Summary: "A band of magicians who served together in World War II
track a killer who's performing deadly tricks"—Provided by publisher.
  ISBN 978-1-62899-768-2 (hardcover : alk. paper)
  1. Magicians—Fiction. 2. Serial murder investigation—Fiction.
    3. Large type books. I. Title.
  PR6107.R534Z35 2015b
  823′.92—dc23
                                                          2015032382

For my mother, Sheila de Rosa,
and in memory of my grandfather,
Frederick Goodwin (stage name: Dennis Lawes).

'I' faith he looks much like a conjuror.'
—Christopher Marlowe, *Doctor Faustus*

PART 1
The Build-Up

CHAPTER 1

'Looks as if someone's sliced her into three,' said Solomon Carter, the police surgeon, chattily. 'We're just missing the middle bit.'

I must not be sick, thought Edgar Stephens. That's what he wants. Stay calm and professional at all times. You're the policeman, after all.

He looked down at the shape on the mortuary table. You couldn't really call it a body, he thought, almost dispassionately. It was more like one of those classical statues, head and shoulders only, hacked through just above the breasts. The beauty of the face and the flowing blonde hair only heightened the sense of unreality. He could be looking at a model head in a milliner's shop. Apart from the clotted blood and smell of decaying flesh, that is. Despite himself, he felt his stomach heave.

'We can't be sure that the head and legs are from the same body,' he said, pressing his handkerchief to his lips.

Solomon Carter laughed heartily at that one. 'There are hardly going to be two dismembered women's bodies floating around Brighton at the same time.'

Edgar shifted his gaze to the end of the table, where the legs lay primly side by side, still clad

11

in flesh-coloured stockings, cut off mid-thigh as if by a prudish censor. It occurred to him that, without the 'middle bit', it was impossible to prove conclusively whether the corpse was male or female.

'Might not even be a woman's legs,' he remarked, just to say something really.

'You're joking,' said Solomon. 'Those are a woman's legs or I'm a Dutchman. Beautiful pair. Long as a showgirl's.'

No, you're not a Dutchman, thought Edgar as he followed the police surgeon from the room. He'd met a lot of Dutchmen during the Norway campaign and they'd all been rather pleasant.

Later, in the pub, he managed to joke about this to his sergeant, Bob Willis. Bob never really laughed at Edgar's jokes, but sometimes his ears went pink. Edgar thought that Bob considered laughter somehow lacked the dignity appropriate to a policeman. Bob was sensitive about being only twenty-one and not having fought in the war. He would never have been a sergeant at this age if it wasn't for the men who did fight, of course.

'Solomon Carter was just about to proposition the girl,' he said. 'I promise you, he wouldn't be put off by a little thing like her middle section being missing. Probably likes his women like that.'

Bob's ears reddened and he took a suspicious sip

of his beer. They do a good pint in the Bath Arms, but it was part of Bob's policeman persona to be suspicious of everything.

Edgar took a more generous swig of his drink. He knew that he shouldn't really be drinking with his sergeant on a Friday night. His own father would have left work sharply at five, brisk walk home, whisky and soda, nice little mixed grill, evening listening to the wireless with the family. But Edgar had no one to make him a mixed grill and the thought of returning to his digs was too depressing. He wondered if Bob had someone to go home to, some clean-looking girl from the perfume department at Hanningtons, a doting mother frying spam fritters, desperate to hear of her son's adventures on the dark side of the law.

But it appeared that Bob had been thinking. Always dangerous.

'Where do you think the rest of her is, then?' he asked, almost fretfully.

'I don't know,' said Edgar. The legs and torso had been found in the Left Luggage office at Brighton station, individually concealed within plain black cases, the kind that house the less interesting orchestral instruments, a French horn, maybe, or a tuba. It had been the smell which had alerted station staff. It was a cold grey August, but still warm enough to make a dead body smell pretty bad after a few days.

'Who would do a thing like that?' said Bob. Again, he sounded personally affronted at the sheer cheek of a person who would cut a woman into pieces and leave them scattered untidily around the place.

'Someone very strange,' said Edgar. He thought of the mortuary room and the head and legs with the gap in-between, the sickly smell, the marble skin. 'Tell you something,' he said. 'I was almost sick today just looking at what they'd done.'

Bob seemed shocked at his boss's frailty. 'Surely you saw worse in the war?'

'I saw a lot of odd things in the war,' said Edgar. 'You wouldn't want to know.'

Bob looked as if he heartily agreed with this sentiment.

'I can't believe nobody saw anything at the station,' he said, sounding aggrieved again.

The two boxes had been deposited on Monday morning and it was now Wednesday. But it seemed that none of the station staff remembered who had left the boxes and why they didn't pick them up again on Monday evening. The only description they had was pitiful in the extreme: 'It was a man. I think he was wearing a hat.' What sort of hat? wondered Edgar now. A pirate's tricorn? An errand boy's cap? A top hat? For some reason— perhaps it was because of the music case connection—Edgar could imagine a top hat.

'We'll go and see them again tomorrow,' he

said. 'Ask at the shops around the station. Someone must have seen something.'

'No one's ever seen anything,' said Bob. 'It's this town. It's a hotbed of vice.'

Bob wasn't from Brighton, and it showed. He had been brought up in a small village on the Kent coast. His parents were Methodists and sometimes that showed too.

'It's not too bad,' said Edgar. He liked Brighton. When he first joined the police force, he had been stationed in Croydon. Brighton was definitely a step up. He liked the cheerful anonymity of the town although, as Bob said, sometimes that had its drawbacks. But surely a man who could cut a woman in two must have left a trail behind him.

'In three,' said Bob, when Edgar voiced this thought aloud. 'He cut her into three. We haven't seen the middle bit yet.'

That was the thing about police work, thought Edgar as he watched Bob go up to the bar to order more drinks. There was always something to look forward to.

As he walked home, Edgar thought again about his father and the mixed grill. What would his dad—long dead now—have thought about having a son who was a policeman? On one hand, the job surely deserved his parents' most prized epithet, 'respectable', but on the other it hardly matched their other major criterion, 'nice'. Edgar had spent the morning looking at dismembered body parts, the afternoon trying to trace someone—anyone— who might know how they came to rest in the Left Luggage office at Brighton station, and the evening drinking beer with a lad who should be looking up to him as a superior officer. No, nice it wasn't.

Edgar's digs were in Hanover, the steep hill that stretched from the Pavilion almost to the racecourse. The houses were mostly small and run-down, but on a clear day you could see the whole of Brighton spread out before you, a series of tottering white terraces until you reached the pier and the sea. As Edgar stomped up the worst part of the hill, he reflected how his mother would have considered the area 'common'. Edgar's parents had graduated from a terrace to a semi-detached bungalow in Esher and had thought themselves the most fortunate people on earth. Edgar's father had not lived long to enjoy the suburban bliss. He had died barely a year after the move to Surrey. But Edgar's mother, Rose, lived on, polishing her silver and ironing her table-cloths as if preparing for a banquet that never quite materialised.

Edgar thought of his childhood as being dominated by the pursuit of respectability. His father, Bill, had worked at the Post Office and, though it was a struggle at times, it was his boast that Rose had never had to go out to work. Edgar and his brother and sister were never allowed to play in the street with the other children. They had to stay inside, doing their homework and practising the piano. This joyless self-betterment had its results. All three siblings won places at the grammar school although, when Edgar later got into Oxford, this was considered rather showy and unbecoming. 'People like us don't get degrees,' his mother said. 'Just when Dad's got you a nice little berth in the Post Office.' But Edgar went to Oxford and enjoyed two delirious terms before Hitler spoilt it all and he found himself, almost without knowing it, on a troop ship bound for Norway. His younger brother, Jonathan, had further ruined the party by getting himself killed at Dunkirk. Lucy, his sister, was now the only regular visitor to the bungalow, where she reported that Jonathan and Edgar were both spoken of in the same hushed, regretful tones. They had both let their mother down. Jonathan dead on a French beach and Edgar in the police force.

Edgar's flat was on the ground floor of a house painted a rather virulent shade of pink. As he let himself in, he smelt the familiar musty smell that never seemed to get better no matter how much he left windows open or tried to spring-clean. He had once gone as far as complaining about it to his landlady, who had sniffed the air and said 'nasty, isn't it?' as if it had nothing to with her.

Mice, Bob had said, when he'd mentioned it at the station, and he was probably right. Edgar frequently heard scurrying and squeaking in the skirting boards and, once, when he had left a biscuit out over-night, he had woken to find that it had been chewed by sharp rodent teeth.

Trying not to think about the mice, Edgar cut himself some bread and searched for something to spread on it. He thought he had some sardines somewhere, but a trawl through the larder produced nothing better than some rather mouldy jam and a half-open tin of spam which he hastily threw away (maybe that was responsible for the smell?). He scraped off the thin layer of green and spread the jam on the bread. Then he took the sandwich and a bottle of beer and repaired to the front room for the best part of the day. The cryptic crossword.

He didn't know where his love for crosswords started. Maybe it was sitting at the kitchen table trying to do his homework and being distracted by the tempting black and white squares on the back of his father's evening paper. His father never did the crossword and his mother could hardly even bring herself to touch a newspaper (news was rarely nice or respectable). All evening the clues would tempt and tantalise: 'fare to be cooked over first part of Sunday . . . I, for one, am reflected . . . ruminate, stuck in ales perhaps.' He couldn't remember the first time that he had taken the discarded paper and tentatively filled in the blanks, but even now, even after completing a crossword had indirectly led him to the Magic Men and some of the worst experiences of his life, he still saw an unfinished puzzle as a treat, something to be savoured at the end of the day.

He sat down now and chewed his pen. 'Turn to important person making a comeback.' Five letters. 'Comeback' often meant that the word was reversed. Important person? VIP. Turn that and you get 'piv'. Oh yes, 'pivot'—turn to—an anagram of 'VIP to'. Edgar filled in the answer in neat black capitals. It was a point of honour never to use a pencil. Two down: 'Christmas visitors include conjuror (8)'. Well, Christmas visitors are always 'Magi'. Magi . . . Edgar stopped, looking down at the paper.

He heard Solomon Carter saying, 'Beautiful pair. Long as a showgirl's'. He thought of the boxes in which the body parts had been found: wooden, black, fastened with brass clips at the back, exactly the same size. And he saw, not the dingy walls of his flat, but a variety show at the end of a pier—the velvet curtains, the wheeled cabinet and the white face of the magician as he proceeded to saw a woman into three.

CHAPTER 2

Max Mephisto stared up at the damp spots on the ceiling. Five and two. Seven-card brag. Find the Lady. Hearts, clubs, diamonds, spades. The darker spots could be spades, if you gave them the benefit of the doubt. Queen of spades. The Dark Lady. One of his best table tricks. You could pluck the baleful-looking queen from a lady's hair, from her evening bag, even from her cleavage if it was the right kind of club and she was the right kind of girl.

The girl beside him sighed in her sleep. Max had no idea what kind of girl she was and, as this show was only a weekly, he wouldn't have a chance to find out. Vanda, he thought. Or was it Tanya? One of those Russian-sounding names. Their act was vaguely Russian, he seemed to recall, lots of squatting with arms crossed and legs kicking out. The costumes too had lots of unnecessary fur, though they were skimpier than those generally worn by peasants in the Urals. To be honest, though, the Majestic Theatre, Eastbourne, was probably colder than Siberia, even in August. Where was he going next? Southport, he thought. Or maybe Scarborough. Somewhere beginning with S. Please God, don't let it be Skegness.

'Mr Mephisto!'

Mrs Shuttleworth's bell-like tones. Did she suspect that he had a woman in his room? Well, she knew him so she probably did suspect. But her voice had sounded excited rather than reproving.

'Yes?' he shouted, unhelpfully. Vanda/Tanya pulled the pillow over her head.

'Gentleman to see you.'

Gentleman must mean that he wasn't a theatrical. Max rejected the idea of coming down in his dressing gown. It might be an agent, someone with news of a really good show, a Number One, somewhere like the Finsbury Park Empire or the Golders Green Hippodrome. He dressed in shirt and trousers, no tie, a respectable-looking tweed jacket. Before he left, he handed the girl her clothes.

'Better get dressed,' he said kindly. 'Landlady'll be up to do the rooms in a minute.' Old Mother Shuttleworth never stirred herself to clean the rooms before midday, but the girl wasn't to know that.

She sat up, trying to stretch in a seductive way. She was pretty enough, even in the daylight, a sort of cut-price Betty Grable. 'Are you coming to the last-night party?' she asked. 'After the second house.'

'Of course,' said Max hoping that a better offer would come his way. Maybe he'd be dining with the agent at the Grand.

'See you later, Max.'

'Bye Vanda.'

'Sonya.'

Sonya. That was it.

Mrs Shuttleworth had shown the visitor into the front room, rather than the dining room where some of the pros were still having breakfast. Coming softly down the stairs, Max could hear the unmistakable tones of Ronaldo the Sword Swallower and Walter Armstrong the Impressionist. He crossed the hall without looking round. Ronaldo was more than he could stomach in the morning—swords, it seemed, were the only things he could swallow without spraying the room with crumbs—and Armstrong was tediously devoted to imitating inanimate objects. Max felt that his day could quite comfortably start without hearing a cork being pulled from a bottle or a lavatory cistern gurgling.

Max prided himself on his double-takes, it was a classic way to distract the audience. Open the cabinet door and the girl is . . . *gone*. Stagger downstage, look wildly up at the royal circle, clutch throat. But stepping into Mrs Shuttleworth's over-stuffed parlour, he did, in fact, take a genuine step backwards.

'Ed. Good God.'

'Hallo, Max.'

Mrs Shuttleworth, hovering in the background,

seemed to feel that this exchange lacked something.

'This gentleman has come to see you specially, Mr Mephisto.'

'So I see.'

'I wondered if there was somewhere we could have a chat,' said Edgar. It was nearly five years since he'd seen Ed. The last time they met was at the end of the war. The Magic Men had been disbanded and they had met at Victoria Station, each on their way to another posting. They had argued, Max remembered, some ridiculous conversation about whether Edgar should go back to university or become a policeman. Well, he had made his choice and here he was, unchanged as far as Max could see. Tall, thin, sandy-haired, looking about him with an air of expectant eagerness. Max knew that in contrast he looked old and seedy. He was ten years older than Edgar, but his eyes had never looked that trusting, even when he was young.

'I'll leave you in peace then,' said Mrs Shuttleworth, after a moment's pause.

'No,' said Max. 'We can go out for a walk.'

'But you haven't had your breakfast yet.'

'I'm not hungry, thank you, Mrs Shuttleworth.'

'Breakfast smells terrific,' said Edgar with a schoolboy grin that would earn him a fortune on the boards in best-friend roles.

'We keep chickens,' explained the landlady,

though Max felt sure that Edgar could have smelt as much. 'And it's easier now bread's not rationed. I can give you some eggs to take home,' offered Mrs Shuttleworth expansively. 'Your wife will be pleased.'

'I'm not married,' said Edgar, grin sagging a little.

'Come on, Ed,' said Max, 'let's get some air.'

Max had lit a cigarette before they had descended the porch steps. He offered his case to Edgar, who shook his head.

'I've given them up.'

'Whatever for?'

'I just didn't like being so dependent on something.'

They walked in silence along the promenade. A cold wind was blowing through the palm trees and the sea was a steely, uninviting blue. They stopped in a shelter so Max could light another cigarette. Breathing in the smoke, he said, 'How did you find me?'

'I looked in *Variety* magazine. "Max Mephisto appearing at the Majestic Theatre, Eastbourne."'

'Are policemen reading *Variety* magazine these days?'

'I don't know,' said Edgar calmly. 'But I looked because I wanted to find you.'

'Why?' Max squinted at him through the smoke.

'Let's walk on a bit and I'll tell you.'

They walked as far as the pier. The floral clock

made Max's eyes ache—all those clashing ranks of Michaelmas daisies, yellow, purple and orange—he must have had more to drink last night than he realised. The wind was turning the deckchairs into mini sailboats, but there were still a few brave families setting up on the beach.

'We've found a woman's body,' said Edgar. 'Cut into three. The top and bottom were found in the Left Luggage at Brighton station. The middle part was delivered to me at the police station yesterday.'

'The middle part?'

'The torso. Breast to hips.'

'Jesus.' Max took a drag at his cigarette. 'And you say this was delivered to you?'

'Yes. In a black case addressed to Captain Edgar Stephens.'

'*Captain* Stephens. Not PC?'

'It's Detective Inspector Stephens. But, yes. They used my army rank.'

They leant on the railings and watched as two children—hardy in striped bathing costumes—built a sandcastle. Max's eyes stung. He hoped it was just from flying sand.

'Well, what's it got to do with me? You chose to join the police. Aren't dead bodies part of the job?'

'The way the body was cut into three, each part put into a black box, it reminded me of a magic trick. One you used to do before the war.'

Max was relighting his cigarette. 'The Zig Zag

Girl,' he said. 'Girl in a cabinet, blades cut through top and bottom. Pull the mid-section out to make a zig zag shape, open a door to show the midriff. Always a crowd-pleaser. The trick is that the cabinet's bigger than it looks. Black strips down the sides make it look narrow and the middle part is actually bigger than the top and bottom.'

'Well this man,' said Edgar. 'He actually cut her into three. I've seen the pieces.'

Max said nothing so Edgar continued. 'The whole thing was so theatrical. The way the pieces were found, the middle part—the key part—being sent to me. I just thought it might be . . .'

'You thought it might be a lunatic magician.'

There was a silence. The hurdy-gurdy started up on the pier. On the beach the children were laughing as they jumped over the waves.

'Yes,' said Edgar at last. 'I thought it might be a lunatic magician. And, if you're looking for a lunatic magician, where else to start?'

Max laughed. It felt like the first time he had laughed for years. He had certainly never laughed at Nobby 'Crazy Legs' Smith, the comedian on the bill that week.

'It's good to see you again, Ed.'

'Good to see you too. It's been too long.'

'Do you see anyone else from the Magic Men?'

At that name, Max stopped laughing. 'No,' he said. 'I don't see anyone from those days. The war's been over for five years.'

'And you can't think of anyone who's per-forming The Zig Zag Girl now?'

Max shrugged. 'I bet magicians are performing it up and down the country. People copy tricks all the time and it's not particularly difficult if you've got a good cabinet-maker.'

Edgar brightened. 'Well, that's a lead for a start. Can you give me the names of the best theatrical cabinet-makers?'

Max turned and began to walk away. Edgar kept pace with him and, after a few moments, Max said, 'All right. I can give you some names. There's a good prop-maker near Brighton, as it happens. But I don't want to get involved. I don't like the police, remember?'

'I remember.'

'We live in different worlds, Ed. You're on your way up and me . . .' he gestured towards the town behind him, the stuccoed hotels, the flags of nations fluttering from the pier. 'I'm on my way down.'

'The Majestic isn't a Number One then?'

Max laughed. 'It's a Number Three on a good day. Variety's dying, Ed, and I'm dying with it. You should see the bunch on this week's bill.'

'I will,' said Edgar. 'I've got a ticket for tonight's show.'

The show wasn't as bad as Max made out, thought Edgar. He'd quite enjoyed the sword-swallowing and the impressions of doors opening and shutting had been mildly entertaining. Max had rightly characterised the comedian, Nobby Smith, as the least funny man in the world, but he seemed to go down well with certain members of the audience. Sonya and Tanya, the exotic dancers, were also popular, though Edgar thought this might be because Sonya's fur bikini kept slipping. From his vantage point in the stalls, he could see their goose-pimples.

Max was the last act, as befitted his star billing. Max might say that he was on his way out, but it was clear that he was the one most of the audience had come to see. In the interval, as Edgar nursed his warm gin and tonic (a woman's drink, Tony Mulholland used to say), there was only one name buzzing through the bar. 'Saw him at the Hippodrome before the war. Incredible . . .' 'They say he escaped from a pyramid in Egypt.' 'Of course he was a spy, you know.' 'I heard he was a Nazi.' 'Touch of the tar-brush . . .' Max was the sort of man who attracted rumours, thought Edgar. It was strange only that some of them were true.

Sonya and Tanya opened the second half with a dance that was vaguely Egyptian in aspiration. Edgar thought about Max and the pyramid. That, too, could be true. He knew that Max had been in Egypt at the start of the war. By the time the Magic Men unit was formed, most of its members had already seen enough action for a lifetime.

Except Tony Mulholland, who had somehow managed to avoid the call-up, and The Great Diablo who was sixty-five if he was a day.

A ventriloquist followed the dancers. He was quite good if you accepted that the puppet had a speech impediment. The audience were charitable about his attempts to sing the national anthem whilst drinking a glass of water. Then there was a female impersonator, Madame Foo-Foo. His (her?) act was absolutely filthy and Edgar wondered how it had got past the Lord Chamberlain's Office. But there was no doubt that Madame Foo-Foo had her fans, particularly in the gallery. She left to what was almost an ovation and the audience settled down to await the great Max Mephisto.

The silence seemed to crackle into expectancy and then almost impatience until, at the last possible minute, Max strolled onto the stage. Edgar hadn't even realised that he was holding his breath until he exhaled with a sigh. Because, if anything was obvious, it was that there was nothing to be nervous about. Max was so clearly in charge. Effortlessly elegant in a dinner jacket with the bow tie undone, he grinned sleepily down at the audience. By the time that he had wandered down into the stalls and removed a watch from someone's ear and a seemingly endless string of pearls from a woman's handbag, the audience were in the palm of his hand. After a few complicated card tricks, enlivened by a stream of patter

29

wittier than anything heard so far that evening, a trestle table was brought onto the stage and Max invited a girl from the audience to lie on it. A delicious tremor ran through the seats around Edgar. This was what they had come for. The faintly macabre sight of a man leaning over a woman and preparing to dispose of her. Edgar thought of the girl on the slab. This girl was blonde too, and Max solicitously tucked her hair under her neck as he pulled the cloth over her face. Edgar had done the same to the poor remains in the mortuary.

He told himself to keep watching the girl but, as usual, he was distracted by Max who, with a clap of his hands conjured two white doves from thin air. As the doves flew, cooing anxiously, towards the royal box, Max removed the cloth with a flourish. The girl had, of course, vanished. Thunderous applause, redoubling as a spotlight revealed the girl back in her seat looking both embarrassed and relieved. Max bowed, kissed his hand to the gallery and disappeared, not emerging even for the cries of 'encore'.

Escaping while the anthem was still playing, Edgar made his way to the pass door, as instructed by Max. The doorman greeted him with a nod. 'Max? Third on the left. Usually I tell his visitors to watch out for him, but you look like you can take care of yourself.' Edgar smiled, guessing that Max's visitors were usually younger and more female. He had never been backstage at a theatre before and he was surprised at how scruffy it was. The Majestic may have seen better days, but the front of house still had a veneer of glamour—red velvet curtains (only slightly moth-eaten), gilded cherubs on the balconies, a chandelier glittering up above the gods. But behind the pass door there were dusty floorboards and pipes running along the low ceiling. There was also a strong smell of damp. Edgar passed a dressing room which was obviously shared by the ventriloquist, the sword-swallower and the impressionist. He heard the sound of a champagne cork popping and wondered if that was Walter Armstrong at work. He couldn't imagine champagne being drunk here otherwise.

Max did, at least, have a room to himself. He was drinking whisky and rubbing cold cream into his face. Edgar found himself staring. He'd never imagined Max using greasepaint somehow. He thought what his father would have said about a man wearing make-up. Well, he didn't want to be like *him* at any rate.

'Great show,' he said. 'You were brilliant.'

Max smiled and pushed the whisky bottle towards him. 'Help yourself. Glad you enjoyed it.'

'That last trick was incredible. How did you do it?'

'I can't tell you. I'd be kicked out of the Magic Circle.'

'You told me that you'd been expelled from the Magic Circle years ago.'

'Oh, all right then. Trapdoor. When I whirl the table round, it's positioned over the trap. The girl just gets down and climbs through the hole. A few drum rolls and she's back in her seat. You can do a version where you set the table alight, but that's against fire regulations here.'

'So the girl wasn't just someone from the audience?'

'God, no. She's the stage manager's daughter. Nice girl.'

Edgar took a sip of his whisky, watching Max carefully removing every trace of grease. What would it be like, he wondered, to do that show twice nightly. Always the same twirl and smile up to the gallery, the same fake surprise as the doves erupted into the air, the same dumb faces tilted towards you.

'Where did the doves go?' he asked suddenly.

Max looked surprised. 'I gave them to Sheila. The girl. Easier to buy another pair when I get to Scarborough. Or I might try something else. A bunch of flowers bursting into flames is always good.'

'Is that where you're going next? Scarborough?'

'Yes. Sunday's changeover day. I've always hated Sundays.'

Watching him in the mirror, Edgar saw Max's face change. A girl was standing in the doorway.

She was one of the dancers, wearing a rather tatty peach satin wrap over her costume.

'Are you coming to the party, Max?' she asked. 'You could bring your friend.'

Edgar watched as the mechanical smile spread over Max's face. His audience smile.

'Wish I could, sweetheart, but Ed and I have business to discuss.'

Max took Edgar to an Italian restaurant that he knew. It was a little place, tucked away in a back street, but the food was wonderful. Max's mother had been Italian, Edgar seemed to remember. It was one of the few facts that he knew about him. Presumably it was from her that Max had inherited his dark good looks, the kind that made people speculate about the tar-brush.

'Bit better than the Caledonian Hotel,' said Max, twirling spaghetti.

'Bet they don't do rock cakes though,' said Edgar. But the mention of the Caledonian, the only bar in the Highland town where the Magic Men had their headquarters, had eased something between them. Edgar found himself telling Max about his job, about how hard he found it having to live up to his reputation as a brilliant ex–secret-service man. 'And most of the time I know less than the lowliest PC. And they know it too.'

Max confessed that the endless parade of

seaside towns was taking its toll. 'I'd pack it in if there was anything else I could do.'

'But you're a brilliant magician.'

'Yes.' Typically, Max did not dispute this. 'But the public don't want brilliant any more. Have you seen all these new NAAFI comics? There was one on at the Palladium the other week. They don't do jokes, they don't do patter. This character—it was like listening to a mad man on the bus, but the audience loved him. Practically ate him up. Have you heard of a chap called Tommy Cooper? Cooper the Trooper?'

'No.'

'He's a magician. Ex-NAAFI too. And his thing is, he gets it wrong. He does the build-up and the patter and then the trick goes wrong. First time I saw it, I couldn't believe it. The watch is under this cup, no this one, no—hang on—it's this one. Brought the house down.'

'Maybe he did just get it wrong.'

'No, that's his act. I've seen him a few times. He's a good magician underneath, I can tell. But audiences don't want good magicians any more. They don't want smoke and mirrors and swirling cloaks. They don't want girls in spangled costumes. They want to see how the trick works. Trouble is, once you tell them how it works, you're done for.'

'Speaking of spangled costumes, why don't you have an assistant?'

Max refilled their glasses. 'Assistants are too much trouble. I had a fantastic girl before the war, Ethel her name was. She knew exactly when to get the audience's attention and when to keep still. Most of them never get it right. They're twirling away when you want the spotlight on you and standing there like a bloody corpse when you want the audience distracted. But Ethel . . . she was a wonder.'

'What happened to her?'

'Got married, like they all do. Married a fireman and lives on the Isle of Wight. She still sends me cards at Christmas.'

Where does she send them, thought Edgar. Max told him that he hadn't had a permanent address since being discharged. He wanted to ask Max about the dancer, about whether there was a woman in his life, but he didn't have the nerve somehow.

But Max, it seemed, had been thinking along the same lines.

'The thing about The Zig Zag Girl,' he said, pouring the last of the red into Edgar's glass, 'is that it's a trick that depends on the girl. You need a very good girl, one that can get into that middle section in double-quick time. She's got to be fast and she's got to be brave.'

'Why are you telling me this?' asked Edgar. The wine was making his head feel fuzzy. The picture of the Bay of Naples behind Max's head was pulsing unpleasantly. Edgar hoped that it wasn't about to erupt.

Max's voice seemed to come from a long way away. 'You wanted my advice about your murder. Well, this is it. Find the girl.'

CHAPTER 3

The station still hadn't got over the shock of the box delivered to 'Captain Stephens'. On the Thursday, the day after the discovery of the head and the legs, the duty sergeant had arrived at Bartholomew Square Police Station to find a black box waiting on the doorstep. None of the night staff had seen it being delivered but, as they had spent most of the night in the basement gathered around a primus stove, this was hardly surprising.

The sergeant, a solid individual called Larry McGuire, picked up the box and carried it to the counter. It was then that he had noticed the smell, a terrible, all-pervading miasma that made him back away, shielding his face. Handkerchief over mouth and nose, he had approached again, seen the typewritten name on the address label, and reached for the phone to call Edgar. By the time Edgar arrived, out of breath from running all the way, there was a small crowd in the reception area.

'Bloody hell,' he'd said. 'What's that smell?'

McGuire had pointed silently to the box. Edgar recognised it immediately—wooden, black, brass clips—the missing triplet that completes the set.

'Get a camera,' he said, 'we should record this. And call Chief Inspector Hodges.'

When he'd opened it, the smell had sent him staggering backwards. He was dimly aware of Sergeant McGuire clicking away in the background and of the chief's indrawn breath. A piece of flesh, roughly hacked at the top and bottom, greyish in colour but still, unmistakeably and horribly, part of a human body. Edgar had heard someone retching and the bile had risen in his own throat.

'There's something in there,' said McGuire, his voice reassuringly matter of fact. 'Looks like a rose. A red rose. It's still fresh.'

So, on the Monday after his visit to Max, when McGuire told him that a flower-seller was asking for him in Reception, Edgar had thought immediately of the rose. The reception area, with its grand mosaic floor, still smelt strongly of bleach and, when Edgar escorted the woman to the interview room, he could see doors opening and people peering out to watch their progress. The weekend papers had been full of the Brighton trunk murders (though the full details hadn't been released), and Edgar knew the pressure was on him, as the detective in charge, to make some progress with the case. Frank Hodges had already had strong words for people who spent their weekends gadding about in Eastbourne when there was a murderer to catch.

The flower-seller was a stout woman with a disconcertingly red face. She looked almost pityingly at Edgar as she said, 'You're the policeman in charge, aren't you?'

Edgar agreed that he was.

'You were asking at the stall about the man that left the packages last week. The ones with the bits of body in them.'

'That's right.'

'Well, I think I saw him. The man.'

'Really?' Edgar leant forwards.

'It was on the Monday. I saw a man carrying two boxes into Left Luggage. Then he came to my stall.'

'Are you sure it was the same man?'

'I think so. He was small, I remember that. The boxes looked too big for him. I remember thinking that he might be one of those theatricals.'

This was interesting. 'Why?'

'The boxes looked like they could have had instruments in them. And he was small, like I said. He looked foreign. Like one of those foreign musicians.'

'He looked foreign?'

'Yes. *Dark*.' She gave the word a sinister emphasis.

'Dark-skinned?'

'No. Dark hair. Except I couldn't see his hair because he was wearing a cap.'

Edgar sighed. 'Witnesses,' Frank Hodges always said. 'You can't trust a witness.'

'He was wearing a cap? Like a sailor's cap?'

'No. More like an errand boy. A peaked cap.'

'Can you remember anything else?'

'He was wearing a long coat. I thought that was funny for August. Still, it's been wicked weather for summer.'

'What did he say to you? Did he buy some flowers?'

'He bought a rose,' said the woman. 'A single long-stemmed red rose.'

Later that day, Edgar sought out the cabinet-maker recommended by Max. His workshop was in Hove, close to the cricket ground. 'D. Fitzgerald,' said the uncompromising sign, 'Propmaker'.

D. Fitzgerald was engaged in putting the roof on what looked like a large kennel. On the side, the words 'Cave Canem' were written in italic script.

'What's that?' said Edgar.

'It's a kennel,' said D. Fitzgerald straightening up. 'For a dog.'

'Oh.' Edgar was disappointed. 'It's not a magic trick then?'

'No. Magic work is thin on the ground these days. I have to take what I can get.'

Edgar thought about what Max had said about variety dying and no one wanting the traditional magic tricks any more. It seemed a shame somehow that there would be no more girls stepping into cabinets and reappearing in the stalls. And, presumably, prop-makers would have to turn to kennels and wardrobes in order to make their living.

Edgar introduced himself. 'I got your name from Max Mephisto,' he said. 'He said you'd made props for him.'

'Ah, Max,' Fitzgerald smiled reminiscently. 'A real gentleman, is Max. A great magician too. Have you seen him work?'

'Yes,' said Edgar. 'Once or twice.'

'I made a few cabinets for him. The ghost cabinet. Have you seen that one? And a couple of sword cabinets too.'

'What about The Zig Zag Girl? Ever make the cabinet for that?'

Fitzgerald looked at him curiously. He was a tall man with curly hair like a bull's poll. There was something bull-like about his stance too. Edgar imagined that he would be a tough customer in a fight.

'Yes,' he said. 'I've made the cabinet for that.'

'I wondered if you'd take a look at this.' Edgar got out one of Sergeant McGuire's photographs. It showed the box—the third box—sitting on the station counter. The actual box was still in the

Evidence Room, but the smell was still so strong that no one would go near it.

Fitzgerald looked up. 'Is this to do with those murders? The body in the trunk?'

'Yes.' Edgar didn't see any point in denying it. 'Have you seen boxes like this before?'

Fitzgerald shrugged. 'Don't know. It's just a box.'

'What about this?' Edgar showed him a picture of the three boxes stacked on top of each other. 'Remind you of anything?'

The cabinet-maker scratched his head. 'It looks like the cabinet for The Zig Zag Girl, but in that case the boxes would all have false bottoms. The girl would have to be able to stand up and the magician would need to be able to get the blades through. Have these got false bottoms?'

'No.' As far as Edgar could see, the boxes were just that—plain wooden cubes painted black. It was just their size and their absolute regularity that brought the trick to mind. 'Have you any idea who could have made them?' he asked.

'Anyone could have put these together,' said Fitzgerald. 'You wouldn't even need to be a carpenter. For a magic cabinet, now, that's different. You need to be a real artist for that. Take The Zig Zag, for example, the middle box is actually bigger, but you wouldn't be able to see that from the audience's viewpoint.'

'So you've no idea who could have made these boxes?'

Fitzgerald shook his head. 'No. Like I say, they're just boxes.' He turned back to his kennel and, as Edgar walked away, he heard the staccato sounds of nails being hammered into wood.

Edgar set off southwards, walking briskly. It was a longish way back to the police station, but the good thing about Brighton was that you couldn't get lost; you just had to head for the sea. He thought about magic tricks and the stage, about cabinets made to conceal bodies, about deception and artifice. The boxes may just be boxes, but the important thing was that someone wanted them to look like something else.

At Bartholomew Square, his boss was waiting for him. Chief Inspector Frank Hodges was a large man with a drooping moustache given to pessimistic pronouncements about the police force, crime and life in general. He was nearing retirement age, but frequently said that he expected to 'die in harness'. 'And with a knife in your back,' Edgar had heard someone mutter when Hodges last made this comment. The Chief Inspector was not popular with the younger officers.

Today, though, he looked not so much gloomy as enraged.

'Where have you been?' he demanded as Edgar entered the Incident Room.

'Following a lead,' said Edgar. He tended to

assume a calm, professional tone with his boss, knowing that this infuriated him still further.

'What sort of lead?'

'A cabinet-maker. Someone who may have known who made the boxes.'

'And did they know?'

'No,' Edgar admitted.

Hodges' face turned an alarming shade of red. Edgar hoped that this wasn't the harness moment.

'The boxes looked as if they might be theatrical props,' he said soothingly, 'so I went to see someone who specialised in that sort of carpentry.'

Hodges did not seem even slightly soothed, although his colour faded a little. 'What's this obsession with the stage?' he said. 'I hear you went to Eastbourne to see a magician, of all people. Get this straight, Stephens. This is a murder inquiry. The biggest murder case this town has ever seen. It's not some bloody silly university review.'

Edgar's two terms at Oxford were a source of never-ending irritation to Frank Hodges. Edgar both resented this and realised that it gave him a certain power over his boss.

'The boxes reminded me of a magic trick,' he said. 'One where it looks as if a girl is cut into three. I saw it performed before the war and I know the man who invented the trick. He's called Max Mephisto and he was performing in Eastbourne last week.'

'Max Mephisto.' Hodges chewed his moustache

thoughtfully. 'He's quite a big name, isn't he? Think I saw him in Blackpool once. Performed a hell of a turn with a burning table.'

'He's the best-known magician in Britain,' said Edgar. 'I served with him in the war.'

'You *served* with him?' Frank's voice suggested that he thought theatricals should have been interned along with the Italians and Jews.

Edgar sighed. He had hoped not to have to go into the whole history of his friendship with Max. 'You know I was seconded to MI5 in the war,' he said. This was a pretty fancy way of saying that he was spotted by Colonel Cartwright doing the cryptic crossword on a train. 'Well, I ended up in this special unit, based near Inverness. Our job was to create false trails for the enemy, to trick them if you like.'

Max, he remembered, had claimed to be able to make ghost fleets ride the north seas. The fact that he had ended up sailing into enemy waters in a dinghy, accompanied only by Edgar and an aged desperado called The Great Diablo, was nobody's fault really.

'Well, Max was part of this unit,' he concluded. 'He was an expert at camouflage. He'd worked in North Africa, in the desert. He created these decoy tanks made from wood and canvas. He even painted an aerodrome on canvas. From the air it looked like the real thing.'

Max had created tanks that folded up and could

be stored in a suitcase. He had placed one on the front lawn at the Caledonian ready to greet Major Gormley when he opened his bedroom window.

'This is all very well,' grumbled Frank. 'But it doesn't get us much further with this case.'

'I suspected that the killer had links to the theatrical world,' said Edgar. 'I asked Max if he knew of any specialist cabinet-makers. That's all.'

'And did you get anywhere?'

'No, but I've got a possible description of the killer.' He described the visit from the flower-seller.

'So we're looking for a foreigner?' Frank brightened perceptibly.

'Not necessarily,' said Edgar. 'The florist just thought he might be foreign because the boxes reminded her of music cases—it's that theatrical link again. But I asked if he had a foreign accent and she said no. She said he had a soft voice, soft and young.'

'The man was small, though.' Frank wasn't letting that go easily. 'Foreigners are often small.'

'Smallish,' said Edgar. 'That's all we have really. A small man wearing a cap and coat.'

'Could be anyone. Could be bloody Max Miller,' said Frank.

'I suspect Mr Miller has an alibi,' said Edgar.

Frank glared at him. 'We're no further forward at all then. Any luck with identifying the girl?'

'No. I've been through the Missing Persons list.

45

Nobody there answering to our girl's description.'

Five foot ten, long blonde hair, a beautiful figure now cut into grotesque pieces. No, nobody like that had been reported missing in the Brighton area.

'I'm making inquiries in private lodging houses,' he said. 'The sort used by theatricals.'

'The bloody stage again,' said Frank. 'What makes you think the girl was . . . well, that type?'

Edgar hesitated. He didn't like to admit that it was Solomon Carter's phrase about the girl having legs 'as long as a showgirl's' that first put the idea into his head.

'It's just a theory,' he said. 'But actors live a nomadic life, here one week, gone the next. It's possible that someone could disappear and not be missed for a while.'

Frank chewed the end of his moustache. He didn't like the word 'nomadic', it had a slippery, foreign sound.

'Solomon Carter said there were marks around her head which could be consistent with wearing a headdress of some kind,' said Edgar. 'The kind worn by an exotic dancer.' He thought of Sonya and Tanya in their fur bikinis and Sonya's face when she had looked at Max. He thought of Max saying, 'You need a very good girl.'

Frank made the snorting sound again. 'She could have been a prostitute. Have you thought of that?'

'Yes,' said Edgar. 'We've made inquiries in the red light district.'

'Well, make more inquiries. The press are onto it. We don't want to look like idiots.'

'We certainly don't, sir,' agreed Edgar.

Max enjoyed the drive to Scarborough. Sometimes it felt as if his Bentley were the only thing in his life to have escaped from the war unscathed. It (however much he loved the car, he refused to think of it as 'she') had passed the war years hidden in a barn on a farm belonging to an ex-girlfriend. Max would never forget the moment when Joan pulled back the tarpaulin to reveal his treasure, covered in straw but still with tyres and headlamps intact. He could have kissed her. He *would* have kissed her had not her husband, a taciturn farming type, been hovering with a pitchfork.

He had left early, in order to avoid saying goodbye to anyone at the digs. Thank God, none of them were going on with him to Scarborough. He tried to remember who was on the bill with him there. One of the new comedians, he thought, and a singer who had made it big with patriotic numbers during the war. 'There'll Always Be an England', that sort of thing. Still, the Alexandra was a nice theatre and he was going to stay with an old friend, a girl who had once been part of a double act and now ran a boarding house. What was her act called again? Sometimes he saw the names on a never-ending playbill in his head: the Great Supremo, Leandra's Feats with the Feet, Lou Lenny and her Unrideable Mule, Raydini The Gay Deceiver, Petrova's Performing Ponies. He'd got it. The Diller Twins. Though they hadn't even been sisters, let alone twins. They didn't even look alike. Pretty enough girls, though. He and Brenda had enjoyed one memorable summer in Scarborough and had kept in touch even after Brenda had married a man who could rip telephone directories in two. What was *his* name? The Mighty something or other. He could never remember the men.

He made good time and reached Scarborough just before eight. As he drove along the seafront, he saw the towers of the Grand looming over the town. Once he had stayed in the Grand for a whole season. Now he was reduced to boarding houses and he could see a time when he'd be sleeping in the Bentley, a shambling figure standing on street corners taking flowers out of his hat and begging passers-by to choose a card. He shook his head, irritated at this self-pitying theme. He needed a holiday, that was all. After Scarborough he was back down in Brighton, then he had a two-week break. He'd go away, somewhere civilised like Le Touquet. There was still some money for that. He wasn't quite reduced to busking yet.

Brenda met him at the door. She was still attractive, with creamy skin and red hair, but marriage to the strong man and the birth of two children had enlarged her contours somewhat.

'Max!' She kissed him on the cheek. 'You look exactly the same. You'll never get older.'

'I feel a hundred,' said Max.

'That's just the drive. You'll feel just dandy after a rest and a glass of sherry.'

'You're a wonderful woman, Brenda.'

And he did feel better after a hearty meal and two glasses of (disgustingly sweet) sherry. Larry, the strong man, turned out to be an affable fellow and they spent a pleasant hour reminiscing over old names.

'Raydini! What happened to him?'

'Heart attack at the Wood Green Empire.'

'What a way to go.'

'What about your twin?' Max turned to Brenda, who was looking quite alluring in the light from the gas fire. 'The other Diller girl?'

'Peggy? I don't know. I lost touch with her. Last I heard, she was down in Brighton.'

'I'm there next week,' said Max easily. 'I'll look out for her. Is she still in the business, do you know?'

'Yes.' Brenda gave her full-throated laugh. 'Actually, last I heard she was following in your footsteps, Max. She was a magician's assistant.' Larry opened the door to let the cat out, but this wasn't the only reason for the small, cold chill that ran through the room.

CHAPTER 4

'What makes you think it was her? Peggy?'

Edgar heard Max sigh down the phone.

'I just thought it might be a possibility. She was last heard of in the Brighton area.'

'What did she look like?'

'Tall, blonde, good legs.'

'How old?'

'Mid to late twenties, I suppose.'

Edgar stared at the wall opposite, which was dominated by a poster telling him to put on his lights while driving at night.

'Have you got a photo?' Max was saying.

'We took pictures, but I can't show them to you. I'd need special permission.' He could just imagine what Frank Hodges would say.

'You never used to care so much about the rules, Ed.'

This was below the belt. Edgar remembered that Max always fought dirty.

'The pictures are pretty disturbing,' he said at last.

'I'm a big boy. I can cope.'

'All right. I'll put a photo in the post tomorrow. Ring me as soon as you get it.'

'Aye, aye, Captain.'

There's nothing more annoying, mused Edgar,

putting the phone down, than being addressed as 'captain' by someone who technically outranks you.

It was nearly the end of the day. Edgar sat at his desk listening to the now-familiar haunted-house noises as the old building settled down for the night. The police station at Bartholomew Square was built in the classical style. Outside it was imposing, with monstrous pillars two storeys high. The reception area boasted an Italian mosaic floor and marble busts of Brighton luminaries. But, as you descended the steps to the CID headquarters, you entered a different world. Tiled walls dripped with moisture and sometimes, turning a corner in one of the subterranean corridors, you could hear mice—or worse—scuttling ahead. Frank Hodges had told Edgar that this part of the building had actually been condemned in the 1930s, but the police stuck stubbornly to their gloomy suite of rooms.

Naturally, the police station had its resident ghosts. The site was once a medieval monastery—St Bartholomew's and it was said that sometimes a monk could be seen moving casually through the thick stone walls of the basement. The monastery well was still under the floor somewhere, you could hear it gurgling away on stormy nights. But Edgar usually found himself thinking of a more recent spectre. Brighton's first chief of police, Henry Solomon, was murdered at the station in the eighteenth century, killed by a petty thief he had brought in for questioning. Edgar often imagined the scene. Apparently Solomon had seated the man in front of the fire, attempting to calm him down. He had turned his back and the felon picked up a poker and battered him to death. The room where it happened was cold, even in summer, and a dark figure was sometimes seen standing by the marble mantelpiece or descending the steps to the cells. Edgar didn't believe in the ghost, but he did think that the story contained a few important policing lessons. Don't be too nice to suspects was one. Don't turn your back on them was another.

The Incident Room was empty, so Edgar was able to find the file marked, uncompromisingly, 'Mutilated Girl', and extract a photograph. Despite his words on the phone, Edgar decided to spare Max the worst. He selected a picture that showed the girl from the neck up. He was struck again how, despite the pallor and the closed eyes, it could be a glamour shot. Her face was symmetrical and perfect, full lips closed in what was almost a smile. In life she must have been a very beautiful woman. He put the photo in a brown envelope addressed, as instructed, c/o The Alexandra Music Hall, Scarborough.

He decided to post the letter on his way home. After an overcast day, the evening was soft and mild. When he got to the top of the hill, Brighton was already lost in the summer smog. It was like walking through the clouds. Edgar thought about Max's telephone call. Was the dead girl really Peggy Ollerenshaw, once part of a double act known as The Diller Twins? He wondered why he was so sure that the girl had theatrical connections. Partly it was the way the body had been found—*presented* was the word that came to mind—cut into three like a macabre version of Max's famous trick. Partly it was her appearance, the long blonde hair, the legs. She wasn't that young, though. Late twenties, Solomon Carter thought, which would tie in with Peggy again. Had this girl fallen on hard times, no longer young enough for the chorus line, desperate enough to become involved with a dubious character who turned out to be not so much seedy as murderous?

When he reached his digs, his neighbour, Mrs Finneghan, was standing in her front garden. Having once seen Edgar talking to the traffic policemen on the seafront, she had become convinced that this was his job.

'How are the cars, Mr Stephens?'

'There seem to be more of them every day, Mrs Finneghan.' He had given up trying to tell her his real profession and, besides, it was soothing to think of a parallel existence where all he had to do was stop cars crashing into each other.

'There ought to be a law against it,' said Mrs Finneghan comfortably. She went back to feeding the seagulls.

Edgar let himself in and went straight for the whisky. One of the benefits of living on the ground floor was the use of a dusty square of garden. Edgar took his drink and sat on the back step, watching the birds swooping down to avail themselves of Mrs Finneghan's soup kitchen. Seeing Max again had brought back all sorts of memories; memories that, for five years, he had sought to expunge by working his way through the police ranks and trying not to antagonise Frank Hodges. Now he knew that if he let them, they would take him over and he would be there again, drifting on the open sea with Max and Diablo, watching Charis die.

It had been odd seeing Max in his own milieu. He had known, of course, that Max was a magician and it was the memory of seeing him on stage that had sparked the idea about The Zig Zag Girl. But it had been strange seeing him in his backstage world of greasepaint and showgirls and men doing sword-swallowing impressions. Seeing Madame Foo Foo in the corridor, dressed in basque and stockings and smoking a pipe, he hadn't been able to stop himself trying to imagine what his mother would have said. He wondered if he was drawn to Max because he was the antithesis of everything his parents stood for. Max, who had thrown off his upper-class background and replaced it with a showman's cape. What would have shocked his mother most about Max? The Italian mother (reputedly an ex–opera singer), the titled father or the life spent in seedy boarding houses, a different woman in his bed every night and the same woman disappearing on the stage every evening? 'Rich people are all very well,' his mother had said once, 'as long as they keep in their proper place.' Max, performing on stage at the Alexandra Music Hall, was about as far from his proper place as you could imagine. Or perhaps he was in it? Edgar couldn't imagine Max stalking grouse or taking tea in drawing rooms (he admitted that his view of upper-class life was rather limited). Even during the war, in the wilds of Inverness, there had been a showbiz glamour about Max.

Who had taken him to the end-of-the-pier show where he had seen Max perform the The Zig Zag Girl trick? It couldn't have been his parents. Maybe it was his rather raffish Uncle Charlie, who had grown rich from the black market and now drove a purple Rolls-Royce. He did remember that they had eaten fish and chips afterwards and Jonathan had been so excited that he'd been sick. 'Things always go to Jonny's stomach,' their mother said when they got home. When Edgar heard that Jon was at Dunkirk, his first—ridiculous—thought was to worry that he would be seasick. What wouldn't he give to have him here now, his smiling, sensitive brother who had never lived long enough to have a job or a woman or even a proper shave?

That was the problem with whisky. It made you maudlin. He wouldn't think about Jon or the war and certainly not about Charis. That part of his life was over. Edgar went back indoors to search in the cupboard for a tin of corned beef.

When Max arrived at the theatre on Wednesday, the letter was waiting for him. At first he didn't recognise the handwriting and the brown envelope looked ominous. He put it aside and carried on with his make-up. Wednesday first house was always tough. Max knew he'd get them in the end, but they were sticky. He had to work hard to get the laughs and the gasps and the 'how did he do that's'. When he finally pulled the cloth away revealing the empty table and Brenda's cousin's daughter was discovered smiling back in her seat, the audience applauded with a kind of groan as if they resented being impressed. Back in his dressing room, Max took off his greasepaint and drank cold coffee (whisky would have to wait until after the second house). It was only then that he remembered the letter, propped up against the mirror.

He opened it carelessly, getting a smudge of five and nine on the envelope. The photograph fell to the floor and he had to scramble for it in the dust (the dressing rooms at the Alexandra were filthy). Eventually he held the picture under the bright mirror lights. What he felt was a kind of lurch, as if he'd missed a step or had opened the cabinet to find the girl still there, staring at him. He put a hand to his head and realised that he was shaking. The room spun like the Wall of Death at a fair-ground, but the girl stayed at the still centre of it, eyes closed, pale as death.

'My God,' said Max aloud.

The years were spinning too. Max was back in Hastings before the war and his assistant was twirling in the footlights, knowing exactly when to divert the audience's attentions to her charms.

Ethel.

CHAPTER 5

Brighton had always been one of Max's favourite towns. In some vague way, he thought they were alike. Like him, the town was classless, raffish, slightly secretive. The hotels on the seafront (he was staying at the Old Ship) presented a smooth, well-bred façade, but at the back, where the kitchens spilled out into the alleys, all was chaos and decay; rats scuttled past overflowing bins and tramps fought the seagulls over the remains of flounder fillets *à la moutarde*. Edgar said there was a lot of crime in the town.

But, as Max walked through the Pavilion Gardens towards the Theatre Royal, he wasn't thinking about Brighton or about the week's show. He was thinking about Ethel. How had she ended up here, the victim of some random sadist? He had been sure that Ethel was living in married bliss on the Isle of Wight. But now he saw that the Christmas cards, 'with best wishes from Ethel and Michael', concealed a darker truth. Because, if one thing was for certain, it was that happily married women didn't end up chopped into three and their body parts scattered around seaside towns. Something must have happened to Ethel and, given their past connection, he couldn't help wondering if he was somehow to blame.

He was meeting Ed after band call. Would Edgar the supersleuth be able to solve the mystery? He had his doubts. He knew Ed was clever (apparently he had scored off the scale on the intelligence tests for MI5), but Max had always felt that Edgar was somehow too innocent for police work. If ever a chap had been suited to going back to Oxford after the war and finishing his degree, it was Ed. Max had fought hard to convince him of this, but Edgar seemed fixated on some stupid public service ideal, probably connected with his brother's death and what had happened to Charis. They had argued in a bar in Victoria station, Ed protesting almost tearfully that Britain had to change and everyone had to 'do their bit'. 'Suit yourself,' Max had said. 'I'm going back to my old life and I'm never going to think about anyone else ever again.' Except that his old life—champagne, dancing girls, delirious audiences—didn't exist anymore and now here he was, not only thinking about his old partner but coming damn close to vowing to track down her murderer. Steady on, Max, he told himself sternly, you're not Dick Barton, you're a stage magician. Ethel's killer was probably some down-and-out who got his thrills from mutilating beautiful women. Except, said the voice in his head, she was your assistant and her torso was sent directly to your friend.

The pillars and archways of the Theatre Royal were sparkling in the sun. It was a snug little venue, somehow managing to be both grand and welcoming at once. 'Max Mephisto' screamed the billboards. Max pulled his hat down over his eyes and headed off to find the stage door. The last thing he wanted was to be spotted looking admiringly at his own posters.

The stage door was in a side street. It was open and the narrow hallway full of boxes and trunks. Max recognised his own stage kit and some boxes labelled AM. Who the hell was AM? He tried to remember who was on the bill with him this week. A comedian, but then there are comedians everywhere these days. A juggler that he last saw—pissed out of his head—trying to get off with a waxwork in Blackpool. Some girls, of course. After a while all the girls merge into one—feathers and headdresses and lipsticked smiles. All except Ethel. She was different.

He saluted the commissionaire (a huge man who seemed wedged into his booth) and made his way towards the auditorium. He was slightly late and knew he'd have to wait his turn. Monday band calls operate on a strictly first-come-first-served basis. Max might be top of the bill, but as he hadn't got his music in front of the orchestra first, he would be condemned to a morning of listening to 'The Chocolate Soldier' played (fortissimo) by a gaggle of amateur musicians. As he made his way through the stalls, he saw that the process had already started. A sharp-suited young man stood on stage tapping his foot and from the pit came the sound of two violins and a cello tuning up half-heartedly. A voice behind Max said, 'Lot of bloody upstarts in the business these days.'

Max turned and looked into the watery eyes of Geronimo the Juggling Genius, aka Bert Hoskins from Hartlepool.

'Hallo, Bert.'

'Good to see you, Max, you old bastard.'

'Likewise, Bert.'

'Do you know smarty-bloody-pants up there?' Bert gestured towards the stage with an unlit cigarette.

'Yes. I'm afraid I do.'

He had recognised him immediately. Tony

Mulholland. And he remembered almost the last time he'd seen Tony, standing on a beach watching Max's great invention burn to ashes. With Charis inside.

Max didn't get a chance to speak to Tony until after the band call. Tony took a long time going through his music, speaking in a low, expressionless voice that didn't carry into the auditorium. When he had finished, he didn't go into the stalls to join the other pros. He stalked out, watched resentfully by the orchestra. Max too viewed his retreating pinstriped back with dislike. What the hell was Tony doing here? They all thought that he had given up the stage. Besides, Max had a clause in his contract saying that he would always be the only magician on the bill. Tony had quite a name before the war. He specialised in card tricks and mesmerism, ending his act by hypnotising a member of the audience. It was a different kind of magic from Max's, but there was no doubt that Tony was an extremely polished performer, smooth and slightly dangerous. Max had seen him work once and there was something chilling about watching Tony staring into a young woman's eyes and then leading her onto the stage where she would bark like a dog at his command. Tony had been brought into the Magic Men to concentrate on what Major Gormley called 'mind-games'. And in this he had certainly succeeded.

After Tony, a comedy dance troupe practised tapdancing to 'Colonel Bogey'. Then a woman with a voice like a corncrake trilled her way through 'Cherry Ripe'. Max took the stage still shaking her top notes out of his ears.

'Hello, Max. Good to see you again.'

'Hello, Franz. How are you?'

The musical director at the Theatre Royal was a once-famous violinist, a German Jew who had been interned during the war. He had always been good to Max (a conductor can ruin a young pro's act—starting too late or too early, drowning out his gags) and now seemed genuinely moved to see him again. Max felt a stab of guilt. He had always meant to write to Franz on the Isle of Man, but had got no further than buying a postcard of a Stradivarius, which he had never got round to sending.

'The usual tab music, Mr Mephisto?'

'If you would, maestro.'

Max always came on to a slow arrangement of the 'Danse Macabre'. It was slower than ever here as one violin seemed to be lagging behind the others. Franz grimaced up at Max. 'Vienna Philharmonic it isn't.'

'It's fine. Thank you.'

Max went through the music for each trick—the build-up, the misdirection, raising the stakes, the reveal. He was aware that he was rushing, half his mind on Tony Mulholland. Why was he in

Brighton? He must have known that Max was on the bill, given that his photo was plastered all over the theatre. Was it possible that Tony actually *wanted* to see him again? But, if so, why disappear like that? That was the problem with magicians, thought Max, thanking Franz and exiting stage left: they always knew how to disappear.

Max made his way towards the entrance hall. He was meeting Edgar at a cafe in the Pavilion Gardens and thought he could do with a walk and a smoke first. He passed the bar (which had a convenient hatch that opened onto the stage) and pushed open the swing doors. The foyer at the Theatre Royal sloped steeply downwards. It was like being onboard ship. The little gold chairs on either side of the fireplace seemed almost to be moving, sliding slowly southwards. Max had a sudden vision of the *Titanic* tilting into the sea while the orchestra (hopefully in better tune than this one) played on. As he stood, disorientated for a moment, a man stepped out from behind a potted plant.

'Max. Long time no see.'

'Hello, Tony.'

'Still the same. The Great Max Mephisto.'

Max noted the mockery behind the words, but elected to take them at face value. 'Thank you. I'm surprised to see you here. I thought you'd given up the business.'

Tony shrugged. He looked older, thought Max,

thinner and more wary. It suited him though, and the sharp suit hung elegantly on his spare frame. His voice had changed too. When Max had met him, Tony had been working hard to eradicate his Cockney accent. Now it was back with a vengeance, almost a swagger.

'Well, you can't get the business out of your blood. You know that, me old china.'

Me old china. Was this some kind of a nightmare?

'Are you doing a magic act?' If so, Max added silently, I'll sue you.

'Magic. Nah!' Exaggerated shudder. 'Magic's old hat, mate. I'm a comedian now.'

'You must tell me some jokes some time,' said Max, edging his way past Tony and towards the daylight.

Tony put out a hand to stop him. For the first time, his voice lost its exuberant edge, in fact now it sounded almost pleading.

'Why don't we get together after the show tonight, Max? Talk about old times.'

Max couldn't think of anything he'd like less, but one thing was certain: he wasn't going to suffer alone.

'All right. We can ask Edgar too. Edgar Stephens. Did you know he was living in Brighton?'

Now Tony looked quite delighted. 'No! Good old Ed. What's he doing these days?'

'He's a policeman,' said Max and, as he walked

through the swing doors, he was still smiling at the look of sheer incredulity on Tony's face.

So Tony Mulholland had reinvented himself as a comedian. That explained a lot. It explained why Tony could share the bill with him, it explained the Cockney accent and the sharp suit. It even explained the boxes at the stage door (AM for Anthony Mulholland). But it didn't altogether explain why Tony was in Brighton in the first place.

CHAPTER 6

Edgar watched Max walking across the grass towards him. You'd know he was a theatrical at once. Was it the well-cut jacket or the fact that he was wearing a cravat rather than a tie? Perhaps it was just his height and general air of well-being. Men in 1950s England didn't, in general, look tanned and healthy. There was something unEnglish too about Max's jet-black hair and the gleam of his white teeth. He strolled through the picnicking families like Moses crossing the Red Sea. Moses in Italian shoes.

Max sat opposite Edgar and ordered coffee from the hovering waitress.

'Guess who I've just seen.'

'The Theatre Royal ghost?'

'Tony Mulholland.'

'My God.' Edgar leant back in his chair. 'What was he doing?'

'He's on the bill with me.'

'No! I thought he'd left the stage. I thought he was busy being a captain of industry somewhere.'

'He informs me that he's become a comedian.'

Edgar pulled a face. 'Can't say he's ever made me laugh.'

'No, nor me. But, like I was saying in Eastbourne, the money's in comedy these days. And Tony always wants to be where the money is.'

'Wonder what his act's like?'

'You can see it tonight if you like. Tony suggested that we all go for a meal after the show.'

'A Magic Men reunion. Very jolly.'

'Very.' Max lit a cigarette. 'So, what have you found out about Ethel?'

'I contacted the husband,' said Edgar. 'He said that he hadn't seen her for a year. He identified her from the photographs.'

'She didn't mention anything on her Christmas card about being separated.'

'Well, it's not the sort of thing you put on a card, is it?'

'I suppose not. Have you any idea why she was in Brighton?'

'I tracked down her lodgings. She was staying up near the station. We searched the rooms and found this.'

He smoothed out a crumpled piece of paper torn from a newspaper and pushed it towards Max.

It was an advertisement, carefully cut out. 'Girl Wanted' was the headline.

> Girl wanted for magic act. Must be supple and strong. Contact PO Box 4700.

Max looked at it in silence for a moment. 'Is this from *Variety*?'

'That's the interesting bit,' said Edgar. 'It looks as if it's from a paper, but we checked *Variety* and the advertisement never appeared there. If you look closely, you'll see that the typeface is different.'

'What does that mean?'

'It means that this advertisement was specially written for Ethel. Probably pushed through her front door. We didn't find an envelope. Doesn't mean there wasn't one though.'

'What about the PO Box?'

'We contacted the Post Office,' said Edgar. 'The PO box was arranged and paid for by letter. Signed Hugh D. Nee.'

'He's a class act, our bloke.'

'We don't even know that it is a bloke.'

'Come on. You have to be pretty strong to cut a girl in three. And Ethel would have put up a fight, believe me.' Max was silent for a few minutes, shielding his eyes with his hand. Then he said,

'Girl Wanted. She was better than that. She was a star, Ethel.'

'Whoever wrote this advertisement must have known that she'd been in a magic act.'

'Who would want to kill a girl from a magic act?'

'That's what we're asking ourselves,' said Edgar dryly. After a pause he said, 'We think she may have been drugged. Our medical chap said her eyes were dilated. He thought she could have been given drops containing deadly nightshade. Belladonna.'

'Belladonna,' repeated Max. Then, almost pleadingly, 'If she was drugged, she wouldn't have suffered, would she?'

'No,' lied Edgar. They sat in silence for a few minutes as the pigeons pecked the crumbs around their feet. Outside the theatre someone was playing the accordion. 'The Rose of Tralee'. Then Edgar said, 'We found this in her room too.' He took out another newspaper cutting, this time carefully folded, and offered it to Max.

It was a newspaper review, dated November 1949. The yellowing paper showed Max grinning as he pulled roses from his hat. *Max Mephisto Mesmerises in Manchester.*

Back at the Old Ship, Max was informed that 'a lady was waiting for him'. He wasn't surprised. He needed a new girl for his act and a fellow magician had suggested someone who had once worked as his assistant, a Miss French. It struck Max that he could so easily have placed a 'Girl Wanted' advertisement in *Variety*. This thought didn't exactly put a spring in his step as he walked towards the lounge where the girl was waiting. No, not a girl, a 'lady'. *That* was what had surprised him.

His first glance corroborated the porter's judgement. Well-cut suit, good shoes, tasteful hat. She looked like a conventional well-brought-up girl: convent school, Pitman's typing course, perhaps even a year in Switzerland. In short, not at all the sort of girl who usually applied to be a conjuror's assistant. Ethel, for instance, had been a fishmonger's daughter. Like Molly Malone. Another waif who came to a tragic end.

'Miss French?' Max doffed his hat.

'Yes. Are you Max Mephisto?'

'At your service.' To his own ears he sounded like a parody of himself.

'You look older than in your posters.'

'That's magic for you.'

She smiled, a wide grin that suddenly made her look much younger. She seemed to regret this unbending because she composed herself again immediately, eyes downcast.

'May I?' Max took the seat next to her. Good hands too, he noticed. Well-kept nails.

'I understand that you've had some experience

with Ray Fellows.' Aka The Great Raymondo.

'Yes,' she said. 'I did a season with him in Hastings.'

'What did you do?'

'Various box tricks. Sawing in half, disappearing, that sort of thing.'

'The Selbit?'

'Yes and The Bowsaw.'

'Selbit was the first person to use a girl, you know. Before him, assistants were always men.'

A glimmer of that smile again. 'Girls bring in the crowds. That's what Ray used to say.'

'Ever do The Zig Zag Girl?'

'No. Is that what you're going to do in your act?'

'No.' If Max was sure of one thing, it was that he'd never do that trick again.

'What are you going to do?'

'It's a version of The Blade Box. Have you ever done anything like that?'

'No. Ray steered clear of knives.'

'Very sensible. Essentially, it's just another box trick. The cabinet is deeper than it looks. You flatten yourself against the back. I put the swords in one by one and take them out one by one. It can be very tedious, but my way's a bit different.'

'Ray said you always had a special way of doing things.'

'Very kind of him. Well, Miss French, are you interested?'

'Oh yes,' she said composedly.

By now he was definitely intrigued. 'Tell me a bit about yourself. What's your first name?'

'Ruby.'

'How old are you, Ruby?'

'I'm twenty.'

'Unlike me, you look younger than your years.'

He had wanted to make her blush, but she continued to meet his gaze calmly. Her eyes were brown with very white whites.

'What have you been doing since you left school?'

'This and that. I lived in France for a while. Now I'm a secretary for an insurance company.'

I was right about the Pitman's, he thought.

'And you want to be a magician's assistant?'

This time the colour did flood her cheeks and she lifted her head defiantly. 'No. I want to be a magician.'

CHAPTER 7

Max couldn't bring himself to watch Tony's act. From his dressing room he could hear some fairly decent laughs, but with satisfyingly long pauses in between. The audience obviously didn't know quite what to make of Tony's cheeky chappy persona. Max half-expected Tony to appear at his dressing room door, boasting of how well he had done, and was very glad when his solitude remained undisturbed. He heard the music for Geronimo start up (loud enough to drown out the sound of crashing clubs), and went back to playing Patience.

Once again, Max was the last act on the bill. Waiting for his entrance, he watched the chorus girls high-kicking their way through the can-can. The stage was small, so the end girls were almost completely hidden from the audience. A good thing too, from what Max could see. The girls clattered past, panting and giggling. As they ran up the stone stairs, Max could see Tony standing in the shadows watching them. He was just the sort of man to stare at chorus girls. The 'Danse Macabre' started up, floating hesitantly across the footlights. Max waited for his bar and then strolled on stage, adjusting his bow tie. They were the same as any audience anywhere, an amorphous mass who could be made to breathe and think as one. Monday first house was notoriously tough because that was when the landladies got their free tickets. An audience full of landladies was enough to reduce seasoned pros to tears. But in Brighton it was always a slightly more cosmopolitan and forgiving crowd. Certainly, Max felt himself riding on what was almost a cloud of goodwill. He knew that he was working well. The laughs came easily and, when he pulled the pearls from the handbag of a stout dowager in the front row, there was a genuine 'ooh' of delight.

He had decided that the girl in the audience trick had become a bit tired. If people came to more than one show, they would be sure to notice that it was always the same person pulled from the audience, a 'stick' they were called in the trade. So he had asked Ruby to come on stage with the cabinet. She still had her old costumes, she said. They had run through the act that afternoon with Ruby in her little blue suit, as efficient as the secretary she claimed to be. So Max's double-take as the sequinned, fish-netted figure pirouetted onto the boards was completely unstaged. And she was good. As Max twirled the cabinet round and plunged the swords into the floorboards, she was always in the right place. A wiggle of feathers disguised the moment when the false back was facing towards the audience, a sidestep allowed Max to place the cabinet exactly on its mark. She knew the trick, Max realised. Was she planning to perform it herself one day?

Max had seen The Sword Cabinet performed in Italy when a magician cut through a melon to show the sharpness of his blade. It worked very well, the texture of the fruit and the fact that it was about the size of a human head added to the fear factor. But melons were in short supply in England, so Max used an apple. He liked the whole Adam and Eve connotation, but it did

73

mean that you had to get your slice right. Ruby placed the apple on the stage and Max raised his sword. He saw the blade flash in the lights and then it came fizzing down through the apple to crash into the boards. 'No drum roll,' he told Franz. 'I need the sound of the sword on the wood.'

Ruby pranced into the cabinet. Her last smile to the audience was nine-tenths composure and one-tenth fear. Max didn't know if the apprehension was acting or not, but it was very effective. Now the drums rolled and Max plunged in the swords one by one. He knew Ruby was in place because she had tapped twice on the side of the cabinet (inaudible beneath the crashing timpani). Even so, he felt a sudden unreasonable fear for her, thinking of Ethel—so trusting, so desperate— offering herself to a man who actually did cut her into pieces. Glancing into the wings, he saw that Tony Mulholland was still there, watching. What was he playing at? It was an unspoken rule that you never watched a magician work from backstage. Was Tony trying to steal his act after all? When all the swords were in place, Max spun the cabinet, showing that the long foils had gone all the way through. The tips at the back were fakes, added from the inside by Ruby. The audience gasped, the orchestra reached a crescendo and Max started to withdraw the swords, one by one, stretching the moment to breaking point. When Ruby emerged, smiling and waving, she caught his eye and winked. For a second, just for a second, he felt completely at a loss.

'I like your new assistant,' said Tony. 'She's cute.'

'Cute?' said Max. 'Did you make that trip to America after all?'

'She was good,' said Edgar hastily. 'Where did you find her?'

'She worked with another magician,' said Max. 'He recommended her. She's not a permanent fixture though. Just for this week.'

'Love 'em and leave 'em, eh, Max?' Tony downed his drink. 'You haven't changed.'

They were in a small French restaurant. It had been recommended by Franz, the conductor at the theatre, so, predictably, the food was bad but the band was good. Tony hardly seemed to notice what he was eating. He was knocking back the wine and boasting about his prowess on stage and off. Though from what Edgar had seen of his act, Tony wasn't quite ready to storm Hollywood just yet. Tony declared himself 'in the vanguard of comedy', and certainly the audience at the Theatre Royal hadn't known quite what to make of the angry young man in the American suit who refused to tell them any jokes. The most successful part of his performance had been when he had performed mind-tricks on members of the audience. 'What colour are you thinking of?' That sort of thing. Max looked irritated and said that

75

this was classed as magic, but Edgar thought that it was more like being stuck with a bore on the train. Tony was asking the questions, but he was only really interested in his own responses. 'Red!' he cried out triumphantly. 'He's thinking of red.'

'It's always red with the men,' he told them, 'blue with the girls.'

'But what if it wasn't red?' asked Edgar. Green was his favourite colour.

'Oh, they always agree,' said Tony. 'The trick is making them think that they were thinking of red.'

'What if they say something surprising?' asked Edgar.

'Ah,' said Tony, 'you must never show you're surprised. That's the magic of it.'

'It's not magic,' Max said grumpily.

The band segued into another little Hungarian number. They were the only diners left in the place and the waiter looked as if he couldn't wait to see the back of them. Tony, though, called for more wine.

'It's a reunion,' he said. 'A Magic Men reunion.'

'Why so nostalgic about the Magic Men, Tony?' asked Max. 'You didn't seem so keen at the time.'

Tony didn't seem to hear him. 'Do you see anything of Bill these days? And what about Major Gormley?'

'Major Gormley's retired,' said Edgar. 'Lives on the south coast somewhere. Bill's married. Lives in London, I think.'

'So old Bill got married,' Tony filled Max's glass, spilling some in the process. 'I thought he'd never get over Charis.'

Edgar didn't look at Max. He watched the wine stain spreading on the tablecloth. It had started as roughly the shape of Italy, but now seemed to be forming the rest of Europe, like one of the maps at the start of the war showing the Nazis advancing.

'None of us will get over Charis,' Max said roughly. 'Let's talk about something else.'

'But Bill really loved that girl,' Tony was saying, his voice thickening with claret-sodden emotion. 'He really loved her. You know, I still can't believe that she's dead.' I loved her, Edgar wanted to say. I loved her and she loved me. But it had been Bill that she had chosen in the end. Bill who, when Charis was killed, had had the status almost of widower. Now he was a husband.

'It was a long time ago,' said Max. 'A lot has changed since then.'

'Yes,' said Tony, 'I'm a comedian and Edgar's a policeman. But you're still a magician.'

'I'll always be a magician,' said Max, lighting a cigarette. 'I don't know how to do anything else.'

'You'll have to think of something soon,' said Tony. 'Variety's on its last legs. When I was in the States . . .' He shot a sidelong glance at Max. 'It was all about television. Have you heard of Milton Berle? He's a comedian, a huge television star. That's where the money is these days, believe me. But magic would never work on television. People need to watch magicians up close. No, you're finished, my friend.' He lapsed in silence.

'Television will never take off in Britain,' said Edgar. 'I can't imagine people gathered round one of those boxes watching fuzzy little shapes. It's not like the wireless.'

Tony's burst of eloquence seemed to have exhausted him. He slumped in his chair, ash from his cigar dropping on the floor. Max gestured for the bill.

'Let's get the great television star home,' he said. 'I've got a hard day's magic ahead of me tomorrow.'

Edgar got out his wallet, but Max waved him away. 'I may be finished,' he said dryly. 'But I can still pay the bill.'

CHAPTER 8

The view from the cemetery was spectacular: gently rolling fields, a perfectly positioned windmill, the houses making a soft smudge in the valley. And the sea, the picture-postcard sea, encircling them, making the outskirts of Brighton feel like Amalfi or some Caribbean island. Max was pleased that Ethel would rest in such a lovely place, a location suited to her mysterious exoticism, so unexpected in a fishmonger's daughter from Margate. It was less fitting though that her only mourners should be Edgar and Max. Max who hadn't seen Ethel in twelve years and Edgar who never knew her at all.

It was Wednesday morning, halfway through the run at the Theatre Royal. In only a few days, thought Max, I can leave this place and never come back. I can leave England and never come back. He had forgotten that he identified with Brighton's raffish glamour. Just at this moment, Brighton was the town where Ethel had died. And who would visit her grave, up here on the lonely hillside?

Max had paid for the headstone. 'I haven't the money to spare,' said her husband, when Max had telephoned him. Nor the time, apparently. It was from the husband, though, that Max had obtained the bare biographical details inscribed on the stone.

Ethel Williams (née Townsend)
1920–50.
A Shining Star.

He had added the 'née' because he wanted to remember her before she had met Michael Williams and buried herself in the Isle of Wight. Why had she left Williams? Why had she ended up in Brighton, answering 'Girl Wanted' advertisements? If she was in trouble, why didn't she come to him? She'd kept the cutting from Manchester, she must have known that he was still on the circuit. Maybe she thought that he had lost interest in her. That was what hurt most of all.

'Maybe she was ashamed,' said Edgar as they stood looking out over the sea. The entire service and burial had taken less than half an hour.

'Ashamed of what?'

'That her marriage failed, that she wasn't a success. All sorts of things.'

'She was only thirty,' said Max. 'What a waste.'

'My age,' said Edgar.

'Thirty's still young,' said Max, lighting a cigarette. 'Believe me, I'd kill to be thirty again.'

He wished he hadn't put it quite like that, but Edgar didn't seem to notice anything amiss. He was breathing in the hill-top air like a man who spent his life indoors. For his part, Max could never see what was so great about the country-side. Give him a London club any day, a whisky in his hand and the promise of a show in the evening. And mornings were overrated too. Like all pros, he was a creature of the night.

They walked back towards Max's car, looking absurdly opulent beside the vicar's rusty Morris.

'Where to?' asked Max, getting behind the wheel.

'The station,' said Edgar. 'We're following up possible sightings of the man who left the boxes at the station.'

'Do you think you'll find anything?'

'No.' Edgar sighed. He was fiddling with the window handle. Max wished he would stop. 'Too much time has gone past. They can all remember a tall, short, thin, fat man who might or might not have had a German accent.'

They were passing the racecourse, two horses jogging along by the side of the road, their quarters swinging out as if they couldn't bear the slow pace for a moment longer.

'Ah, the old German accent,' said Max. 'Some things never change. What about the handwriting on the letter, the letter to the Post Office? The one signed Hugh D. Nee.'

'It was typed. We can even track down the make of typewriter, but it doesn't get us very far.'

'Did Ethel have any visitors at her digs?'

'No. The neighbours all said that she was a very respectable lady. Kept herself to herself. No gentleman callers.'

Max felt oddly relieved to hear this. Ethel may have fallen, but not into the abyss. Yet, if she had been a prostitute, maybe she would have had someone to protect her. Maybe it would have been better if she wasn't respectable to the end.

'What about the husband?' he asked. 'Does he have an alibi?'

'He was the first person we thought of,' said Edgar. 'It's usually the husband, that's what my boss always says. But he's got an alibi. He was on duty that day.'

'Still a fireman then?'

'Yes. Calls himself Leading Fireman Williams.'

'Idiot,' said Max. He had never met Williams, but this didn't stop him from disliking him cordially. He disliked him even when all he knew of him was his name scrawled on Christmas cards.

'I'm going to see him tomorrow,' said Edgar. 'See if he can tell me anything about Ethel's last movements. He was pretty reluctant to meet me.'

'So he might have something to hide.'

'Maybe just doesn't like talking about his private life. He seemed the taciturn type.'

'They're just the types that become murderers,' said Max.

They drove down Bear Road, back into Brighton. There was another crematorium here and they stopped to let a hearse go by. 'The dead centre of town,' Bob Willis called it.

Max crossed himself, a gesture that suddenly made him look completely alien. He saw Edgar looking, and grimaced. 'Catholic reflex.'

'I didn't think you believed in God.'

'The question is,' said Max, putting the car into gear, 'does he believe in me?'

'I'm sure he does,' said Edgar. 'Everyone believes in you.'

Max grinned, registering the irony. 'Well, we did get good reviews last night.'

'So the Brighton *Evening Argus* believes in you. That's something.'

'It certainly is. Did you see what they said about Tony?'

'I didn't read it.' Bob had shown him the review that morning, but for some reason Edgar didn't want to admit this.

'Mr Mulholland clearly believes himself to be psychic,' quoted Max. 'It's a pity that he couldn't have predicted the audience's reaction at the Theatre Royal last night.'

'Gosh. Do you think Tony saw that?'

'Of course he did. All pros read their reviews, even if they say they don't.'

As Edgar remembered, the paper had rhapsodised over Max's 'thrilling stage presence' and his 'effortless manipulation of the audience'. He felt sure that Max must have read the piece several times over.

'What's next?' he asked. 'Where are you going next week?' He wondered what it was like, not having a real home, changing your backdrop every week, like stage scenery. To be honest, it sounded pretty damn enticing at the moment.

'I'm going to take a holiday,' said Max. 'Go abroad for a few weeks.'

'It's all right for some.'

'Come with me,' said Max lightly. 'See something of the world.'

'I can't,' said Edgar. 'I've got to make some

progress on the case. According to my boss, no woman in Brighton can sleep safely until he's caught.'

'Oh, he won't kill again,' said Max, accelerating smoothly. 'A trick like that, it's a show-stopper. What an earth can he do for an encore?'

'I don't like to think,' said Edgar.

Max dropped Edgar back at the station. After the air up on the race hill, descending the stairs to the CID offices felt like entering a tomb. Bob was sitting at Edgar's desk, doing a crossword.

'Haven't you got anything better to do?' asked Edgar.

'It's my lunch hour.'

Edgar itched to have a go at the crossword. It was only the quick version, but it seemed to be giving Bob some trouble. He was stuck on one down, 'devil of a cut', four letters.

'I'm going to the Isle of Wight tomorrow,' said Edgar. 'Can you get someone to look up the ferry times for me?'

'All right,' said Bob.

'Yes, sir,' Edgar corrected him, but silently. Somehow people never seemed to call him sir.

He could see Bob wanted to ask him why he was going to the Isle of Wight. Was it just a day trip, or something to do with the case? The silent scrutiny was starting to get to him.

'I'm going out,' he said. 'Get some fresh air.'

You've been out all morning, said Bob's body language.

At the door, Edgar paused. 'Nick,' he said.

'Pardon?'

'One down. Nick.' And he made for the stairs.

Edgar walked briskly through the Lanes. Then he remembered that it was his lunch hour too and stopped at a Lyons Corner House for a roll and a cup of tea. The place was packed and he had to share his table with a holidaying family, complete with buckets, spades and quarrelsome mongrel. The children were arguing about whether they could go on the Volks Railway. 'But you *said* . . .' Edgar couldn't remember arguing with his parents, though he supposed it must have happened. Lucy went in for occasional explosions and stompings upstairs, but he and Jonathan had been quieter, more secretive about their emotions. Anyway, theirs had not been a family that talked much about its feelings. He could barely remember any holidays, come to think of it. There had been a trip to a bed and breakfast in Weston-super-Mare, but his mother had been so worried about them 'being in the way' (they had to leave their rooms after breakfast and not return until supper-time), that this too had been an oddly furtive affair. Trips with Uncle Charlie had been more fun. He would have allowed them to go on the railway and eat candy-floss too. Edgar smiled apologetically at the family, removed his trouser leg from the dog and made his way out of the cafe.

He walked back along the seafront. He still couldn't get used to the daily miracle that was the sea, its rushings and rustlings, the white-topped breakers in the winter, the days when water and horizon merged into one. Today, the beach looked almost inviting, the tide out to reveal a thin band of sand. Children were paddling in the shallows and adults sat in deckchairs, trying not to notice the wind that sent the occasional newspaper flying into the air like a demented seagull. Edgar had been swimming once since coming to Brighton, an icy plunge from the breakwater. He had emerged almost paralysed with shock, wondering if he was going to have a heart attack. Was that what it had been like for Jonathan in Dunkirk? he wondered. Had the cold numbed the pain? He hoped so.

As he stood looking out over the scene, he was aware of a young woman standing near to him. Something in her pose, straight back, head tilted slightly, seemed familiar. He had actually started to walk away before he realised who she was. He backtracked.

'Ruby?'

She turned. She obviously didn't recognise him, but she was smiling all the same. For some reason this struck him as incredibly endearing.

'Ruby? We met on Monday after the show. I'm Edgar Stephens. Max's friend.'

'Oh yes,' said Ruby, smiling more widely. 'The policeman.'

That wasn't quite how Edgar wanted to be remembered. PC Plod, eternal figure of fun. But he smiled and said yes, he was a policeman.

'Max said that you'd served in the war together.'

Was it his imagination or did she blush when she said Max's name?

'That's right. It seems a long time ago now.'

'I can't imagine Max in the army.'

'He was exactly the same then as he is now.'

People said that actors were chameleons, all things to all men, but what always struck Edgar was their ability to remain unchanged whatever the circumstances. Put Max or Diablo in the desert or the jungle or adrift on the open sea and they would always remain exactly themselves.

'Are you walking that way?' said Ruby. 'I'll go with you.'

Edgar was surprised at the rush of pleasure that came over him at the thought of walking with Ruby. He hastened to fall in with this plan and was only slightly disappointed when, skipping along at his side, she proceeded to talk about Max.

'Is it true that his father is a lord?'

'Yes,' said Edgar. He didn't think that this could be a secret, it was common knowledge in the press after all ('The Hon Max swaps stately home for a life on the boards').

'What does he think about Max being on the stage?'

'I don't think he's too keen.' Edgar had never met Max's father, but from Max's occasional comments he gathered that Lord Massingham was not a fan of showbusiness.

'It's funny,' said Ruby, looking up at him in a way that made Edgar wish that they could change the subject. 'Max isn't what I expected. People in the business talk about him as if he's some sort of dark genius, as if he's Count Dracula or something. There are all these stories going round. I was terrified at the thought of working with him. But he's really nice, so polite and considerate.'

Polite and considerate. At least it didn't sound as if she were in love with him.

'How long have you been on the stage?' he asked. He hadn't missed the self-conscious pause before 'in the business'.

Ruby laughed. 'This is only my second job. I worked with a magician called The Great Raymondo before. He wasn't that great, to be honest, but I've always been fascinated by magic. I used to do card tricks for my mum. I sent away for this conjuring set, exploding cigarettes, handkerchiefs tied together, that sort of thing. I'm sure I drove everyone mad.'

She said this with the breezy confidence of one who has been adored all her life.

'So you want to be a magician.'

'Yes.' A defiant tilt to the head. 'You probably think it's impossible for a girl to be a magician.'

'No, I . . .'

'There was this woman called Eusapia Palladino in Italy at the end of the last century. She was married to a magician, but she became famous in her own right. She could levitate tables and play instruments without touching them.'

'Amazing,' said Edgar politely. He imagined that evenings at Eusapia's house were a riot.

'But she did all this mediumistic stuff. I wouldn't do that. I'd concentrate on pure magic.'

Pure magic. It sounded both innocent and rather terrifying. Edgar imagined Ruby in the world described by Max; a different boarding house each week, changeover on Sunday, the endless round of dressing rooms and band calls.

'It's a tough life, being on stage,' he said.

'That's what my mother says.' Ruby was silent for a moment. She was so much smaller than him that he could look down on the top of her head. It made him feel protective.

They had reached the Grand, where Edgar usually crossed the road. He hesitated, not wanting to end the walk, but Ruby said, 'Are you crossing here? I'll walk on a bit further.'

'Goodbye then.' Edgar went to raise his hat and realised that he wasn't wearing one. 'Good luck for the rest of the week.'

'Thank you,' said Ruby. 'It's not easy, being stabbed to death every night.'

Something in the way she said this made Edgar feel suddenly afraid. He wanted to tell her not to go back to the theatre, not to enter the cabinet and face the shining swords. But Ruby was smiling so he had to smile too, raise his non-existent hat and say that he hoped they'd meet again some day.

It was only as he was nearly back at the station when he remembered that, in the theatrical world, the words 'good luck' are considered extremely unlucky.

CHAPTER 9

Edgar enjoyed the ferry crossing. It was a bright day, but the wind was strong. He stood on deck and felt the salt spray on his face, forgetting everything except the still surprising pleasure of being alive. After Jonathan died, he had assumed that he was next. Even when he was sent up to Scotland, to the sinecure that was the Magic Men, he had thought that a stray bullet would get him. An exploding top hat perhaps, or a man-eating rabbit. To have survived the war still seemed wrong somehow. Why should he be out in the sun and the wind when Jonathan and Charis were buried? Actually, he didn't have a grave for either of them, which somehow made the whole thing harder to believe. Edgar gripped the deck rail and tried to forget the past.

Leading Fireman Williams had given him an address in Newport. Edgar was surprised to find that it was quite a big town. His view of the island was coloured by a long-ago school trip, and he remembered only stripy cliffs, a gift shop and a house that belonged to Queen Victoria. He remembered trailing around the house and gardens with a lot of other bored schoolboys: rooms with high ceilings and glittering objects in glass cases, formal gardens and a fountain where Tomkins Minor took an impromptu bath. The place seemed frozen in the nineteenth century. Hadn't Tennyson lived on the Isle of Wight too? He imagined them all drifting about, in their frock coats and crinolines, writing poetry to each other. So Newport, with its bustling high street, was a shock. There was even a policeman directing traffic around a statue of Queen Victoria (at least she was still in residence).

The Williamses lived above a haberdashery. Edgar climbed the narrow stairs wondering about Ethel. He knew nothing about her, this woman he'd known only in death. Max had said that she was a star. Would a star have been happy, living above a shop in Newport High Street? And what about the man who'd lived there with her?

Michael Williams, a short belligerent-looking man with a high colour, was waiting for him in the spotless sitting room. He may have missed his wife, thought Edgar, but he'd obviously got someone else in to do the cleaning.

'I'm sorry,' Edgar began. 'I know it must be difficult talking about Mrs Williams.'

Williams shrugged. 'She left me, didn't she?'

Edgar got out his notebook. 'I wonder if you could tell me when she left? I'm trying to account for Mrs Williams' movements up until the time of her death.'

'Mrs Williams,' said the fireman. 'Can't believe she was still using my name. Wanted to forget all about me, that's what she said.'

'When did she say that?'

'A year ago. It happened last summer. When *he* came to the island.'

'He?'

'Him,' Williams glared at Edgar as if he were being deliberately obtuse. 'Max Mephisto.'

'Max came to visit Ethel?' Edgar was shocked into first names, but Williams didn't seem to notice. He was clearly being driven mad by Edgar's stupidity.

'No, of course not. Why would he come here? A man like that. No, he was appearing at the Pavilion on Sandown Pier. We went to see him. That's what a fool I was. I didn't know.'

'What didn't you know?'

'About her and him. Oh, I knew she'd been in the theatre. I knew she'd been his assistant. I was prepared to overlook that. We've never had anyone showbusiness in the family. My family are chapel, very respectable. But Ethel was young. She would learn, my mum said. She'd learn to be a good wife.'

'And did she?'

Williams snorted. 'What do you think? She hadn't the faintest idea about keeping the place nice. I did all that.' He looked round the room complacently. 'It's a darn sight cleaner now than when she was here, I can tell you. But she was a pretty little thing. She didn't have much of a childhood. Never knew her mum, her dad threw her out when she was sixteen. I thought I'd give her a proper home.' For the first time his voice softened.

'How did you meet Ethel . . . Mrs Williams?'

'I was on holiday, staying at a place just outside Brighton. Butlin's Ocean Hotel. Ethel was the pro.' He saw Edgar's look of enquiry. 'The professional dancer.'

'She wasn't working with Max Mephisto then?'

'It was the summer. She was going to go back to do the Christmas season with him, but I got there first.' There was a real sound of triumph in his voice. 'I asked her to marry me and she said yes.'

'How long had you been married when . . . when she left?'

'Ten years.' He gave a bitter laugh. 'Ten years. Bloody tin anniversary, according to my mum.

Things hadn't been easy. There was the war. We were totally cut off here on the island. I wasn't called up.' He shot a look at Edgar. 'Reserved occupation.'

'Can't be an easy job being a fireman.'

Williams seemed to relax slightly. 'You can say that again. The things I've seen. I was in London in the Blitz.'

'So Ethel was here on her own?'

'Yes. My mum was always good to her, but I think Ethel was a bit lonely. Like I say, she wasn't the domestic type.'

'And after the war?'

'We tried to start again. That wasn't easy either. We wanted to start a family. When Ethel got pregnant, I really thought things were going to be better for us. Then she lost the baby.'

'That must have been hard.'

Williams looked away. 'Ethel was really cut up about it. That's why I took her to the show on the pier. I thought it would cheer her up. That's how much of a mug I was. There was no travel during the war, you see, so there were no shows on the island, just amateur stuff. When the restrictions were lifted, the big names started to come. I thought it'd be a treat for Eth. She kept in touch with him. Mephisto. She used to send him cards every Christmas. Put both our names on them, sweet as pie, but you have to ask yourself, why's your wife sending cards to another man?'

Edgar thought that he'd better not answer this. Instead he said, 'So you went to see Max Mephisto on Sandown Pier.'

'Yes.' Williams sat back and crossed his arms, looking more pugnacious than ever. 'He was a fair magician, I'll give him that. Very fair indeed. He did this trick where he put a girl into a box, just an ordinary cardboard box, then he stuck swords through it.'

Edgar thought of Ruby on the stage at the Theatre Royal. He was glad that Max had used a traditional cabinet and not a box. He didn't think he could stand the thought that it was only cardboard that protected Ruby from the blades.

'It upset Ethel,' said Williams.

'Seeing the swords go into the box? That upset her?'

'No.' Once again that jeering note. 'It upset her to see another girl performing with Mephisto. She kept saying, "That used to be me. I used to be his girl." That's what she actually said. "I used to be his girl."'

Despite himself, Edgar felt sorry for the angry little man. He had tried to cheer up his discontented wife, only to have her hankering after the man on the stage. Williams had loved her, he thought. He hadn't missed the significance of the 'Eth'. He thought of Ethel, the glamorous showgirl imprisoned on the Victorian island, like a princess in a tower. What must it have been like for her, stuck on the Isle of Wight for the duration of the war with only her mother-in-law (who sounded a bit like Edgar's own mother) for company? Then to lose a baby and, maybe, her last grasp at a happy marriage. What would have happened if Ethel hadn't seen Max on stage and been reminded of her other life? Maybe she would have had another baby and settled down with Williams. It was impossible to tell. But Ethel had ended up in Brighton, the victim of a sadistic killer. Brighton was the place where she had met her husband. What had drawn her back there?

'She left the next day,' said Michael Williams. 'Left a note saying that she was going back to the stage. Said she wanted to forget all about her life here.'

'Did you hear from her again?'

'No. Not till you telephoned to tell me she was . . . to tell me that you'd found her. I assumed she was with him.'

'She wasn't.'

'But there was something between them, wasn't there? He paid for the headstone and everything. Why would he do that if he didn't feel guilty?'

Max did feel guilty, thought Edgar. He knew that he was to blame, even if he didn't know the details of it. He knew that Ethel had died because of her connection to him.

'Max Mephisto isn't a bad man,' he said. 'He didn't even know that Ethel had left you. He was terribly upset when he found out that she was . . .'

'That she was murdered,' finished Williams grimly. 'There you are again. People like us just don't get murdered.'

'Anyone can get murdered,' said Edgar. 'Believe me.'

CHAPTER 10

Edgar thought about Ethel a lot over the next few days. The trip to the Isle of Wight, though illuminating in some ways, hadn't really got him much further in the investigation. Ethel Townsend had met Michael Williams at Butlin's Ocean Hotel in the summer of 1938. The next year war broke out, and Williams went to fight fires on the mainland. Ethel had stayed on the island in the company of her religious and disapproving mother-in-law. After the war, she and Williams had tried to 'start again'. Ethel had got pregnant, but had lost the baby. In a doomed attempt to cheer her up, Williams had booked tickets to see Max Mephisto perform on the pier. The next day, Ethel had left him. A year later, she turned up in Brighton again, cut into three.

'She never got in touch with me,' said Max, when they met for a quick drink before the first house on Friday night. 'I wonder why.'

'We don't know what she was doing between leaving Williams and answering that advertisement. We've checked and there's no record of her appearing in any shows.'

'How long had she been in Brighton?'

'Just a few weeks, her landlady said.'

'And you've no idea where she was before?'

Edgar bristled slightly at Max's tone. 'It's harder than you think to trace someone. We contacted her father in Margate, but he said he hadn't seen her for years.'

'No. They weren't close.'

'Her landlady thought she might have been up north somewhere. And there was that clipping from Manchester.'

'You think she was there in the audience? Watching me?'

Edgar thought about how Max put this. *Watching me.* Was that what he thought it was all about, Ethel watching him? Perhaps he thought that was what everyone in the audience was doing, watching him to the exclusion of everyone else. And he could be right at that. Certainly, Ethel had left her husband the day after seeing Max on stage. Had she spent the next year following him around the country? It was possible, but Edgar didn't think that Ethel was in love with Max. Because, if so, wouldn't she have contacted him before? She certainly would have contacted him once she had left her husband. No, the truth was more complicated than that.

'The clipping was from November,' he said. 'She turned up in Brighton at the beginning of July. We've no idea what she was doing between those dates.'

Max sighed and drained his glass. 'I'd better go. Are you coming to the show tonight? I could get you a comp.'

Edgar shook his head. 'I'm exhausted. I'm going to head home.'

'I don't blame you. Life's too short to watch Tony Mulholland trying to guess people's star signs.'

As he walked home, Edgar wondered why he hadn't accepted Max's invitation. All he knew was that the last few days had given him a slight distaste for the theatre. Its lure had led Ethel to her death, that much was certain. Also, he felt obscurely irritated that Max was disappearing off to France in two days. There was nothing to stop Max going on holiday, but it just felt rather callous in the circumstances. It was all very well Max paying for a headstone and standing beside it looking sad for ten minutes, but, when all was said and done, it was business as usual. Another week, another town. Edgar had often felt, during his Magic Men days, that pros were the hardest-hearted creatures on earth and, now, here was more proof. Ethel was dead, but the show went on. Edgar had an uneasy suspicion that the only person to visit the grave on the hill would be DI Edgar Stephens. PC Muggins himself.

As for Tony, he certainly never expected to hear from him again. He and Max had poured him into his digs on Monday evening and Max reported (rather gleefully) that a vicious hangover had not improved his act. He wondered if Tony was regretting his return to the boards. Would he now fix his sights on America and television, the ultimate magic box? Edgar didn't know. He doubted whether Tony would bother keeping in touch with him. Max was one thing; Tony still courted his approval, wanted to surpass him. But Edgar, he was a nobody, a provincial police-man. He would probably appear in a future Tony Mulholland monologue as a creature of monumental stupidity, saying 'well, well, well' and bending his knees a lot.

So, all in all, he was surprised when, on Saturday morning, he was greeted by Bob with the news that a Tony Mulholland had called in. 'He wants you to meet him at his digs at one-fifteen,' said Bob, in the wooden voice he used for official messages. 'He said that he wanted to talk to you about the Magic Men.' Lapse into his normal voice. 'Who are the Magic Men?'

The precision of the timing struck Edgar as odd. He knew from Max that pros are punctual to the second when in the theatre, but are otherwise casual about time. One-fifteen was a businessman's appointment, the choice of a person so important that they measured their hours in quarters. He determined to be slightly, but pointedly, late.

Max spent Saturday lunchtime with Ruby. They had got into a routine of eating at a different restaurant every day, Max choosing places that he thought Ruby would appreciate, places off the tourist trail—or off the trail of the respectable secretary. They had eaten minestrone in subterranean Italian restaurants, sauerkraut and dumplings in Franz's kitchen and cockles from a stall by the West Pier. But today, their last day, Ruby had said there was only one thing she wanted to do. 'Eat fish and chips on the Palace Pier.' So that's what they did, sitting in deckchairs, Ruby in her neat green dress and Max in his best summer suit, taking care not to get grease on his trousers. Seagulls perched hopefully on the railing in front of them but, in Ruby's case, they were unlucky. She ate every last mouthful, popping each chip carefully into her pink-lipsticked mouth and even moistening a finger to chase the last crumbs from yesterday's *Argus*. When Max threw a piece of fish in the birds' direction, she rebuked him. 'I would have eaten that.'

'Are you starving, Miss French?'

She smiled, folding the newspaper into a perfect square. 'I have to keep my strength up, you know.

It's hard work having swords stuck into you every night.'

Max didn't respond. He was looking out towards Newhaven and Seaford. In two days' time he'd be on a ferry heading to France, the seagulls chasing in his wake. And, the way he was thinking, he might never come back.

He turned to Ruby. Her hat had blown off and she hadn't put it back on. It was a sunny day, but the wind was strong. The sea was navy-blue with white-crested waves.

'What will you do now?' he asked.

She smiled. She had one slightly chipped front tooth. 'Try to find another booking. I can't see myself going back to typing and making tea.'

'What do your parents think about that?' Max was yet to meet these mythical beings. They had a house in Hove, but Ruby didn't live with them. She shared a flat with another girl. Max had never met her either. Now she shrugged. 'I'm over eighteen.'

Ethel was thirty, he thought, but that didn't stop her being murdered.

'I'll try to help you find work,' he said, 'but promise me one thing. Promise me you'll never answer an advertisement in *Variety*.'

She laughed, not really listening, and the wind blew her dark hair around her head.

'Promise me,' he said and his tone made her look at him in surprise.

'All right,' she said. 'If it means that much to you.'

Edgar really was late by the time that he left the station. He had been held up by a woman who claimed to remember a sinister man carrying a black box into the station. The man, who was apparently small and dark, bought a bunch of flowers from the woman's stall. Edgar promised to look out for a murderous flower-loving midget and set off for Tony's lodgings at one-thirty.

He took the most direct route, along the seafront, but soon regretted this as the promenade was absolutely packed. It was a Saturday lunchtime in August and the world seemed to have come to Brighton for the day. Edgar pushed his way through the strolling, aimless bodies. He envied them. They knew nothing of murder or mutilation, these smiling, happy people. Families ate ice creams, lovers posed for photographs and an eccentric with a billboard handed out leaflets prophesying the end of the world. As he forced his way through the crowds, Edgar found himself more and more in tune with the doomsayer: 'The world will end in 1951. This is a FACT.' He wondered why the man had fixed on 1951 instead of the neater 1950. It seemed oddly arbitrary, like Tony's appointed meeting time. As he turned the corner by the Albion Hotel, another swarm of people seemed to be crossing the roundabout by the aquarium. The policemen directing the traffic had white helmets—a sure sign that it was summer—and they were having trouble clearing a space for cars. An open-top bus floundered amidst the sea of humanity. As Edgar watched, he saw a couple running across the road. They stood out, even amongst the throng. The man wore a cream-coloured suit—lighter and smarter than any other suit on the seafront—and the woman's green dress fluttered against her legs. Max and Ruby, laughing, hand in hand. Edgar watched them until they passed under the archway welcoming visitors to the Palace Pier and were lost from view.

For a moment he forgot his appointment as he stared after them. Ruby and Max. They worked together, there was no reason on earth why they shouldn't be sauntering along in the sun together. He thought of Ruby walking beside him talking about that woman magician who could levitate tables. How far would Ruby go to further her career? Polite and considerate, that was how she had described Max. He certainly looked more than polite now, holding her hand, smiling down at her. He remembered what Max had said that evening with Tony: *She's not a permanent fixture. Just for this week.* Like Ethel, like all the other girls. Edgar stood so long that the man with the bill-board was able to walk right up to him and thrust a leaflet into his hand. The world will END. We are all going to DIE.

Edgar remembered Tony's lodging house from Monday night. It was in a row of fisherman's cottages leading up from the Steine. Tony might be destined for great things but, in terms of digs, he was still mid-way down the hill. The door was opened by a young girl—barely fifteen—who told him that Mr Mulholland's room was upstairs. 'Third on the left. But I don't think he's in. I haven't seen him all day.'

She seemed to have no objection to Edgar's climbing the stairs and opening Tony's door, which wasn't locked. The room was small, just a single bed, a desk and a large wardrobe. This last was remarkable only for the large sword which had been thrust through the wood.

Edgar and the girl stood in the doorway. As they watched, blood seeped through the wardrobe door and ran along the uneven floorboards until it formed what was almost a lake around their feet.

PART 2
Misdirection

CHAPTER 11

'I don't understand. Why would someone want to kill a bloody comedian?'

'I don't understand either, sir.' Frank Hodges was glowering at Edgar as if the whole thing were his fault but, even so, Edgar found himself feeling sorry for his boss. Frank was a straightforward man: burglary, fights in dance halls, even the odd murder (a shooting, say, or a robbery gone wrong), he could cope with all that. But these killings—these elaborately staged *tricks*—it was all too much for him. He gazed at Edgar almost with entreaty; his moustache was wet where he had chewed the ends.

Averting his eyes from the facial hair, Edgar said, 'At least we've got a few leads. Tony left a message at the station saying that he wanted to talk to me about the Magic Men. I think we should look at the possibility that this murder was linked to the girl in the trunk. That's the link—the Magic Men.'

'The Magic Men. Was that the damned silly war outfit you were telling me about? The one with Max What's-his-name?'

'Max Mephisto. Yes. He's appearing at the Theatre Royal this week. Tony Mulholland was on the bill too.'

Frank's eyes bulged. 'Well, then he's our main suspect. Didn't you say he was linked to the girl, too?'

'Yes. She used to be his assistant. But Max has got an alibi for today.'

Edgar had left a message for Max at the Old Ship. When Max had called him back, he'd told him about Tony. He hadn't tried to soften the story, just told him the facts. Max was tough; he could take it.

'Jesus. Poor old Tony. What a way to die.'

'Yes.'

'Will you tell them at the theatre? I assume they'll want to know.'

'Yes. Yes, of course I will.'

'Thanks. Max?'

'What?'

'Where were you at midday today?'

Max had laughed. 'So now I'm suspect number one, am I? Well I was with Ruby all morning. We rehearsed from about ten to twelve, then we strolled down to the pier for a bite to eat.'

I saw you, Edgar wanted to say. I saw you strolling along as if you hadn't a care in the world. Even now, he felt a sour jealousy at the memory.

'Well, check his alibi,' Frank Hodges was saying. 'These showbiz types always stick together.'

They do stick together, thought Edgar, remembering the many times in Inverness when he had felt an outsider: the terminology, the in-jokes, the 'do you remember old so-and-so's'. But these chummy old memories could also conceal real resentments. Tony was hardly a likeable man, but who could possibly have hated him enough to kill him in such an awful way?

'Has Stephenson looked at the body?'

'Yes. I've just come from the mortuary.'

It was only three o'clock, but Edgar felt as if Tony had been dead for years. The discovery of the body, the screams of the landlady's daughter, the frantic call to Bob, the wait for the undertaker's van, more telephone calls, the terrible silence after he'd broken the news to Tony's mother ('Mrs Mulholland, are you still there?'), the moments when he remembered the look in Tony's eyes— shocked, scared, accusing. It all seemed to have taken forever, but it was only mid-afternoon. Max would be on stage in a few hours. 'The show must go on,' he'd said, with only a trace of irony.

'What about the girl? The landlady's daughter?' said Frank. 'She must have seen something.'

But the girl, who rejoiced in the name Desdemona, had proved to be a poor witness. 'She said she was listening to the wireless and didn't hear anything. But she admitted that the front door wasn't locked. Anyone could have just walked in and gone up to the room. There were two cups by the bed. Whoever it was, Tony drank tea with them.'

'Must have been someone he knew.'

'It's possible.' Tony hadn't been afraid of his visitor, not at first. When had the fear started? When the assailant stood up? When he brandished the sword?

'Have you sent the cups to the lab? The girl was drugged, wasn't she?'

'Yes. My bet is that they'll find the same drug in one of the cups. Tony was a strong man. It wouldn't have been easy to overcome him without drugging him first.'

'What about the sword?'

'Ornate. Looks like an antique. I'll have my men going round the shops on Monday.'

'This is Brighton. Bloody antique shops everywhere.'

Frank was a Londoner. In his view, the capital, den of vice though it undoubtedly was, was preferable to this shifty, seedy seaside place, full of actors and foreigners and men wearing perfume.

'I'll get on to it as soon as I can,' Edgar said. 'Pity it's Sunday tomorrow.'

'Have you spoken to Mulholland's parents?' asked Frank.

'Yes. They're on their way.'

Now that was an interview he wasn't looking forward to.

Max was with Roy Coulter, the theatre manager, in his office. Roy was wearing a dinner jacket, ready for the night's show. Eddie Bowen, the stage manager, was there too, more prosaically attired in overalls. It was an unwritten rule of showbusiness: only the theatre manager gets to wear a bow tie.

'We'll announce it at the start,' said Coulter. 'Mulholland was on at the beginning of the second half, wasn't he?'

'Yes,' said Max, 'Just before Geronimo.'

'I remember now,' said Coulter. 'He wanted to close the first half, but I wouldn't have it. I don't go much on comedians myself and I was right. Bloody awful act, I thought.'

Coulter stared gloomily at the playbill in front of him. He was a lugubrious man at the best of times and the gruesome murder of one of his acts hadn't made him any more cheerful. On the other hand, he didn't seem much more depressed than usual.

'We'll be short on time,' he said. 'Can you do a few more minutes, Max?'

'I suppose so.'

'I'm not asking Geronimo. He spends half his act picking up the clubs he's dropped as it is. I'll get the girls to do an extra spot.'

From what Max had seen of the chorus line, another performance from them didn't seem designed to raise the general spirits. But Coulter was right about Geronimo: by the second house the clubs would be raining down on the unfortunate orchestra.

'Who'll make the announcement?' he asked.

'I'll do it,' said Coulter. 'I don't think we'll have them asking for their money back. Mulholland wasn't much of a name anymore. Good job it wasn't you.'

'Thank you,' said Max politely.

Eddie Bowen spoke for the first time. 'It's an odd business, isn't it? I mean, Mulholland could be a bit of a bastard, but who would want to kill him? Did you say he was stabbed?'

'Yes,' said Max. Edgar had asked him not to share the details about the sword and the wardrobe, and he had been only too happy to comply. As it was, in an hour he'd have to go on stage and perform that trick.

'Maybe it was a girl,' said Coulter, 'or a jealous husband. He had an eye for the ladies, Mulholland.'

'If it's a jealous husband,' said Eddie, 'Max should watch out.'

'How's your little assistant?' asked Coulter. 'How's she taking the news?'

Max didn't like the way that Coulter's mind was working.

'I haven't told Ruby yet,' he said.

Tony's parents were a surprisingly small and timid couple. Edgar led them into the mortuary and they stood there, holding hands. Tony looked a lot better with his eyes shut and the undertakers had covered him with a sheet so you couldn't

114

see the stab wounds. The sheet was purple. Edgar supposed this was because it wouldn't show the blood, but it gave Tony a surprisingly noble look, as if he were a Roman emperor lying in state.

'It's him,' said Mrs Mulholland in a whisper. 'That's Anthony.'

The name struck at Edgar's heart. Tony—brash, confident, America-loving Tony—would never have used his full name, but to his mother he was still Anthony.

'Would you like some time alone with him?' he asked.

The Mulhollands looked scared. 'No thank you,' said Tony's father, as if Edgar had offered him a cup of tea. But, as Edgar was ushering them out, Mrs Mulholland suddenly turned and went back to the table where her son's body lay. 'Goodbye, Anthony.' Her lips brushed his forehead. Her husband didn't move from his position by the door, but he lifted his hand in a kind of farewell. Edgar led them out of the room.

In his office, he offered them drinks and tried to make things as easy as possible. He explained that he had known Tony in the war and that he would do his very best to bring his killer to justice. In the meantime, there were just a few questions he had to ask.

'Anthony had a very important job in the war,' said Mrs Mulholland. 'He was with the Secret Service.'

'I know,' said Edgar, thinking, as he had thought at the time, that the Magic Men was the least secret secret mission that he had ever encountered. Everyone in Inverness knew all about them. Tony kept himself in free drinks—and worse—by telling the locals that he was part of a crack commando team.

'When did you last see Tony?' he asked.

'Just before he came down to Brighton,' said Mr Mulholland. 'He didn't really keep in touch much. We hadn't seen him since he'd come back from America, but he called in that Saturday, all dressed up in a flash suit, box of chocolates for Mother, and told us that he was top of the bill in Brighton.'

Edgar wished Max could hear that. 'Did you come to see the show?' he asked.

'No,' said Tony's mother. 'We don't go much on Variety.'

'I'm sorry,' said Edgar, 'but I have to ask. Did Tony have any enemies? Do you know of anyone who might have threatened him?'

'No,' said Mrs Mulholland, dabbing her eyes with a handkerchief. 'I mean, Anthony always rubbed people up the wrong way, but all the same . . .'

'We didn't expect anyone to murder him,' finished her husband. 'I mean, you don't. Do you?'

Ruby took the news quite calmly. Max told her as soon as she arrived at the theatre. She was on her way to the dressing room that she shared with the chorus girls. Max stopped her on the stairs beside a giant model of Dick Whittington's cat which had prowled across the theatre roof during the panto season.

'Don't say too much to the others,' he said. 'They'll be told that Tony's dead but not how he died.'

'You haven't told me how.'

'Believe me, you're better off not knowing.'

Ruth looked at him, her brown eyes round. Max had never told her about Ethel, but he was sure that she must have read about the gruesome Brighton Trunk Murders. She might even know about Ethel's connection to Max. Word travelled fast backstage, and he was sure that the chorus girls would have filled her in on every detail of his past. But he couldn't tell her that Tony had been murdered in a gory approximation of the trick that he was about to perform on her.

'How do you know?' she asked.

'Edgar told me. He found Tony's body.'

'Edgar? Oh, your policeman friend. Poor him.'

'Yes,' said Max. 'Poor him.'

'And poor Tony, of course.'

Max had tried to ensure that Ruby and Tony didn't meet that often. He wasn't sure why. Ruby didn't seem to be particularly interested in any of the other acts on the bill, although she was friendly enough with the chorus girls. Perhaps it was just the memory of Tony's face when he'd said that Ruby was 'cute'. Tony had quite a reputation in the old days, and Max knew that nothing would please him more than to seduce Max's little assistant from under his nose. He would assume, wrongly of course, that he had succeeded where Max had failed. But it wasn't just that, it was the thought of Tony with his practised leer bending over Ruby's hand and complimenting her on her stage presence . . . No. He couldn't stand it. So he had never introduced Ruby to his one-time colleague. They had met once and, although Tony had been unctuously polite, Ruby remained pleasant but distant. She didn't look sad now, though she had composed her features into an appropriately serious expression. She was young and nothing matters much when you're young.

'Anyway,' he said, 'don't think about it tonight. It's our last show. Let's make it a good one.' He found himself absent-mindedly patting the cat's head.

'Yes,' said Ruby. 'It's our last night together.'

He wished she hadn't put it quite like that.

Edgar arranged for a police car to drive Tony's parents back to north London. They waited at the back entrance to Bartholomew Square, watching as the taxis weaved their way through the narrow streets up to the station. Edgar had offered to escort the Mulhollands to Tony's lodgings, but they had refused, looking terrified again. Edgar had been relieved. He didn't think he could stand looking at the splintered wardrobe again. He had told the Mulhollands how their son had died and had been relieved when they had received the news in stunned silence. 'We think the killer drugged him first,' Edgar had said. 'He won't have suffered.' He had promised to send Tony's belongings on to them.

It was still light, but the air was chilly. Mrs Mulholland pulled her scarf round her neck. It was an incongruously cheerful affair in red and pink silk. Edgar wondered if it had been a present from Tony.

He willed the car to arrive quickly. He couldn't think of anything else to say to the bereaved couple and they, for their part, looked as if they might never utter a word again. But, just as the squad car rounded the corner, Mr Mulholland said, 'Were you a friend of Anthony's, Inspector Stephens?'

Edgar would never have described himself as Tony's friend, even during the Inverness years. Tony had always looked down on him, had never lost an opportunity to tease him or pour scorn on his army career, his respectability, his supposed cleverness. It had always been Max that Tony had wanted to impress and, consequently, Max whom he had wanted to surpass. He remembered

Tony saying to Max, that evening at the French restau-rant, 'I'm a comedian and Edgar's a policeman. But you're still a magician.' He remembered the exact look on Tony's face as he said this. A sort of calculated malice.

'Yes,' he said to Tony's father. 'I was his friend.'

'In that case,' said Mr Mulholland, 'we'd be grateful if you could come to his funeral. It wouldn't seem right, just being the two of us there.'

On stage at the Theatre Royal, Ruby flashed a smile up at the circle before disappearing behind the wardrobe door. Franz pointed to the per-cussion section and the drums began to roll. Max raised his sword in the air. Its blade gleamed dully in the footlights. One more performance, he thought, and then I can escape for two weeks. Two weeks of drinking Pernod and eating in seafront restaurants and talking to French girls with sly, dark eyes. He looked across at the audience and wondered what they would do if he just threw the sword down onto the boards and walked off stage.

The drums grew louder and louder.

Max plunged the sword into the cabinet.

CHAPTER 12

Max met Edgar on Sunday morning at a cafe by the aquarium. At first sight, Max thought his friend looked dreadful. Edgar always had a rather rumpled look, but this morning he looked almost dishevelled: unshaven, tieless, sandy hair standing up in an uneven crest. Max watched him with a mixture of amusement and disapproval. He hadn't slept that well himself—images of the sword cabinet kept scrolling through his head like one of those dioramas you get on the pier—but he prided himself on not having a hair out of place.

'You look like hell,' he said.

'Thanks.' Edgar ordered coffee and, as an afterthought, a bacon sandwich. 'I feel like hell.'

'You've had a tough time.'

'Yes,' Edgar took a gulp of tea and winced. 'I saw Tony's parents yesterday.'

'I can't imagine Tony having parents somehow.'

'They were sweet. Sad. A nice old couple. His mum called him Anthony. I kept thinking of him as a child. I mean, even Tony might have been quite nice as a child.'

'I doubt it.'

'I mean, nobody expects their child to grow up and be murdered by some madman with a sword.'

'Is that who you think it was? Some madman?'

'No.' Edgar looked at Max across the table. Max was surprised to see that he suddenly looked quite formidable. 'I don't think it was a random madman. I think this has to do with the Magic Men.'

They were the only people in the cafe, but even so, Max looked round to see if they could be overheard. The owner was picking his teeth at the counter and a fat seagull stood on the window ledge outside.

'I got a message from Tony yesterday,' said Edgar, 'asking me to meet him at his digs at one-fifteen. When I got there . . .'

Max watched as a greasy hunk of bread was placed in front of Edgar. Tomato sauce was leaking from the sides. 'Another black coffee please,' he asked faintly.

Edgar took a bite of his sandwich. He seemed lost in thought.

'Did Tony say why he wanted to see you?' said Max.

'He said it was to do with the Magic Men. I didn't see him myself. My sergeant took the message.'

'Are you sure it was Tony who called in?' Max was half-joking, but Edgar took the question seriously.

'Description sounded like him. Thirties, dark hair, loud suit. He made a lewd remark to one of the policewomen.'

'That does sound like Tony.'

'But what did he want to talk about? And why one-fifteen? It's such a weird time to choose. I keep thinking about it.' Edgar ran a hand through his hair so it stood up even higher. Max wished he wouldn't.

'Why didn't he come straight in and talk to you?' asked Max. 'Why make an appointment?'

'I don't know,' said Edgar. 'Maybe he wanted to make an occasion of it. You know what he was like.'

Max nodded. He understood all right. Set the stage, prepare the props. But who was orchestrating this particular trick?

'What time did you get to his place?'

'I was late. About one-thirty.'

'But someone got there before you.'

'Yes.' Max looked out of the window. The seagull had flown and he had an unimpeded view over the dark-grey sea. The clouds were black on the horizon. This time tomorrow, he thought, I'll be in France.

'Anyone see who Tony's visitor was?' he asked. 'What about the landlady?'

'She was out. Her daughter was in charge, but she claimed not to have seen anyone. She's not the sharpest tool in the box.'

Not as sharp as the sword that pierced the wardrobe door, thought Max. He remembered slicing though the apple on stage, Ruby's slight expression of alarm, the audience's intake of breath.

'There was no sign of a struggle in the room,' said Edgar. 'Bedclothes creased as if someone had sat on them, the chair pulled out beside the bed, two cups of tea on the table.'

'So it looks as if he knew his killer?'

'Yes. Or at least that he didn't feel threatened by them. Until it was too late.'

'Any other clues? In books the villain always leaves clues lying about the place.'

Edgar smiled. Max remembered that he used to be rather a fan of detective stories. Maybe that was what made him take the ludicrous step of becoming a policeman.

'There's the sword,' said Edgar. 'It looks quite distinctive. I'll have my men go round the antique shops on Monday.' He looked at Max. 'By which time you'll be on your way to France.'

'Yes,' said Max. 'I must say, France is looking better by the second.'

'When will you be back?'

'In two weeks' time. I've got a booking in Hastings for the first week of September.'

'What about Ruby? Has she got another job to go to?'

Max had said goodbye to Ruby after the second house last night. It had been rather an awkward moment. Ruby never allowed him to walk her home to her digs. She said that it was because her flatmate went to bed early and she didn't want to disturb her, but Max thought that maybe she just didn't want him to see where she lived. So they had said goodbye under the portico at the Theatre Royal.

'I hope we meet again,' he'd said.

Ruby had smiled. Her hidden half-smile, instantly suppressed. 'Maybe.'

'Goodbye, Miss French.' He had wanted to kiss her, but had kissed her hand instead. He wasn't sure why he had hesitated. It wasn't like him, but something seemed to stop him making the usual moves towards Ruby. Maybe it was just because she was so young.

'Goodbye, Max,' she'd said. He had walked away, leaving her standing there. He hadn't looked round, but it had been a close thing.

'I don't know what she's doing now,' he said to Edgar.

'I wonder if we should keep an eye on her, given what happened to Ethel. Do you have her address?'

Max looked up sharply, but Edgar's face showed only kindly, professional concern.

'I don't have her address,' he said.

Edgar pushed his plate away. 'Do you fancy a walk?' he said. 'This place is depressing me.'

'I think it's going to rain,' said Max.

They walked along the seafront. It was late morning and the promenade was almost deserted.

The threatening clouds had descended even lower and the sky had a fractured, hazy look like a religious painting. Out at sea it was already raining.

'We're going to get soaked,' said Max. He hadn't brought an umbrella, but then he had his umbrellas professionally furled and rarely used them to keep off the rain.

'Let's head back towards the station.'

They crossed the road and started to make their way through the streets of Kemp Town. At Black Rock Gardens, the first fat drops of rain began to fall. Soon they were fighting their way through what felt like a tropical downpour. The bushes in the gardens were flattened by the onslaught and shop awnings bent and swayed under the weight of water.

'Let's get out of this,' said Max, raising his voice to be heard.

'In here,' shouted Edgar.

Max shook the water out of his eyes but, even before he could see, he knew they were in a church. It was the smell. The heady scent of incense and candle wax. It was triggering a rare memory of his mother. A church, his mother holding his hand, someone bending over him, tweaking his cheek. The adult voices had a foreign, operatic quality. Were they talking Italian? Was this remembered church in Italy or just a gathering of Italians in England? Max had visited Italy several times as an adult but never, as far as he knew, as a child or with his mother. It wasn't something he could ask his father.

'There's no service going on anyway,' said Edgar.

'Mass,' said Max. 'This is a Catholic church.'

'How do you know?'

Max gestured towards the Lady altar, the statue of the virgin mother with arms held out, the banks of candles guttering in front of it. A nun was kneeling at the altar rails.

'Mary,' he said. 'Lots of pictures of dead saints, holy water, tabernacle on the high altar, light showing the sacrament is in residence. How much more evidence do you need?' But he'd known immediately. He'd known by the smell.

'Well let's sit down for a moment,' said Edgar. 'It's still pouring outside.'

They could hear the rain battering against the roof. There was a dripping sound too, water falling into some metal container. The roof, like all ecclesiastical roofs, obviously leaked.

'Jesus,' said Max, taking off his wet jacket. The nun glanced round disapprovingly.

'It's funny,' said Edgar, 'I can't remember the last time I was in a church. A proper church like this. Not just a chapel at a crematorium.'

'Nor can I,' said Max. He wasn't about to share his childhood memories with Edgar. Friendship only went so far.

'Might have been some sort of remembrance service at the end of the war.' Edgar seemed to be talking to himself.

There had been a service for Charis, but neither of them had attended. Edgar because he couldn't bear to and Max for reasons of his own.

Edgar lapsed into silence, leaning forward as if he were praying. Max looked up at the ceiling which featured a fresco of God sitting in judgement, sheep on the right, goats on the left. Some of the goats had disturbingly human expressions. He wondered where he would go when the last trump sounded: into the Elysian Fields with the sheep or into the fiery depths with the goats? Now that was quite some conjuring trick. He turned towards the Lady altar. Mary with her billowing cloak, arms outstretched. As a child, he had dimly associated Mary with his own, absent mother. He had even had his own little figurine of her which he had kept under his pillow until his father had found it and thrown it away. 'None of that popish nonsense in my house.' Max's schools had certainly been chosen as much for their breezy secularism as for their academic achievements. As Max watched, the nun stood up, genuflected and crossed the church to exit by a door at the side of the altar. The stage door, he thought.

Edgar spoke, his voice oddly resonant even though he was almost whispering.

'Tony's father asked me to go to his funeral.'

Max said, still staring at the statue of Mary, 'I can't imagine that'll be much fun.'

'No. He said it wouldn't be right if it was just the two of them. He wanted one of Tony's friends to be there.'

Max said nothing. He had often imagined his own funeral: who would make speeches, which of his former girlfriends would cry and which would look merely expectant. Although, apart from the Bentley, he didn't have much to leave.

'Poor old Tony,' he said. 'He didn't have much of a life really.'

'No,' said Edgar. 'I don't think he was very happy, for all his boasting.'

'He was a good magician really,' said Max. 'All that mesmerism nonsense, it covered the fact that he was really observant. He knew how to work an audience.'

Never show surprise, Tony had said. Had he been surprised, he wondered, when he opened the door to his murderous visitor? He thought of Ethel, her easy charm, her ready laugh. Had she too sat down to drink tea with her killer?

'Do you think the same person killed Tony and Ethel?' he asked.

'Yes,' said Edgar. He turned to look at Max. The rain had slicked down his hair and this had the effect of making him seem younger; guileless and innocent. 'I do think it was the same person. And I think there's a link to me. To us. The box was sent to me, to my army rank. Your assistant was murdered. And now someone who served with us has been killed in a way that mirrors one of your tricks. A trick you're performing this week. It all comes back to us, to the Magic Men.'

The rain was still drumming on the ceiling. Drip, drip, drip. Backstage, the water fell into the bucket.

'Well,' said Max, 'what's our next move?'

'You're going abroad,' said Edgar.

Max sighed. He thought of the beach and casinos at Le Touquet. Drip, drip, drip. 'No,' he said. 'I know when I'm beaten. I'm staying here. You'll never solve this thing without me. This guy's a showman and I know about showmen.'

Edgar said nothing, but as he turned away, Max caught his smile of satisfaction. That was the trouble with guileless people: they could be very cunning.

Edgar took a folded sheet of paper from his pocket. 'We need to trace everyone connected to the Magic Men.'

'That shouldn't be too difficult. Most of them are dead.'

Edgar shook his head. 'Bill's in London, Major Gormley's in Worthing.'

'What about Diablo?'

'God knows.'

Max looked up at the ceiling, at the sheep bound for the sunlit pastures and the goats heading for the fiery trapdoor.

'Let's start with the Major then.'

CHAPTER 13

The Major always had an obsession with tidiness, remembered Edgar. During the war, his disparate band of soldiers, none of whom seemed capable of wearing a uniform correctly, had been a source of real pain to him. Now, looking at the lawns and flowerbeds that surrounded the Worthing bungalow, it seemed that perfect order had been achieved at last. Flowers stood in colour-coded ranks, pale blues merging into violet delphinium. Max and Edgar walked carefully over the close-cropped turf, so green as to be almost fluorescent.

'Lot of rain this summer,' said the Major laconically. 'Good for the grass.'

Max smiled rather thinly. Edgar knew that he hated rain—and gardens too for that matter. In fact, he hated the countryside in general. Max said it was because he'd been sent away to school 'in the middle of nowhere', but Edgar thought it was more to do with an actor's need of an audience. Hedges, trees and fields can't applaud when a trick goes well.

The reason for the tour of the garden was that the Major's wife ('poor Elsie') was in fragile health and shouldn't be disturbed. But Edgar thought that it was also an attempt to diffuse the horror of the story by setting it in the context of the flowers and the rose bower and the butterflies flying in and out of the lavender.

'Poor old Mulholland,' said the Major, coming to a stop by a rustic seat. 'Never had much time for him, but he didn't deserve that.'

'Before Tony died,' said Edgar, 'he said that he wanted to talk to me about the Magic Men. I wondered if he'd tried to contact you.'

The Major shook his head. 'Haven't heard from him in years. Haven't heard from any of you. Got an invitation to Bill's wedding a few years ago. After that, nothing.'

Edgar, who had also received an invitation (declined), said nothing. Max asked, 'Who did Bill marry?'

'Oh, some WAAF,' said the Major dismissively. 'They all looked the same to me.'

'What about Diablo?' asked Edgar.

'Probably dead,' said the Major, echoing Tony a few days earlier. 'He must be over seventy by now. He was a wreck even when we knew him, the amount he drank.'

Edgar wondered how old the Major was. The old soldier was as upright as ever, but his hands had shaken when he'd made them tea earlier and now he sank on the bench as though standing were an effort.

Edgar sat next to him, but Max remained standing, frowning at an apple tree as if he expected it to attack him.

'Has anyone else been asking about the Magic Men?' asked Edgar. 'Anyone at all?'

'A few journalists over the years,' said the Major. 'Mostly asking about *him*.' He gestured at Max. 'Massingham.'

Edgar saw Max's cheek muscle twitch. He remembered that Major Gormley always addressed Max by his birth name rather than his stage name.

'Anyone recent?' Edgar persisted.

The Major bent down to uproot a tiny sprig of clover. 'There was a reporter. A woman. A *girl* really.'

Edgar and Max exchanged glances.

'When was this?' asked Edgar.

'A few weeks ago. During Wimbledon.'

'Around the beginning of July?'

'That's right. She turned up at the house, don't know how she got the address, asking all sorts of questions.'

'What sort of thing?'

'Oh, the usual thing. Magicians at war, all that rubbish. Lots of questions about Acting Major Massingham.'

'It's Max Mephisto,' said Max.

The Major turned to look at him. 'I heard you'd gone back to the stage,' he said.

Max shrugged. 'What else could I do?'

'You could have stayed in the army. Colonel Cartwright thought the world of you.'

Max smiled, but said nothing.

The Major turned to Edgar. 'And you're a policeman. I couldn't believe it when you telephoned. I was always sure that you'd go back to Oxford.'

'This reporter,' prompted Edgar. 'Can you remember her name?'

'No,' said the Major. 'Does it matter?'

They were all silent for a long minute. The bees were buzzing in the hollyhocks and there was a heavy, drowsy feeling to the air. It was the first really hot day of the summer. Then the Major spoke and his voice brought everything back: Inverness, the Caledonian Hotel, mornings so cold that there was ice on the inside of the windows.

'There was a spy, you know. Amongst the Magic Men.'

Edgar stared at him. 'What?'

'There was a spy. Someone in the group was passing intelligence to the enemy. Cartwright and I were convinced of it.'

Max leant forward. 'Do you know who it was?'

The Major gave a short laugh. 'If anyone knows, it's you.'

• • •

'What did he mean by that?' They were driving back in the Bentley. Even the sea looked better from such a luxurious viewpoint, thought Edgar. It sparkled like the Mediterranean itself. He wondered if Max was regretting his decision to stay in England.

Max shrugged, a gesture which seemed to involve taking both hands off the steering wheel. 'Who knows? I never knew what the old fellow was going on about half the time.'

'At Inverness he seemed to spend most of the time with his head in his hands, groaning.'

'I didn't go through the Boer War just to spend my life babysitting a bunch of namby-pamby actors.' Max imitated the Major's parade ground rasp.

'Do you remember when Diablo dressed up as a gypsy woman and offered to tell his fortune?'

'No one is ever likely to forget the sight of Diablo in drag.'

Edgar watched as the pier, seaside villas and hotels slid past. Worthing gave way to Shoreham, grey and industrial. Once places like this had seemed frozen in time, untouched even by the war, but change was coming, even to pleasant seaside resorts. Theatre was giving way to cinema, the wireless to television, Variety to comedy. The Major was an old man and Tony was dead.

'Do you think there was really a spy in the Magic Men?' he asked.

Max shrugged again. The car swerved slightly. 'I wouldn't think it would be worth any spy's time, hanging round with a group of magicians in a god-forsaken Scottish town.'

'But Tony had something he wanted to tell me,' Edgar argued. 'Maybe it was about the spy.'

'But why now? Five years after the war is over. I don't think so. If anyone lived in the present, it was Tony.'

'I don't know. He got pretty nostalgic that night at dinner.'

'He was just trying to get under your skin. Going on about Charis like that.'

Or yours, thought Edgar. As he remembered it, Max had been more disturbed than he was.

'And there was that journalist asking questions about you,' he said. 'What was all that about?'

'Journalists are always asking questions.'

That might be the case if you're Max Mephisto, thought Edgar. Max might say that he was on the way out, but the great magician was still news. Fewer people, though, were interested in Acting Major Massingham. Why would a journalist be asking about Max's war years?

'I'm sure the Major wasted no time in telling her what a scoundrel I was,' said Max. 'How I spent the war drinking and womanising.'

'Don't forget playing poker.'

'Yes. And playing poker. And performing the odd conjuring trick or two.'

Edgar said nothing. It was one of Max's conjuring tricks that had killed Charis.

CHAPTER 14

In May 1940 Edgar had been part of the Allied expeditionary force sent to Narvik in Norway. The idea was that the land troops would take advantage of the naval success of HMS *Warspite* and repel the invading German army. The reality, though, had been very different. Edgar would never forget his first view of Norway. From the deck of the troop ship the jagged, icy landscape seemed like something from another planet. He had seen snow before, had made snowmen in his Esher front garden, had sledged down hills on a tin tray with Jonathan yelling in his ear. But this, this slogging march through snow that came up to his waist, was something else entirely. The Norwegian troops had skis and, to Edgar, they seemed liked mythical creatures, a snowy form of centaur. The French troops seemed almost as unprepared as the British, and the so-called Polish mountain specialists had had no cold-weather training at all. They marched on, watching war planes take off from frozen lakes, finding their way blocked by snowfall and by glaciers and fjords whose existence seemed to come as a complete surprise to their commanders. For all of them it was their first experience of war and, for many, it was also their last.

Edgar was eventually evacuated by an aircraft carrier. He was lucky; the aircraft carrier *Glorious*, carrying returning troops and evacuated Hurricane bombers, was torpedoed and sunk. All in all, the Norway campaign was considered a complete failure and led to a vote of no confidence in Prime Minister Neville Chamberlain. In fact, Edgar liked to say, without Norway and that first shock of actual battle, Winston Churchill might never have become prime minister. Ironic, really, as Churchill had been one of the major architects of the Norway debacle. Edgar himself was sent to hospital with severe frostbite and was fortunate to escape with nothing worse than the loss of a toe.

After Norway, Edgar was determined never to fight on land again. He decided to volunteer for the RAF. He liked the idea of being in the air, free and clear amongst the clouds, and never getting his feet wet. He had never even been in a plane, much less flown one, but how difficult could it really be? Besides, Jonathan had just been killed, and nothing seemed very important any more. Helped by a sympathetic commanding officer, Edgar applied to Victory House and was told to present himself for interview.

Edgar was recuperating at a hospital in Kent so

he took the train to Charing Cross, planning to walk to Kingsway and the RAF headquarters. The train was full of evacuees, so a kindly guard told him to have a seat in first class. He still remembered the slight thrill of pleasure as he took his seat in the compartment, empty apart from one other man, and opened his paper at the cryptic crossword. One down: Hankers after a name in time. Edgar wrote the answer in block capitals. YEARNS. It was a fairly straightforward puzzle that day, and his pen flew across the paper.

'Excuse me?' Edgar looked up and saw the man opposite smiling at him. He was tall, with iron-grey hair, the sort of person who looks military even when dressed in civilian clothes.

'I couldn't help noticing,' said the man, 'that you've almost finished the crossword and we're not out of the station yet.'

Edgar remembered feeling rather embarrassed, as if doing the crossword were a sign of a useless, dilettante life. 'I've been convalescing,' he said. 'I suppose I've had rather too much practice.'

Under the man's sympathetic gaze, he told him about Norway, about the RAF, even about Jonathan.

'Have you ever thought about the Secret Service?'

Edgar remembered that he had laughed aloud. The Secret Service? People didn't just join the Secret Service: you probably had to put your name down at birth like you did for Eton.

'Why not?' said the man mildly. 'You told me

that you were studying at Oxford and you've obviously got an eye for code-breaking.' He gestured at the crossword. He leant across and presented Edgar with a card. Colonel Peter Cartwright, MI5.

Two days later, Edgar sat in a dingy room near Shepherd's Bush, being briefed about his new assignment.

'It's an experiment really,' said Colonel Cartwright. 'The enemy are in Norway. Well, you know that better than anyone. They may well turn their eyes to the Highlands of Scotland. Remember the attack on the Firth of Forth at the start of the war? And there are some important armament factories in Scotland. We have to make them think that the coast is defended, that we're prepared for an invasion. I'm sending you to the RAF base at Inverness.'

'*Are* we prepared for an invasion, sir?'

Colonel Cartwright had laughed. 'No, of course not. But it's your job to make them think that we are. There'll be a special team to help you.'

'What sort of team?'

Another laugh. 'I think I'd better let you discover that for yourself.'

Edgar first saw them from the train. Coming into Inverness, tired and travel-stained after the long journey, he had looked out of the window and seen two men on the platform. Though it was nine in the morning, one of the men was in full evening dress. The other, who was considerably older, was wearing a private's uniform topped by a straw hat. The two WAAFs who were sharing Edgar's carriage cheered up immediately.

'That's Max Mephisto, the magician.'

'Isn't he staying at the Cally? Part of that hush-hush team.'

The first girl laughed crudely. 'I don't know, but he can saw me in half any time.'

Edgar had looked curiously at the dinner-jacketed man. He was drinking from a hip flask now. The older man said something, and Max Mephisto passed him the flask with a laugh. Then, to Edgar's surprise, he took a pack of cards from his pocket and shuffled them casually, without looking. The older man sat down, rather abruptly, on a bench. Then he took off his hat and wiped his brow. Edgar's first thought was that they both looked rather seedy. He hoped they wouldn't be part of the team. The top-secret team that was, it seemed, known to everyone.

But, as Edgar hauled his heavy case along the platform, Max put the cards away and strode towards him.

'Captain Stephens? We've been sent to meet you.'

Edgar took the proffered hand and found himself looking into a pair of amused brown eyes.

'I'm Max Mephisto. This is Stan Parks, otherwise known as The Great Diablo.'

'Charmed, I'm sure.' The older man remained seated. 'Excuse me if I don't get up. Max and I had rather a heavy night last night.' He took a deep swig from the flask.

'Get up, you old reprobate,' said Max. 'We've been told to make a good impression on Captain Stephens.'

He smiled sardonically as Diablo limped forward to shake hands. Edgar was taken aback when the old man leant in close and asked, with a powerful blast of brandy breath, 'Are you one of us?'

Edgar looked at him blankly.

'One of the *fraternity,*' mouthed Diablo.

'He means are you a magician?' said Max, picking up the case.

'Oh,' said Edgar. 'No. Regular army.'

'Fascinating.' The old man peered at him as if he were an interesting—though potentially repulsive —specimen.

'Come on,' said Max, over his shoulder, 'you're staying at the Cally. I've got transport.'

As they followed Max to the front of the station, where a jeep was waiting, Diablo whispered loudly in Edgar's ear, 'Word of warning, my boy. If you're playing cards with Max, never take your eyes off his hands.'

The team convened in the bar that evening. Max was in uniform and Edgar was surprised to see that he was a captain. Diablo, silk scarf rakishly round his neck, was deep in conversation with a young man in civvies. Everything about the man, from his wide pinstripes to his trilby, screamed 'spiv', so Edgar was surprised when he was introduced as 'Private Tony Mulholland, another member of our merry band.'

'Are you a magician too?' asked Edgar.

Tony Mulholland drew himself up as if affronted. 'I was only top of the bill at the Liverpool Empire. Tony "The Mind" Mulholland.'

'I'm sorry,' said Edgar humbly.

'Don't mind him, dear boy,' said Diablo. 'He's a civilian.' This was said without apparent irony.

They were soon joined by Major Gormley and a thickset man introduced as 'Sergeant Bill Cosgrove, he's our carpentry whizz-kid. Massingham has the ideas and Cosgrove puts them into action.'

'Or into wood,' added Diablo in a stage whisper.

The Major organised drinks with brusque efficiency and there, in the lounge bar, with the stag heads staring sorrowfully down at them, he outlined the mission ahead.

'Enemy are in Norway, only a few miles away. We can't attack, we haven't even got the sea power to have a warship on patrol. But we've got to persuade them that, not only are we bristling with guns and boats, we're weeks away from invasion. So the idea is to employ some *deception*. Sleight of hand, I believe you fellows call it.' He glared round at the group: Max shuffling his cards again, Diablo picking his teeth, Tony smoking, Bill watching calmly.

'Captain Massingham here . . .' it took Edgar a few moments to realise that he meant Max, 'has had some success with camouflage in North Africa. Private Parks,' he gestured towards Diablo, 'knows about stagecraft and suchlike. Private Mulholland is to help with the psychological aspects. Sergeant Cosgrove is in charge of construction.'

Edgar thought that it was time to say something that had been on his mind for several hours.

'What am I here for, sir?'

'You,' said the Major gloomily, 'are the brains of the outfit.'

Tony Mulholland let out a guffaw. Max grinned into his card-deck.

'What shall we call ourselves?' said Diablo. 'Better think up a dashed good name.'

'I don't care,' said the Major, having exhausted his eloquence. 'As long as you don't call yourselves the bloody Magic Men.'

Much later, after Max had produced a rabbit from Diablo's straw hat and won five pounds from Edgar playing cards, Major Gormley announced that he was going to bed.

'Don't stay up drinking until all hours. And you, Massingham, don't play cards with the locals.'

The only other occupants of the bar were an elderly man and a dog. Max looked across at them. 'I think the locals are safe.'

'Watch the dog,' said Diablo. 'It's probably a plant.'

With the departure of the senior officer, the atmosphere swiftly became raucous. Diablo told Edgar that he'd once been a serious actor, 'People still talk about my Hamlet.' He then juggled with three ashtrays, breaking one. Tony, whisky in hand, embarked on a long story about a WAAF and an orange. Edgar remembered watching them with a mixture of dislike and envy. What did these men know about fighting? About Jonathan, dying on the beach at Dunkirk. About Norway and the endless march through the snow, soldiers falling to freeze to death where they lay. They were tricksters, charlatans. They had never done a useful day's work in their lives and now they had secured this cosy little berth where they could sit out the war, drinking all day and carousing all night. There was about as much chance of this bunch being able to think up a decent plan to trick the enemy as there was of Edgar being able to work out how the hell Max had produced the rabbit. And where was the animal now? He looked round, feeling confused and disorientated. He would not have been surprised to find the rabbit sitting next to him, checking the time on its pocket watch.

But the occupant of the next seat was Bill. He smiled at Edgar as if he knew something of what he was thinking. 'Rum bunch, aren't they?'

Edgar agreed that they were.

'Mulholland's a spiv, of course. Apparently he's meant to be able to read minds. Don't know about that. Never seen him read anything. Diablo's an old soak. They say he was a good magician once, but he's all washed up now. Don't know what he's doing here, to be honest.'

'What about Max Mephisto?'

'Ah, Mephisto. He's a hell of a fellow. In Egypt there was this imam, a whirling dervish or some such thing. The imam controlled the route from Cairo through Palestine to Syria. He was refusing to let our troops set foot on his land, said he'd start a holy war if necessary. Mephisto met with him and apparently levitated the imam's servant right up to the ceiling. The old dervish was so impressed he let our chaps through. That's how Mephisto got to be a captain.'

Hearing his name, Max looked round. After a few moments he came to join them, placing a fresh whisky in front of Edgar.

'Thanks,' said Edgar stiffly. 'But I've had enough.'

'You've had enough of all of us, I imagine,' said Max. 'The only answer is to have another drink.'

'I'm sorry,' said Edgar. 'It's just that it all seems crazy to me. How can we stop the Nazis by . . . by magic?'

Max didn't answer. Instead, he leant forward and cleared a space on the table, brushing away the remnants of Diablo's ashtray. Then he took the cards out of his pocket, placed one in the centre of the table, face down. Then, a little way away, he placed four more cards, also face down.

'Which is the important card?' he asked.

Edgar pointed at the centre card. Max turned it over. Two of hearts. 'No,' he said, pointing at one of the four others. 'Put something in the centre, create a space around it, and it becomes important. This card, one of the outer ones, is the important one.' He turned it over. Ace of hearts. 'By putting it with others, it loses significance. Misdirection. We can make the enemy look where we want him to look. And that's important.'

How? Edgar wanted to ask. But Bill, who was obviously deeply impressed by Max, asked, 'Is it true that Hitler actually mentioned you personally, Max?'

Max laughed. 'Yes. When I was in Egypt, he apparently said that he wanted to make me disappear in a puff of smoke. And, to be fair, he did try to blow me up once or twice.' He looked across at Edgar. 'The Germans believe in magic. They've got a word, "*Fingerspitzengefühl*". It means being able to feel something in your fingers, to sense it before it happens. Hitler's superstitious—the man employs five astrologers, after all—but he also knows the power of totemic objects and symbols. The swastika was an ancient fertility symbol and the SS badge is modelled on the mythical runic alphabet. Have you heard of the Spear of Destiny?'

Edgar and Bill shook their heads. Edgar was aware that the dazed feeling was back again.

'It was supposedly the lance that pieced Christ's side. It was kept in a church in Austria, but when the Germans invaded Austria, Hitler went to the church and took the spear. The legend is that whoever possesses it controls the destiny of the world.'

'It's very Wagnerian,' said Edgar.

'Very,' agreed Max. 'And Hitler loves Wagner, as well as myth and magic.'

'Do the Germans really believe all that?' asked Bill.

Max shrugged. 'People will believe any-thing, especially in wartime. Why do you think Goebbels published all those Nostradamus prophecies saying that the Nazis would conquer Europe? Only after he'd rewritten them first, of course.'

'And how's this going to help us make the Germans think that we're invading Norway?' asked Edgar. He realised that he'd used the word 'us'.

'Be careful,' said a voice behind them. 'Careless talk and all that.'

Edgar turned and saw a woman in WAAF uniform. She had dark-red hair tied back in a bun and was the possessor of a face of such perfect beauty that Edgar could only gape at her.

'Who's going to overhear?' asked Max, gathering up his cards. 'Bambi's father up there?' He gestured at the stag.

The woman smiled. 'Just be on your guard. I've never met such a lax crew.'

She moved away to speak to Tony and Diablo. Edgar tested his voice to make sure that it still worked. 'Who's that?' he croaked.

Max was also watching the woman, but his expression was hard to read. 'Captain Parsons,' he said. 'Charis Parsons. Our commanding officer.'

CHAPTER 15

Bill and his wife lived in Wembley, a district close enough in spirit to Esher to make Edgar feel nervous. But where Esher was still toy town, Wembley was vast, expanding in every direction. The Bentley glided past sprawling estates of new social housing, each with their small square of garden. Children played hopscotch and the chimes of an ice cream van sounded in the distance. Edgar sank lower in his seat.

'What's the problem?' asked Max with a malicious smile. 'Suddenly realising that domestic bliss isn't up your street after all?'

'It just reminds me of the place where I was brought up.'

'You've never told me where that was.'

'It's in Esher in Surrey. My mother still lives there.'

Max shot him a glance. 'Do you see her much?'

Edgar shifted uncomfortably. 'I try to see her as much as I can, but I'm pretty busy and she . . .' His voice drifted away.

'You should see her,' said Max. 'You're lucky that you've still got your mother.'

Edgar looked at his friend's profile. He knew that Max's mother had died when he was very young. He probably couldn't understand what it was like to have a mother with whom you had nothing in common, someone who never failed to make you feel obscurely guilty about everything, even the fact that you had survived the war when your brother hadn't. Still, Max was right. He should visit Rose more often.

'I don't like places like this,' he said, to change the subject as much as anything. 'They make me feel nervous.'

'Wembley's a boom town,' said Max. 'Lots of new businesses and houses. They had the Olympic Games here, after all. The Athens of north London.'

But Max liked lots of people around him. People meant audiences, new towns meant new theatres, crowds to entertain. As he often said, it was the countryside that made him feel nervous. Too many open spaces, too much silence. But, for Edgar, cities meant crime. Who knew what was hiding in these newly tarmacked streets, each named after a First World War general. Allenby Avenue, Haig Drive. Each one of these little houses might be housing a murderer. Besides, he'd never been to Athens, but he couldn't imagine that it included a greyhound stadium.

Bill and Jean didn't live in one of the new estates. Their street was obviously a step up: net curtains at the windows and cars parked in driveways. Edgar knew that Bill had a good job with the General Electric Company. Clearly things were going well.

'Now this,' said Max, coming to a halt in front of a semidetached house with a wishing well in the garden, 'is charming.'

'I can't see you living here,' retorted Edgar.

'No. I'm a vagabond. It's a sad life.' He sighed heavily, but Edgar thought he looked rather smug all the same.

Edgar had called to say they were coming, and it seemed that Bill was waiting for them. He flung open the door before they had time to knock.

'Ed! Max! It's great to see you again. Is that your car, Max? What a beauty.'

Edgar noticed that Bill didn't assume for one second that the Bentley could be his. Bill hadn't changed, he thought. Still tall and good-looking with an open, friendly face. ('What does Charis see in him?' he had once asked Tony in a fit of drunken despair. 'What, you mean apart from the classic good looks and the bulging muscles,' Tony had replied.)

But now Bill was ushering them into the house and saying, 'Of course, you remember Jean.' Edgar *did* remember, as a matter of fact. Oh, not her name, but he remembered the face—pretty, symmetrical, small blue eyes. She could have been any one of the girls at the WAAF base in Inverness. Why had Bill married her? How could he stand looking at her face after Charis's?

But, as Bill led them into a sitting room dominated by a vast playpen, it seemed that his overriding emotion was pride.

'And this is our son and heir, Barney. You wouldn't have thought such a petite little thing could produce such a huge baby, would you?'

'Oh, Bill!' Jean aimed a playful slap at him.

'Would you fellows like tea?' Jean put her head on one side coquettishly. 'Or something stronger?'

Edgar and Max assured her that tea would be perfect.

On the phone Edgar had told Bill that he wanted to discuss Tony's murder but now, in this pink-

and-white room, he found it almost impossible to raise the subject again. He caught the baleful eye of the baby and looked away again. He really was huge.

It was Bill who said, sinking into an armchair, 'Poor old Tony. Who would do such a terrible thing?'

Edgar and Max sat side by side on the sofa. It was covered by a fabric so fiercely floral that Edgar felt as if the tendrils were about to wrap themselves round his legs, imprisoning him in a deadly chintz embrace. Max, on the other hand, seemed perfectly at home.

'I don't know,' said Edgar. 'But I think it could have something to do with the Magic Men.'

He explained about The Zig Zag Girl murder and Tony's last message.

'He said he wanted to talk to me about the Magic Men, but he was killed before I could see him.'

'Maybe that was a coincidence,' said Bill. 'Maybe he just wanted to reminisce.'

'Maybe,' said Edgar, 'but the theatrical nature of the murders . . .' He looked at Max. He hadn't told Bill exactly how Tony was killed. 'And the fact that there seem to be links to both me and Max makes me think that this could be someone from . . . well, from those days.'

'You think the killer could be someone from Inverness?' Bill's voice rose in disbelief. 'Who?

Major Gormley? Old Diablo? Me? Perhaps you think it's me?'

Jean, frozen in the doorway with the tea-tray, said, 'Why are you shouting, dear?'

Edgar, who'd been wondering the same thing, said, 'It's OK, Jean. Just discussing the old days.'

Jean carefully put the tray on the table. 'Oh, I expect you're talking about her. Charis. Well, she was no better than she should be. Everyone knew that.'

The baby let out a sudden and terrifying guffaw.

Edgar had fallen in love with Charis immediately. In those desperate days of the war, there seemed no point in waiting for anything. Jonathan was dead, London was still being pounded by German bombs every night, there seemed little chance that the raggle-taggle soldiers with whom Edgar had served in Norway could ever defeat the mighty Axis powers—even with the help of the Americans. Their little unit seemed cut off from the war, cut off from ordinary life. 'Massingham has the ideas,' Gormley had said and, in this, he was certainly right. Max had about fifty ideas a day and it was Edgar's job to decide which could be turned into life—or into wood and canvas. One of Max's first suggestions was an army of dummies that would make the base look as if it were stuffed full of troops, ready for an imminent invasion.

'They tried dummies on the south coast,' said Diablo, 'when everyone was worked up about an invasion after Dunkirk. They wouldn't have fooled a child.'

'That was because of the shadows,' said Max. 'Get the shadows right and, from the air, they'll look just like real soldiers.'

'If we have them lying around smoking cigarettes and playing cards they will,' said Tony.

In the end, Bill only built a few members of Max's dummy army. One of these, a corpulent sergeant with a cigarette butt in his hand, was positioned on the first-floor landing of the Caledonian and never failed to give Edgar a shock when he visited the lavatory in the night.

The dummy tanks were more successful. They were stage props really, wooden frames covered with painted sackcloth. From a distance, with the right lighting (Diablo was an expert at lighting), they looked incredibly realistic. The problem was that there was really no reason to have tanks at Inverness. Edgar knew that Max had created whole squadrons of tanks in Egypt ('the shadows are wonderful in the desert'), but here there was only room for one or two. It was one of these tanks which, positioned on the front lawn of the Caledonian, had given the Major such a shock when he opened his bedroom window to commence his morning stretches.

Building the props was quite fun. Bill did most

of the skilled carpentry work, but the others all helped with painting and what Diablo called 'dressing'. The trouble was that this left a whole lot of time when there was nothing much to do. Days when Edgar walked by the river thinking about his brother, shot down as he struggled for his boat at Dunkirk, and wondering if anyone had ever spent a more useless war than Captain Edgar Stephens.

Charis, though nominally in charge, kept her distance from the physical work, those long hours spent in the barn workshop, angling lights at cardboard flats and working out the exact colour to paint a slightly bullet-damaged tank. Nobody knew much about her. She had joined the WAAFs as soon as war broke out. 'The interview was ridiculous,' she told Edgar. 'All they wanted to do was check that we could hold a knife the right way.' She had been a plotter, one of these steadfast girls working in the Operations Room, mapping both British and enemy planes and reporting their movements to the Filter Room. She worked through the raid on Dieppe, Edgar knew, and people still spoke about the way she had remained calm throughout the dreadful night, her hands remaining completely steady as she put down the arrows, over a hundred losses. The command of the Magic Men had meant promotion, but Edgar thought that Charis was often bored by the long days discussing camouflage and sleight of hand.

'I'm not one of the Magic Men,' she would say with her trademark teasing smile, 'I'm not magic and I'm certainly not a man.' She sometimes took a rather competitive tone with the magicians, as if to prove that she was as clever as they were. And she was clever: she could play cards almost as well as Max and spoke three languages. She could swap badinage with Tony and quote Shakespeare with Diablo. Once she had filled in three clues on his cryptic crossword while he was at the bar getting drinks. In his darker moments, Edgar wondered if she'd only had an affair with him to stave off the boredom.

It was certainly the situation—the isolation, the boredom, the sense that the rest of the world might have been swallowed up by one of the sea frets blown in from the Firth—that led to Edgar's uncharacteristic boldness in making the first move. He had desired Charis from the first and, as the months wore on, he found himself becoming obsessed with her: her face, her hair, her walk, her bold appraising glance. Finally, almost driven mad by boredom and frustration, he had grabbed hold of her as they stood looking over the Ness one evening and pressed his lips against hers. He had expected her to break away, to cry, to slap his face. Instead, she had responded to his kiss and, when they finally broke apart, had leant forward to murmur her room number in his ear.

She wasn't his first girl, but she was the first

girl that mattered. They went to great lengths to keep their affair secret—not least because she was his commanding officer—so it was a real shock to Edgar when he realised that everyone knew about it. It took a snide comment from Tony about his 'magic powers' to alert him to the fact.

'You couldn't expect us not to find out,' said Max. 'We're magicians, we're used to reading body language, picking up unspoken clues. Besides, you keep staring at her.'

Charis was a constant wonder to him. She didn't tell him much about her past. In fact, looking back, they didn't really talk much at all. She was born in Wales, but her father was dead and she didn't get on with her mother. She had been to boarding school, she said, and she certainly had the kind of cut-glass accent that would have made Edgar's mother swoon with delight if he had ever taken her home to Esher. She had spent a couple of years abroad and this, to Edgar's inexperienced eyes, imbued her with a mysterious foreign glamour. Sometimes she would roll her eyes at him and accuse him of being 'typically English', something which Edgar could not really deny. Apart from his time in Norway, he had never even been out of Britain. Charis had left school at sixteen, but she knew about art and opera, she could play the piano and occasionally used an amber cigarette-holder. And she was effortlessly, exotically beautiful. Watching her walk across the saloon bar at the Caledonian could move Edgar almost to tears.

Edgar never quite knew what she felt about him. She called him 'darling', but she never talked about a future together or suggested that they formalise their relationship. In fact, she seemed to expect nothing more from him than frequent and energetic sex. Edgar tried to convince himself that they were somehow engaged, that after the war they would settle down together and produce a series of beautiful, red-haired children. 'I love you,' he said, whenever he got the chance. And now, years later, he was tormented by the fact that he could not remember whether she had ever said it back.

Predictably, it was Tony who told him that Charis was sleeping with Bill. Although Charis was always nice to Bill, congratulating him on his carpentry prowess and calling him her 'wood-working wizard', Edgar had never really considered him a rival. Max was the one that the WAAFs swooned over, the one whom Edgar's mother would have called (disapprovingly) 'a ladies' man'. Even Tony, fast-talking and smooth, had his successes. Bill—steady, hard-working, always slightly behind on a joke—was easy to overlook. Afterwards, Edgar wondered if it was, after all, simple snobbery. Bill was the sergeant, the worker. How could he aspire to a woman who was not only a goddess but also a commissioned officer? But aspire he did, and one day, about six months after their arrival at Inverness, Tony leant forward in the bar of the Caledonian and said, 'How does it feel to be second best to Clueless Cosgrove?'

'What do you mean?' Edgar had asked.

Tony pointed up at the rafters. 'You've been replaced in La Parsons' bed by Bill. Didn't you know?'

Edgar remembers turning to Max and seeing him, momentarily, look away. That was how he knew.

CHAPTER 16

'What do you think?' asked Edgar as the Bentley eased away from the street of little houses. Bill and Jean, standing waving on the doorstep, were growing smaller too. Soon they were lost to view.

'What do I think?' asked Max. 'That is one hell of a big baby.'

'You know what I mean.'

Max was silent as he edged into the traffic on the main road. Edgar almost missed the days when there were hardly any cars on the road. Now it seemed that every Tom, Dick or Harry had a car. Except him.

'He was hiding something,' Max said at last. 'But I don't know what.'

'Maybe he just didn't want to talk about the Magic Men in front of Jean.'

'That could be it. She looked the jealous type.'

'Jealous of Charis, you mean?' It still hurt to say her name, Edgar realised.

'Jealous of all of us. Of something she didn't share. She's got him now. House, baby, respectable job. She doesn't want us dragging him back into the mire.'

The mire. The Magic Men had certainly enjoyed an unsavoury reputation at Inverness. There were rumours of black magic, of WAAFs who went into the Caledonian for a quick drink and were never seen again. Even Max, the WAAF's pin-up, was not immune to these rumours; indeed he might even have been said to encourage them, wafting around the town in top hat and cape like the phantom of the opera. Tony, who liked to imply that he had supernatural—possibly devilish—powers of deduction, did not help matters. Even Diablo, amiable drunk that he was, gave off a faint whiff of necromancy, of dusty potions and forgotten incantations, of a different, darker world. Edgar liked to think that he was the only normal one amongst them (except Bill, of course, Bill was the epitome of normal). Then, one day, he had heard two WAAFs talking about him. 'There's something odd about that Edgar Stephens,' said one, 'he just goes around trying to be so *nice* all the time.' 'Gives me the creeps,' agreed the other.

Now he said, 'Do you remember Jean from Inverness?'

Max shrugged, taking both hands off the wheel. 'How could I? They all looked the same.'

'You sound like Major Gormley.'

'A sterling character.'

'But all the same,' said Edgar, glad that Max was holding the wheel again (even if he was lighting a cigarette at the same time), 'there was something odd about her. Why go on about Charis like that?'

Jean's comments on Charis's character had not stopped at her initial outburst. They had continued as a steady counterpoint to the whole afternoon. A remark that Edgar should find police work easy after the army had elicited, 'I tell you who was easy . . .' A reminiscence about the Norwegian sailors stationed at Inverness had caused her to wonder how many of them Charis had slept with. By the end, Edgar was white with anger, and even Bill seemed embarrassed. It had been left to Max to smooth things over, complimenting Jean on the house and Barney on his immense size. 'He's got the build of an athlete. He could play cricket for England.'

'She was jealous, like I said. Charis was a beautiful woman. I bet a lot of people were jealous of her.'

'You didn't like her, did you?' said Edgar.

Max was silent for a few minutes. The ash on his

cigarette lengthened until it reached his finger. Cursing, he threw the stub out of the window.

'No, I didn't like her,' he said at last. 'She was a woman who enjoyed the power she had over men. I didn't like that.'

'But you were devastated when she died,' said Edgar. They had never spoken about this before and it was easier like this, in the car, both of them staring straight ahead.

'Because it was my fault,' said Max simply.

Major Gormley had got tired of the tanks and wanted them to build a battleship. 'We need them to think we've got a ship permanently stationed off this coast,' the Major had explained. 'Jerry's doing a lot of reconnaissance these days. Planes going over all the time. He's interested in us and we want to keep it that way. If he's looking at us, he's not looking towards France.' The Major always talked about the German army in the singular, as if it were a personal acquaintance.

'Build a boat?' Bill had said. 'From what?'

Even though, by this time, Edgar had barely been able to look at Bill, he had to acknowledge that he had a point. All available timber had been used for beach defences. The coastguard vessels were in constant use. Anything else seaworthy had been requisitioned years ago.

'It's hard to make a battleship appear out of nowhere,' said Max.

'Hard but not impossible,' said Diablo. 'Trust in your powers, dear boy.'

And it was Max who found the boat in the end. Taking a girl on a day-trip to a nearby loch ('Day-trip,' sneered Tony, 'that's a new name for it.'), he had discovered an old cruiser gently rotting away in the shallows. The gallant old ship was towed to Inverness where she was painted battleship-grey and fitted with guns made from beer barrels. She was named HMS *Ptolemy*. Max created a scale model of a real battleship and the men had laboured to make *Ptolemy*'s dimensions match. They added extensions to the bow and stern, lengthening the boat by over two hundred feet. They took down the masts and added gun towers. The main problem was making the ship look as if it could hold aircraft. Eventually, Max and Diablo painted them flat on a vast canvas. 'The Germans will be looking down on them,' Max explained to a sceptical Gormley. 'It'll be fine as long as we get the shadows right.'

Eventually, one September evening, the fake battleship was towed down the Ness towards the Moray Firth. It rode a little high in the water and the canvas flapped in the wind but, in the fading light, the *Ptolemy* was an impressive sight. The WAAFs crowded on the quay to cheer as the grey hulk passed by. Max looked at it through narrowed eyes.

'It'll be better with the right lighting. I'll fix up some arc lights on the beach. Then we can let some flares off from the boat itself. That'll give Jerry something to think about.'

The first attempt to stage the light show went badly wrong. Max, Edgar and Diablo took out a rowing boat one night, intending to let off flares when they were near the *Ptolemy*. But as soon as they reached the Firth, the waters boiled into a sudden storm. Before long, Edgar had lost the oars and the three men were crouched in the bows as the waves broke over their heads. Edgar remembers thinking: so this is it, this is the way I'm going to die, drowned off the coast of Scotland with two magicians in a dinghy. At least it'll make a good obituary. Then, without warning, the seas had calmed and they had found themselves floating in what appeared to be a vast, flat ocean. Dawn was breaking and there was not another living soul to be seen.

'Perhaps we have died after all,' said Diablo. 'And this is the afterlife.'

'It's a bit wide for the River Styx,' said Max. 'Christ, I wish I had a cigarette.'

They were picked up ten hours later by a fishing boat. But, as far as Edgar was concerned, they could have been drifting for weeks, years. He didn't think he would ever forget that time: Diablo singing music hall songs and Max reciting 'The Lady of Shalott' ('I had to learn it at school'), the sun beating down and the uncaring sea as blue as heaven.

'I'm Burlington Bertie. I rise at ten-thirty.'

'By the margin, willow-veiled, Slide the heavy barges trailed . . .'

'I'm Bert, Bert. I haven't a shirt . . .'

'She has no loyal knight and true . . .'

'I stand by the awning while Lord Derby's yawning. And he bids ten thousand and I bid good morning.'

'Who is this and what is here? And in the lighted place near. Died the sound of royal cheer . . .'

They survived with nothing worse than severe sunburn. But Major Gormley wouldn't hear of another attempt. 'Next time, we'll get a plane to drop someone on board. They can let off the flares and we can airlift them off again.' But the problem was that the *Ptolemy* was massively unstable. The original planking was rotten and, underneath the painted canvas, there were gaping holes fore and aft. 'Any of the men will go right through,' said the Major. 'Captain Parsons will have to do it.'

'Delighted,' said Charis, her eyes glittering.

The story was told at the inquest and again at the inquiry. The flare wedged itself in the decking and the canvas went up in a single sheet of flame. Max and Tony, standing on the shore, screamed and shouted, but to no avail. The plane swooped as low as it dared, but was unable to locate Charis in the burning wreck. Diablo, showing unexpected gentleness, broke the news to Bill, but Edgar, who had a weekend's leave, didn't hear until two days later.

When he was told, by a wide-eyed WAAF, that Charis Parsons was dead, Edgar thought of the poem that he had heard whilst drifting in the open sea.

And at the closing of the day
She loosed the chain and down she lay;
The broad stream bore her far away,
The Lady of Shalott.

CHAPTER 17

Max had known that Tony's funeral wouldn't be a barrel of laughs, and he was right. Minutes after entering the sooty church near Shepherd's Bush, he regretted letting his better nature get the upper hand, something that, in fairness, hardly ever happened. He remembered Edgar saying, that day in the church with the rain battering against the roof and the Virgin Mary stretching out her arms to them, 'Tony's father wanted one of his friends to be there.' He had looked so stoical that Max's heart had been wrung. He couldn't let Edgar face the funeral on his own. Neither of them had been Tony's friend, exactly, but they had shared a past with him. It was only right that they should go together and, if that gave Tony's parents the entirely erroneous impression that their son had had two friends, so much the better.

But Tony's parents didn't seem to be noticing anything very much. They sat side by side in the front row, two small figures in black, his mother wearing a hat with a veil that looked as if it were a relic of a happier occasion. Next to them sat a solid man and a defeated-looking woman. Otherwise, the church was empty.

Max and Edgar sat near the back. Tony's mother turned and gave them a timid smile. Edgar raised his hand. Max suddenly felt that his clothes were wrong. His suit was too smart, his tie was too narrow and his shoes were too shiny. He wished he could smoke.

A wheezy breath of organ music and the pall-bearers entered, carrying the coffin. Max averted his eyes. He felt a morbid desire to cross himself. The pall-bearers rested the coffin onto a kind of trestle table in front of the vicar and then filed into one of the pews. Max wondered if they had done this to increase the numbers in the church. It was a nice touch, if so.

The vicar eyed his small congregation with a kind of weary distaste.

'Dearly beloved,' he began, surveying the pews and wincing slightly. 'We are here to mourn the passing of a young man, taken from us in the most brutal way.'

He paused, as if to indicate that none of this tastelessness was *his* fault.

'Anthony was not a churchgoer,' the vicar continued, 'but his mother tells me that he was a boy with a strong sense of right and wrong.'

This was probably true, thought Max. Tony certainly knew the difference between Right and Wrong, which was why he almost inevitably chose Wrong.

'He lived an unconventional life.' The vicar sounded positively disgusted by now. And, was it Max's imagination or did his eyes flicker towards him and Edgar when he said this? 'Some might call it glamorous. Travelling all over the country, even to America. His name in lights. But, in the end, we are all equal before God. His judgement is all that matters.'

What an unpleasant idea, thought Max. He imagined that God would be rather a stern critic, worse even than the *Glasgow Herald*. It was back to the sheep and goats again. He wondered what Tony would have made of the occasion. Granted, he had star billing, but it wasn't much of a venue. And as for the warm-up act . . . He let his attention wander. Words floated towards him, carried by the dust motes.

'I am the resurrection and the life . . . whoever believes in me . . . Man that is born of woman has but a short time to live . . .'

Tony's life had certainly been short. He had

been barely thirty when he died, the same age as Ethel. Her funeral had been grim too, just him and Edgar and the undertaker's men. They really had to stop this before it became a habit.

The pall-bearers were shouldering the coffin again. Tony's parents followed it out, his mother holding a handkerchief to her eyes. The solid man and his wife followed. The man looked like a larger version of Tony, and Max guessed he was his older brother. The wife cast them a scared glance as she passed. Max smiled encouragingly.

They drove from the church to Kensal Green Cemetery, a sprawling city of tombs that reminded Max of Père Lachaise in Paris. He was pretty sure that the comparison wouldn't have occurred to Tony's parents or to the brother.

The coffin was lowered into the grave. Tony's mother threw in a small posy of flowers. One of the undertaker's men then offered around a tray full of soil, like a grisly tray of canapés. Max let his handful trickle through his fingers onto the mahogany lid with its brass name-plate. (Why did it need a name-plate? Who the hell would be asking who was inside?) In an escapology act, this was where the music would swell and the wooden box would shake and the magician would rise, holding the severed handcuffs triumphantly over his head. But, as this wasn't Saturday night at the Palladium, all that happened was that two birds flew overhead, cawing loudly, and the pall-bearers withdrew, leaving Tony's family facing the horrible gaping hole.

Tony's mother turned to Max. 'It was so kind of you to come. Were you a friend of Anthony's?'

'Yes,' said Max. 'We served in the army together.'

'Was that in Scotland?' asked his father. 'We were surprised when Tony volunteered for that. He had a reserved occupation, you know. Journalist.'

Max had often wondered how Tony had managed to avoid military service. Well, now he knew. Tony had been a journalist though, to Max's knowledge, he had never reported on anything other than his own brilliance. Ironic, really, that he had been able to get through the war unscathed, only to die a brutal and violent death.

'You're that magician,' the brother cut in. 'Max Mephisto.'

Max admitted that he was. Incredibly, this news seemed to impress Mrs Mulholland. 'Max Mephisto! Well I never. Think of Max Mephisto coming to Anthony's funeral. He was ever such a fan of yours, wasn't he, Dad?'

'He was,' admitted Mr Mulholland.

'Won't you come back to the house, Mr Mephisto? Have a cup of tea? And you too, Inspector Stephens.'

Max could think of nothing he'd like less, but he couldn't think how to refuse. Edgar was no

171

help at all. He stood staring glumly at a neighbouring gravestone (angel, arms out-stretched, lichened hair streaming down stone back) and seemed incapable of speech.

Edgar had thought that nothing could be more depressing that Ethel's funeral, but this was worse. At least with Ethel nothing had been expected of him, but here the Mulhollands seemed to expect him to play the role of Tony's grieving friend. It had been bad enough in church, with the vicar looking down his nose at them and the sister-in-law acting as though they were about to assault her. And the cemetery had been ghastly, rows and rows of graves, like some terrible housing estate, like Esher in fact. But then, just when he thought they might be able to escape, Max had accepted an invitation back to the house.

'What were you thinking?' he asked, as the Bentley followed the Mulhollands' gleaming Morris with Tony's brother at the wheel.

'I felt sorry for them,' said Max. 'Your son dies in a horrible way and then only two people turn up at his funeral. Was I going to say that we couldn't even bring ourselves to have a cup of tea with them?'

'I feel sorry for them too,' said Edgar. 'I had to take them to see Tony's body, for God's sake. I was the one who volunteered to come to the funeral in the first place. But it's hypocritical to pretend that we were all best pals. Besides, I'm in the middle of an investigation, I oughtn't to get too friendly with them.'

Max's lips twitched as if he recognised the poorness of this excuse. 'Think about it as a chance to pick up some clues,' he said.

Clues may have been thin on the ground, but there was no shortage of childhood anecdotes back at the Mulhollands' neat terraced house. Before they had sat down, Edgar had been shown a picture of Tony at school ('he was ever so bright, but the masters didn't seem to like him') and at Scouts ('he was asked to leave just after this picture was taken') and as a young man on the stage ('he was going to be on television, you know'). Edgar looked at the young Tony, grinning cockily at the camera, and wondered how this timid couple had ever produced such a son. All the same, he was glad they had come. Mrs Mulholland had produced quite a spread: scones, sponge cake and cucumber sandwiches. It would have been too pathetic if there had been no one to eat it.

They sat in what Mrs Mulholland called the 'front room' and tried to balance teacups and dainty plates on their laps. Mr Mulholland sat in what was obviously his chair and made little contribution to the conversation. The brother, whose name was Brian, sat beside them on the sofa and proceeded to hold forth. He had the pompous manner of someone who is used to being listened to. His eyes were bulbous versions of Tony's famous mesmerist orbs. Pauline, Brian's wife, sat opposite and watched him with what could have been either awe or resentment. 'Of course,' said Brian, demolishing a sandwich in one bite, 'Tony should never have got involved with those showbiz types. It wasn't how we were brought up, you know. We used to go to Sunday school and everything.' Max smiled sardonically into his tea and Edgar wondered where Brian Mulholland thought showbusiness people sprang from. He thought of the performers in Brighton last week. Presumably Geronimo and the 'Cherry Ripe' singer and the chorus girls all had parents who had sent them to school and to church on Sundays without knowing that they would one day dress up in sequins in front of a paying audience.

'Of course, you're not one of them, are you?' Brian was saying.

'No,' said Edgar. 'I haven't got enough talent to be on the stage.'

'Talent!' said Brian. 'If you can call it talent. Tony was a clever enough kid. Very quick at arithmetic and things like that. He could have had an office job like me. But, no, he had to become a magician of all things . . .' His voice trailed off as he seemed to register Max's presence for the first time.

'Of course, I don't mean you,' he said, after a slightly awkward pause, 'I mean, you're famous.'

'Oh, I agree,' said Max. 'Performing magic tricks is no job for a grown man.'

'Tony was always so quick with his hands,' said Mrs Mulholland. 'I remember him making a ten-shilling note disappear, just like that. He was only a schoolboy when he did that trick.' She smiled. Edgar wanted to ask if Tony had been able to make the money appear again. He had been notoriously stingy. He thought of Ruby performing card tricks for her mother. Where was Ruby now, the girl who wanted to be a magician in her own right? Max said that he didn't know whether she had another job. Was he really going to let her disappear from his life so easily?

'Tony was clever,' said his father. 'That's why he was picked for that special mission in the war. Top-secret, it was. Very important stuff.' He turned to Max. 'Did you say you served with Tony up in Scotland?'

'Yes,' said Max. 'Excellent cakes, Mrs Mulholland.'

'Thank you.' Tony's mother looked overwhelmed by this praise. Edgar had noticed how she watched Max carefully as he ate, perhaps expecting a rabbit to burst out of his hat and start sharing the cucumber sandwiches.

But Mr Mulholland's mind was still on the war. 'Are you in touch with anyone else from that unit, what did he call it, the Magic Men? The old chap, what was his name? The Great Dynamo?'

'Why do you ask, Mr Mulholland?' asked Edgar curiously.

'It's just, the last time Anthony came to see us, just before he went down to Brighton, he told us that he'd seen him, the old magician.'

'Really?' Edgar and Max exchanged glances.

'Yes. He'd run into him in some godforsaken place, out east somewhere. Said he was on the skids, in a pretty bad way.'

'Can you remember where?' asked Edgar. 'It's just that we're quite anxious to trace Diablo.'

'Diablo. That was his name. I saw him at the Empire before the war and he was on the way out, even then.'

'Can you remember where Tony saw Diablo?' Edgar persisted.

But Mr Mulholland had lapsed back into silence. It was his wife who leant forward, in the act of pressing another home-made cake upon Max, and said, 'It was Great Yarmouth. I remember because we went to Yarmouth for our honeymoon.'

'Yarmouth,' Brian laughed nastily. 'It's a wonder you weren't divorced years ago.'

CHAPTER 18

Edgar surprised himself by enjoying the drive to Norfolk. This was partly because Max had let him drive. If the view from the passenger seat transformed the world into something exotic and wonderful, that was nothing to the view from behind the wheel. He felt like a racing driver, a flying ace, the first of the few; arms braced, foot on the accelerator, the Sussex countryside merging into the London suburbs.

'Take it easy,' said Max. 'You can be fined for speeding, you know.'

'There's not a police car in the country that would catch us,' said Edgar. But he slowed down slightly.

It hadn't been easy, persuading Frank Hodges that he needed two days away from the station. The town was full of rumours about the so-called 'conjuror killer', but the police didn't seem to be any closer to making an arrest. 'You'd think somebody would notice a man walking through the streets carrying a bloody great sword,' was how Frank had put it. But the murderer did seem to be able to walk the streets unnoticed and undetected. Bob had managed to trace the sword to an antique shop in the Lanes, but the owner had only been able to provide the vaguest description of the man who had purchased it. 'I think it was a man, a smallish man. I think he had a moustache.' Was this the same small man who had bought flowers at Brighton station before storing Ethel's dismembered body in Lost Property? Everything pointed to the murders being committed by the same person, but his years with the Magic Men had led Edgar to distrust pointers, especially obvious ones. 'Put something in the centre,' Max had said, 'create a space around it, and it becomes important.' Was this what he was doing with the sword and the flowers, all the peripheral props? What was the important thing here?

He had had some success with tracing Diablo though. On impulse, he had rung Bill, remembering that Bill had invited the Major—and Edgar and Tony too—to his wedding. Had he asked Diablo? Well, no, but it seemed that Diablo had got wind of the event all the same. He had sent a card, delicately balancing congratulations with an appeal for money. The address was a guesthouse in Great Yarmouth.

'Did you send him any money?' Edgar asked.

'A bit,' said Bill. 'Just for old times, you know. There's no need to say anything about it to Jean.'

'But why Great Yarmouth?' Edgar wondered aloud, as they approached the Blackwall Tunnel. 'Diablo wasn't from round there, was he?'

'There's quite a nice theatre in Yarmouth,' said Max. 'The Windmill.'

'Surely he's not still performing?'
'He's the sort who'll go on till he drops.'

Max had heard from Diablo a few times since the war. At first these communications had been fairly convivial: a suggestion that they meet for a drink, followed by a request for a recommendation to an agent or a management. They would meet in dark bars where Diablo was invariably a member. Max would hand over a fiver and write an unblushingly glowing reference. A few years down the line, and the appeals became rather more desperate, money needed to pay for food rather than drink. Diablo stopped suggesting that they meet, but he always sent a forwarding address in neat capitals. But, for the last two years, nothing. Max was ashamed how quickly he assumed that Diablo must be dead. But now, here he was, alive and well in Great Yarmouth. Well, alive at any rate.

Where did old music hall acts go to die? It was a question that had started to bother Max a lot, late at night, lying in some hotel bedroom unsure for a second exactly where he was. Was that the door or the wardrobe? Where was the light switch? What was that odd smell? Was it the plumbing or something more sinister? What the hell was he doing with his life? He couldn't go on forever, like Diablo. Soon people like the Mulhollands wouldn't know his name. He would just be that magician chappie who'd been quite big before the war. He was forty years old and he'd never owned a house, mowed a lawn or fathered a child. What was going to happen to him when he could no longer remember how to perform the cup trick? Would he too end up performing at the far end of a pier at the far end of Britain?

He wondered if he was mad, cancelling his French holiday to go slogging around the country with Edgar, calling on old comrades whom he hadn't liked much the first time, attending funerals and visiting out of the way seaside resorts. At first, despite everything, there had been a kind of excitement about it. Together he and Edgar were going to solve the mystery, bring wrongdoers to justice and lots of other wireless-play clichés. But, at Tony's funeral and afterwards, facing his family across the endless cakes, it didn't seem fun any more. It felt bloody depressing, to be honest.

Still, he was pleased that Edgar had cheered up today. Max knew Edgar was feeling guilty about Tony's death (he was a great one for guilt, you'd think he was the Catholic). Max thought that sometimes he could read Edgar like a book. Tony 'The Mind' Mulholland couldn't have done it better. Edgar was thinking that if he'd caught Ethel's killer, if he'd gone to meet Tony just a little earlier, their old comrade would still be alive. Did he even feel guilty about Charis? Did he think that, if he'd been in Inverness that weekend, he could have stopped her going onto the boat? But Charis was a grown woman. She knew her own mind and she had wanted that mission. Max could still hear her voice. 'Delighted.' She'd looked at him, a glance composed half of challenge and half of amusement. Max thought at the time that she had wanted to assert her authority, she was the senior officer after all. But now he wondered if it was just that she liked danger, whether it was parachuting onto a floating minefield or sleeping with two men at once. Well, either way, she was dead now. Like Tony. Like Ethel. Jesus. Max shook his head to free it from the past. It was going to be a long enough drive without him getting maudlin. Mind you, at the rate Edgar was going, they'd be in Great Yarmouth by lunchtime. Max had made one decision at any rate: he was going to leave Edgar the Bentley in his will.

In fact, they stopped in Cambridge for lunch. They ate at a pub in the shadow of one of the colleges, a lopsided, low-ceilinged place with ties hanging like banners from the ceiling.

'Undergraduate humour,' said the barman when Edgar asked him about this unusual design feature. 'Thank God they're all on holiday at the moment. Cambridge isn't a bad town without the students.'

But Edgar couldn't help imagining himself in the pub, having a pint of beer after lectures and discussing philosophy with a group of like-minded friends. Perhaps he should have stayed at Oxford after all. He could have a scarf and a bike and a basket filled with books about Marx and Hegel. Instead, he had a rented flat in Brighton and a job involving severed body parts. Perhaps he'd even be a don by now, with rooms in college or a cottage by the river complete with a pretty wife who had a lower second in classics.

'Don't look back,' said Max, when Edgar shared this fantasy. 'That way madness lies. We all have regrets, the only answer is not to think about them.'

His face darkened as he said this, and Edgar wondered if he was thinking about Charis.

'I felt sure I'd die in the war,' he said. 'So there wouldn't be any need for all these decisions.'

'Bloody hell,' said Max, raising his glass of red wine to the light. 'You're a bundle of laughs today.'

Edgar was drinking ginger beer (he didn't want to take the edge off his driving). 'Didn't you ever think you were going to die?' he asked. 'Even in Egypt?'

'Never,' said Max. 'Closest I've been to death is first house at the Glasgow Empire.'

Edgar laughed. 'From what you've told me about the Glasgow Empire, that's quite close. But don't you ever wonder why we survived when . . . others didn't?'

Max shrugged. 'It's luck, that's all. There's no

cosmic plan to it. There's no great magician in the sky planning his next trick.'

'But luck's important too. Didn't Tony always say he was born lucky?'

'Well, his luck ran out in that case.'

'Yes, it did.' Edgar thought about Tony 'Lucky' Mulholland, who had been unlucky enough to cross a murderer. Was that really all it came down to in the end? Was Ethel, too, just unlucky?

'Come on,' Max drained his glass. 'Let's get on. The bright lights of Great Yarmouth await. Do you want to drive the rest of the way?'

It was early evening when they reached Great Yarmouth. The shadows were lengthening, donkeys were trudging home across the sands and the fish-and-chip men were putting away their stalls. The town itself, though, was clearly just hotting up for the night. Max hadn't been far wrong about the bright lights. Edgar was amazed at the gaiety of the place. There were amusements and boating lakes and horses wearing straw hats pulling excited visitors along the promenade.

'He might still be performing,' he said to Max. 'There seem to be lots of shows on.' They stopped by a poster for a show on the Britannia Pier. There was no mention of The Great Diablo, though Max snorted to see that Tommy Cooper was topping the bill.

'It's all the new stuff,' said Max. 'Holiday

camps and the Crazy Gang and knobbly-knee competitions. There's no place for an old pro like Diablo.'

'Well, let's keep looking,' said Edgar. 'We know he was here quite recently. If I know Diablo, he'll have found somewhere that'll give him free drink if nothing else.'

Max had booked rooms at the Star on the North Quay. As they drove away from the seafront towards the river, the town seemed to become sadder and more tired. Some of the streets still showed signs of bomb damage and urchins stared open-mouthed at the Bentley. The quay was busy, though, with timber being unloaded and the grey hulls of tankers looming over the terraced houses. Edgar thought of the *Ptolemy* and how long they had laboured over the precise shading of the gun towers. She was at the bottom of the Firth now.

The hotel, though faded, was solid and comfortable. Edgar dumped his suitcase and came downstairs to find Max deep in conversation with a buxom barmaid. He had a whisky in one hand and a cigarette in the other. The barmaid's laughter was rattling the optics. Edgar knew that, given a chance, Max wouldn't move for the rest of the night. He was inches away from starting a poker game.

'Come on,' said Edgar, 'let's go to the address that Bill gave us.'

'What, now?' said Max. 'Can't it wait until morning?'

'Everything can wait until morning,' said the barmaid meaningfully.

'This can't,' said Edgar, propelling Max towards the door.

'You've become awfully officious since you've been a policeman,' grumbled Max.

'And your standards have slipped,' said Edgar. 'That woman was pushing fifty.'

'So am I,' said Max.

'Rubbish. You're forty.' And you weren't above flirting with Ruby, who's half your age, thought Edgar.

According to the barmaid, Diablo's address was only a few streets away. As they walked along the riverbank, the streets became progressively shabbier. Windows were boarded up and many of the houses looked empty. But the guesthouse, though shabby, was obviously clean and cared for. A gnome in the front window sported a sign promising vacancies.

The landlady, a pleasant, exhausted-looking woman in her sixties, seemed happy to answer their questions. Yes, she remembered Mr Parks, a very nice gentleman, she let him off his bill time and time again because he was so polite, but, in the end, well she wasn't Job, was she? Max agreed that she wasn't.

'Do you have any idea where Mr Parks is now?' asked Edgar.

'I'm afraid not. He left in the night, owing quite

a bit, I'm sorry to say. I expect he's gone to London. He had a lot of friends there. He was a brilliant magician once, you know.'

'He was a terrible magician,' said a voice from the back room. A man in his shirt-sleeves appeared in the doorway. The landlady introduced him (with rather touching pride) as her husband.

'He was always trying to do this trick where he passed a coin through a bottle,' said the husband. 'Never got it right. Not once. Drank lots of bottles dry, mind you, but never got the trick right.'

'Poor Diablo,' said Max as they set off through the darkening streets. 'He really was a terrible table magician. And that's where the real skill is. Anyone can do a trick on stage with the right props. But table magic—performing a trick just a few inches away from someone—that takes real sleight of hand.'

'I'm sure you're brilliant at it,' said Edgar sourly. 'But we're no nearer to finding Diablo, are we?'

'Let's go back to the seafront,' said Max. 'We can scout out a few of the shows. And we can get a proper drink.'

'We don't need to find Diablo,' said Edgar. 'You're turning into him.' But he allowed himself to be propelled back towards the centre of town.

On the Golden Mile, the lights were blazing. There were shows on both piers as well as a circus and something called a 'Venetian Carnival' on the boating lake. But none of these attractions featured an ageing magician called The Great Diablo. Eventually Max and Edgar ended up in a seedy 'Private Members' club, chosen because it seemed to be the only place in Great Yarmouth that sold spirits.

Max slouched at the bar, staring into his whisky. He was at his gloomiest and least talkative. Edgar sipped a gin and tonic and wondered whether Diablo was in fact dead. After all, members of the Magic Men seemed to be dropping like flies. Charis was dead, Tony was dead. The Major couldn't have many years left. Soon it would be only him and Max. Oh, and Bill. Bill would live forever, surrounded by Jean and an ever-expanding family of huge children . . . It was a few minutes before he was aware of a disturbance in the background. The doorman, a heavyset Irishman, was making an announcement. For the first time, Edgar realised that there was a rudimentary stage at one end of the room with tables grouped around it. The doorman, now wearing a greenish-looking tail-coat, was standing beside a velvet curtain.

'Ladies and gentlemen,' he intoned though, as Edgar suddenly realised, the clientele of the club was exclusively male. 'For one night only—Suzette de Paris.'

The scratch of a gramophone needle, a blast of Offenbach and a woman appeared from behind the curtain. The music stopped abruptly and, accompanied only by wheezy breathing and the hiss of the gas fire, Suzette proceeded to remove her dress.

Edgar thought that he'd scarcely seen anything sadder than this desolate striptease. He'd been to a strip club once before (with Tony, of course) and then he remembered that there had at least been some semblance of enjoyment from the participants. And the audience had clearly been having the time of their lives, whooping and cat-calling. Here although, with the exception of Max, everyone was watching Suzette, nobody seemed to be enjoying the spectacle very much. The club members stared solidly ahead, occasionally raising their pint glasses to their lips. And Suzette, pulling off petticoat, bra and, finally, pants, could have been getting undressed for bed. No, not for bed (which would presuppose some pleasurable anticipation), for an examination at the doctor's. When, naked, she gyrated half-heartedly in front of them, Edgar almost expected to hear a dispassionate medical voice ask, 'Where does it hurt, dear?'

Edgar turned back to Max, who was staring morosely into his drink.

'God, how depressing. I only hope she gets paid well for this.'

'I doubt it,' said Max.

'Think her name's really Suzette?'

'Who knows. I had a girlfriend called Emerald once. She had a snake-charming act.'

Edgar watched as Suzette parked herself on the lap of a distinctly unenthralled spectator. Suddenly he thought of Charis and her room at the Caledonian, how the pale Scottish sunlight had embraced her as she had stood in front of him, her hair like fire. She liked to walk around naked, doing ordinary things like pulling the curtains and lighting the lamps, teasing him with her beauty.

Almost without knowing it, he stood up.

'Siddown,' shouted a voice at the back of the room.

'I'm off,' said Edgar to Max, 'See you outside.'

But, as he crossed the room, Suzie finished her spot and, gathering up her clothes, disappeared behind the curtain. This time the doorman was saying, with markedly less enthusiasm, 'It's time for Mr Magico.'

And Edgar heard a familiar voice offering to make a coin pass through a bottle.

CHAPTER 19

'Diablo!' said Edgar, before he could stop himself.

The old man peered across the dark room. 'Edgar? It that you, dear boy?'

'Geddon with it,' shouted a voice from one of the tables.

Diablo was still looking eagerly towards the direction of Edgar's voice.

'Edgar? What are you doing here? Is Max with you?'

'I'm here,' Max spoke from the bar.

'Max!' Face wreathed in smiles, Diablo reached out to shake his hand.

'Get on with your act, you old fool,' said the doorman.

'My act, yes.' Diablo looked down at the bottle in his hand in apparent bewilderment. 'I'm now going to pass this bottle through the coin . . . No, the coin through the bottle . . .'

The audience started to boo.

'No, hold on a second,' pleaded Diablo. 'In one hand I have a sealed bottle. In the other I have a coin, an ordinary coin of the realm.' He opened his hand. It was empty. The booing grew louder.

'Do some magic,' hissed the doorman, 'or you're out.'

Diablo still continued to stare at his empty palm. Edgar stood rooted to the spot by the door. He wanted to rescue Diablo, to floor the doorman, to silence the crowd. But how and in which order? While he dithered, Max strode forward. Gently, he took the bottle from Diablo's hand.

'Come on, old chap. Let's get out of here.'

'You're fired,' said the doorman.

'He's been fired from better places than this,' said Max.

He placed the bottle in the doorman's hand, turned it upside down once and then rattled it to show the half-crown that was now inside.

'Consider it a tip,' he said. 'Come on, Ed.'

And the three of them trooped out of the club.

Outside it was dark and cold. Diablo shivered in his thin jacket. He was wearing fairly presentable evening dress, but it looked too big on him. The trousers were held up by jaunty green braces. The shirt was stained with what looked like red wine.

'Let's go back to the Star,' said Max. 'Have a meal, get Diablo a bed for the night.'

'Anything you say, dear boy,' said Diablo, tucking his arm into Max's. He seemed quite unfazed by the events of the night.

After shepherd's pie, served by Max's barmaid friend, Diablo became more expansive.

'What are you two doing here? Bit far from the bright lights, Yarmouth.'

'We came to see you,' said Max, leaning back and lighting a cigarette.

'To see me?' Diablo cocked his head on one side, looking like a rather dishevelled parrot.

'A few things have happened,' said Edgar. 'We think they may be linked to the Magic Men.'

'The Magic Men,' repeated Diablo. To Edgar's surprise, there were tears in his eyes. 'Those were the days, weren't they? The fun we had.'

Edgar had grown used to thinking of the Magic Men years as purgatory. A limbo of tedium, followed by the heaven of his affair with Charis and the hell of her death. It hadn't occurred to him that to Diablo they were halcyon days.

'We did have some fun,' he said, realising that this was true. 'But this is a bit more serious. It's about murder.'

'Murder?' Diablo's still watery eyes were round with surprise.

'Edgar's a policeman now,' said Max.

'A bobby? Bless my soul. I thought you were such a clever chap.'

'I'm not the clever one,' said Edgar. 'That was Max, if you remember. Look, Diablo, this will come as a shock. Prepare yourself. It's about Tony.'

'Tony? What's the young fool done now?'

'Got himself murdered,' said Edgar. He told Diablo the whole story, about Ethel's dismembered body, about Tony and the sword cabinet. He wondered why he was telling Diablo things that he had deliberately withheld from Bill. The old magician was a good audience. He listened attentively, occasionally sipping his wine. The bottle in front of him was almost empty, but he didn't seem even slightly drunk. In fact, the meal and the company seemed to have revived him to an extraordinary extent.

At the end of Edgar's story, Diablo said, 'Poor old Tony. That wasn't the way I expected him to go.'

'How did you expect him to go?' asked Max.

'Oh, heart attack in a penthouse surrounded by dancing girls. That sort of thing. You know I saw him recently? Here in Yarmouth.'

'Yes, we heard that,' said Edgar. 'What was Tony doing in Yarmouth?'

'What do any of us do anywhere?' asked Diablo. 'He was on the bill at the Windmill. He had a comedy act. I went to see him. Just to be kind, you know, but it wasn't my sort of thing at all. I told him, dear boy, stick to magic. The public will never get bored with seeing a rabbit appear out of a hat. But, no, Tony said the money was in comedy. Magic was dead, he said. He was going to make it big in television, be a millionaire in five years, that sort of talk.'

Edgar wondered whether Diablo had persuaded Tony to part with any of his beloved cash. On balance, he thought not. Diablo was a good hustler, but Tony kept his wallet close.

'He was on the bill with me in Brighton,' said Max. 'A comedy act with a few mind-tricks. He was working quite well, but it didn't seem to click for some reason.'

'When you met Tony,' said Edgar, 'did he say whether he'd been in touch with anyone else from the Magic Men?'

'Yes,' said Diablo, much to Edgar's surprise. 'I know he'd seen the Major.'

'Major Gormley? Really?' Edgar looked at

Max. Didn't the Major say that he hadn't seen any of the Magic Men in years?

'Yes. Said he'd seen the Major and he was as stiff-necked as ever. Got the impression that they might have quarrelled.'

'What about?'

Diablo laughed. 'When did Tony ever need an excuse to quarrel? Boy had a positive genius for getting under your skin. Not to speak ill of the dead, of course.'

'What about Bill? Had he seen Bill?'

'I don't think so. Bill got married. Did you know?'

'Yes,' said Max. 'We went to see them. They've got a very small house and a very big baby.'

'He married Jean Whitby, didn't he?'

'Yes,' said Edgar. 'I didn't remember her, but she was at Inverness.'

'You must remember Jean, dear boy. She had a thumping great crush on you.'

Edgar stared at him. 'On me?'

'Yes. Don't you remember? Oh, most of them fancied Max, but little Jean had a real thing for you. She was always hanging round asking questions.'

'I don't remember,' said Edgar again, but even as he said it, a picture flickered in his brain, a tiny flash of light. Coming back from the dock where they'd been working on the *Ptolemy*, a blonde girl walking up the towpath with them, asking endless questions about boats and camouflage, Tony's voice saying, 'Haven't you got a home to go to, Jean?'

'The Major said that he'd been visited by a girl,' said Max, 'a journalist. Has anyone been pestering you, asking about the Magic Men?'

Now Diablo laughed in earnest, wiping his eyes on his napkin. 'Dear boy, it's been years since a girl pestered me: 1921, to be exact. Summer season at the Palladium. Shall we order another bottle?'

Edgar woke the next morning feeling very much the worse for wear. Max, he remembered from old, was able to drink all night without it seeming to affect him at all, and even Diablo had the iron constitution of a hardened drinker. Last night, after the wine, they had moved on to brandy. Edgar dimly remembered sitting in the hotel's parlour under a portrait of Nelson and listening to Diablo reminisce about Vesta Tilley, pantomime dames and girls you didn't have to wine and dine before kissing them. When Edgar had finally staggered off to bed, Max and Diablo were still sitting by the gas fire; Max in shadow, the light glinting off his balloon glass, Diablo performing his famous ashtray routine.

But, when Edgar braved the Terrace Room for breakfast, there was Diablo, bright and breezy, demolishing bacon and fried bread. There was no sign of Max, but that was only to be expected. Max didn't like mornings, never ate breakfast and thought fried bread was the invention of the devil.

'Morning, dear boy,' Diablo greeted him. 'Can I pour you some tea? There's still some in the pot.'

'Thank you,' said Edgar faintly.

Diablo poured the tea, humming 'Mary from the Dairy' under his breath. Last night he had looked a hundred, an old man worn out by drink, poverty and years of touring seaside towns offering to pass a coin through a bottle. But, this morning, though he was still dressed in a crumpled dinner jacket and bow tie, there was a determined cheerfulness about the old magician, a sense that he would rise again another day. God, these old pros are tough, thought Edgar, wincing as he swallowed the lukewarm tea, a year on the variety circuit would kill him, but here was Diablo, who must be at least eighty, homeless and penniless, settling down to his breakfast as if he hadn't a care in the world.

The barmaid from last night appeared with more tea. Edgar requested some toast.

'No bacon?' said Diablo. 'They keep pigs, you know.'

'No thank you.'

Fresh tea revived Edgar slightly. They would have to set off for Brighton that morning. He had already taken too much time off. Had they gained anything from the trip to Yarmouth? Only the knowledge that Tony had met Major Gormley fairly recently and that they had quarrelled. Did that get them any further? As Diablo had said, Tony had been capable of quarrelling with almost anyone. He would have to get a list of everyone who had been on the bill with Tony over the last few years. There was bound to be some bad feeling somewhere. Bad feeling had followed Tony like a cloud. He had to make some progress on this case before anything else happened . . .

But it seemed that Diablo had also been thinking about the future.

'You know, dear boy,' he said, wiping his hands delicately on a napkin. 'I've been thinking. To tell you the truth, Yarmouth is pretty flat at this time of year. I was thinking that I might go back to Brighton with you. Lovely place, Brighton. Always feel years younger when I can breathe in the sea air.' He sniffed hopefully, one eye on Edgar.

'Of course you can come back with us,' said Edgar. 'But what . . . ?' He meant to say, what will you do? Where will you stay? But Diablo waved aside these questions with an airy hand. 'Something will turn up. It always does.'

'Do you need to collect your things?' said Edgar, feeling as though events were moving rather fast. 'Where are you staying?'

'And how much do you owe there?' said a voice behind them. Max had materialised, immaculately dressed as usual, cigarette in hand.

'Good morning, Max,' said Diablo. 'Care for some tea?'

Max shuddered. 'No thanks. I was asking how much you owed at your digs.'

Diablo looked hurt. 'I always pay my way.'

'We called in at the Nelson yesterday.'

Diablo was unabashed. 'Did you? Lovely people. Always enjoyed my magic tricks.'

Max drove Diablo to his lodgings to collect his belongings. 'I'll take my chequebook,' he said to Edgar. 'I'm not sure I'll have enough cash on me to pay the old devil's bar bill.'

Edgar waited for them in the front parlour watched sardonically by Admiral Nelson. He paced the room, feeling obscurely resentful. It was all very well for Max to swan in, paying Diablo's bills, whisking him out of that dive last night, performing the bottle trick as an encore. This was supposed to be Edgar's show. He was a policeman and this was still a police case. He wandered into the bar. The place was deserted apart from the barmaid half-heartedly wiping tables. She seemed to do everything. She'd probably cooked breakfast too. And slaughtered the pig. Edgar said a polite good morning and made his way back to the lobby. There was a public telephone by the reception desk, but, with an odd twist of loneliness, Edgar realised that there was no one who would really welcome a telephone call from him. His mother had a phone, but she viewed it with extreme suspicion. He could just hear her voice, 'But why are you calling, dear? What's wrong?' His sister would be friendly but impatient. She had her own life; doctor's receptionist and mother of three noisy sons. She wouldn't appreciate being interrupted in the middle of some urgent domestic or clerical task just because he was in Yarmouth and feeling sorry for himself. In the end, he telephoned Bob at the police station. Might as well try to do his job well, even if his personal life was non-existent. And Bob was at least paid to be polite to him.

'Who's that?' said Bob. 'Ed who?'

'Your boss,' said Edgar. 'Have there been any developments?'

'What sort of developments?' said Bob cautiously.

Edgar counted to ten. 'Anything you think I might need to know.'

'Well, something was delivered for you yesterday.'

Edgar's heart contracted. He thought of the black box addressed to Captain Edgar Stephens. The stench that had Sergeant McGuire backing away, retching. The sight that greeted him when he opened the lid.

'What sort of thing? A package?'

'No. A letter. Hand-delivered.'

'Who's it addressed to?'

There was a brief pause. 'To you.'

This time Edgar counted to twenty. 'The exact name.'

'Captain E. Stephens.'

'Open it.'

A maddeningly long silence, interspersed with the sound of a letter-opener and Bob telling someone called Cathy that he liked it strong with two sugars.

'For God's sake,' Edgar exploded. 'Forget your tea break and tell me what's in the bloody letter.'

Another silence, an offended one this time. 'It's a photograph,' said Bob.

'A photograph? Of what?'

'A group of people standing by a boat, a battleship. They look like soldiers except one's wearing a straw hat. Oh, one of them's you . . .'

'Me?'

'Yes. You look a lot younger though. There's someone who looks like that magician friend of yours, Max Mephisto. And there's a girl on the end. She's quite pretty.'

Quite pretty? Even after all these years, Edgar bristled at this description of Charis, the most beautiful woman since Helen of Troy.

'Anything else about the photo?' he asked.

'Well, one of the people has a cross over his face. It's the man between you and Mephisto.'

That must be Tony, who often positioned

himself between Max and Edgar as if he resented their friendship. The man in the straw hat must be Diablo, who insisted on wearing this headgear in the face of Major Gormley's rage. 'I need to protect my skin,' he would say, regardless of the fact that Inverness saw roughly one day's sun a year. The boat must be the *Ptolemy*. Edgar felt a moment's pride that Bob had thought she was a bona fide battleship.

'There's something else,' his sergeant was saying. 'Something written on the back.'

'What?'

'It says: "For my next trick, The Wolf Trap".'

CHAPTER 20

They were on their way back to Brighton. Max was driving and Edgar sat next to him. Diablo sat in the back, exclaiming with pleasure over the comfort of the seats and the smoothness of the drive. Edgar had told the others about his telephone call and the delivery of the photograph. Neither of them seemed particularly concerned about the sinister implication of Tony's crossed-out face. They were trying to place the magic trick.

'The Wolf Trap,' said Max. 'I've seen it performed a few times. It's one of those "mind over matter" things. Magician starts with a small trap, shows it snapping a pencil in two. Then a bigger trap, this time it breaks a stick or a branch. Raising the stakes each time. Ends up with a huge trap, the wolf trap. The magician puts his head inside and comes out unscathed. Trick is that this trap might be bigger, but it's the least dangerous, the blades are probably made of rubber. But the audience is fooled into thinking that the traps get more dangerous as they get bigger.'

'I've seen a different version,' said Diablo. 'It's an escapology act. Magician gets into a cage called The Wolf Trap. Darkness, sound effects of wolves howling. Lights go up and—hey presto!—he's free.'

'Well, whatever it is,' said Edgar, 'it's his next trick.' He wasn't sure if he should have told Max and Diablo about the picture, but Max knew so much already that it seemed stupid not to tell him this latest development. And Diablo, well somehow he'd become one of the team. A slightly troublesome member, it was true, prone to performing drunken turns at strip clubs, but one of the gang all the same. It's like a parody of a family, thought Edgar, with Max as the father behind the wheel and Diablo as the whining youngster in the back seat. God, what did that make him? The mother?

'Are we there yet?' asked Diablo, right on cue.

Max ignored him. 'Do you really think that this chap is picking us off one by one?' he asked.

'Bags I be next,' said Diablo brightly.

'It's not funny,' said Edgar dourly. 'We should all have police protection. I'll have to warn Bill.'

'But why Ethel?' said Max. 'She wasn't one of the Magic Men.'

'I don't know,' said Edgar. 'Unless she was an attempt to get at you.'

'But how would anyone know about the link between me and Ethel?'

'It wouldn't be hard to find out.'

'Well, if he's after all Max's old girlfriends,' said Diablo, 'he's got his work cut out.'

'Ethel wasn't an old girlfriend,' said Max. 'I'd never have an affair with an assistant. Too dangerous.'

Dangerous was an odd word to choose, thought Edgar, as he looked out over the grey countryside, land and sea merging into each other (Diablo was right: Yarmouth was very flat). And he wasn't sure if he believed Max's protestations about his assistants. He certainly seemed to be getting pretty close to Ruby that day on the pier. Ruby! Edgar thought of that little figure twirling on stage, at once provocative and vulnerable. He remembered her walking beside him on the promenade, the little skipping steps as she tried to keep up. Could Ruby be in danger? He'd better speak to her, just in case. He realised that Diablo was talking to him.

'All right if I stay with you, old boy,' he was asking, 'just until I get myself sorted.'

'I've only got a small place,' protested Edgar.

'Doesn't matter,' said Diablo kindly. 'I'm an awfully good house guest. You'll hardly know I'm there.'

Edgar found himself agreeing to share a flat with The Great Diablo.

By the time they got to Brighton, Max had had enough of both of them. He wasn't used to spending so much concentrated time with other people. His life normally consisted of audiences—far enough away as to become faceless—the occasional girl and plenty of solitude. He remembered now that this was what he had hated about the army: the enforced camaraderie, the banter, the idea of being part of a team. 'Max isn't a team player,' his headmaster had written on his report. It was meant to be a criticism—that school had *worshipped* team games, that whole 'play up and play the game' rot—but, even at the time, Max had glowed with pride. No, he wasn't a team player. He was better than that.

Max liked Edgar, had sometimes thought that he was like a younger brother to him. Not that he had any idea what it was like to have a brother, what with his mother dying when he was six and his father being too much of an unsociable bastard to find himself another wife. But, even with Edgar, there were times when he just wanted to be left alone with a whisky and a cigarette, not to be constantly talking things over all the time. 'What do you think of Bill? Mrs Bill? Major Gormley?' Christ, these were people he had hoped never to see again. And Diablo. When he had seen Diablo on stage, fumbling with that bloody coin and bottle, he'd been shot through with pity. He had wanted to take care of him, rescue him from that ghastly club, sit him in an armchair and tell him that he'd never have to do another card trick as long as he lived. But now, after having spent the day with the old reprobate, he felt as if he'd willingly sell Diablo to the highest bidder. Not that he'd get many offers. 'To tell you the truth, dear boy,' Diablo had said to him that morning, 'I'm not quite the draw I once was.'

When he'd seen the squalid lodgings and had helped Diablo pack his belongings into a cardboard suitcase tied up with string, the com-passionate feeling was back again. This was no life for an old man. How old *was* Diablo? Seventy? Eighty? He deserved to be sitting at home, surrounded by his family, boring them senseless with stories of his showbusiness youth. But Diablo had no family. 'Never had time to get a wife,' he had confided last night over the port. 'Too late now, of course.' He had leered hope-fully at the barmaid. Was that going to be how Max ended up? Slogging round the strip clubs of Great Yarmouth, trying to do the coin in the bottle trick? God, no. He'd shoot himself first.

After he had dropped Edgar and Diablo at Edgar's digs (trying to suppress a smile at Edgar's obvious dismay at this arrangement), he drove straight to the Old Ship. He wanted to have a hot bath and an evening of complete silence—apart from the words 'a large steak and a bottle of red wine please'.

But, as he crossed the lobby, a voice said, 'Someone to see you, Mr Mephisto.' Christ, who was it this time? Another skeleton about to come crawling out of the cupboard? He honestly felt that he'd seen enough cupboards for one lifetime.

And it was a skeleton of a kind, albeit a rather well-fleshed one, red-faced and uncomfortable after his long wait.

'Hallo, Max,' said Bill.

'Bill! What are you doing here?'

Bill flushed, looking more overheated than ever.

'I wanted to see you.'

Why? was the question on Max's lips, but he realised that this would sound impossibly rude, especially as it transpired that Bill had been waiting for him since eleven o'clock that morning. It was now five, so Max suggested tea in the conservatory, a comfortable English ritual to offset what he felt was going to be a singularly uncomfortable conversation.

As they sat down in the 'sun room'—black and

white tiles, wrought-iron furniture, piano tinkling in the background—Max reflected that this was probably the first time that he'd ever been alone with Bill. 'Salt of the earth,' is what he would have said if anyone had asked him about the ex-sergeant, but earth had never been Max's favourite element. At Inverness, he was aware of Bill only as an excellent craftsman and, later, as the man who—unwittingly or not—broke Edgar's stupidly breakable heart. He was happy to talk to Bill about refinements to the *Ptolemy* or the construction of dummy tanks, but in the evenings —if nothing better was on offer—he had always sought out the company of Edgar or Diablo. Even Tony had more to say for himself.

But now, it seemed, Bill had something to say.

'Hope you don't mind me tracking you down like this,' he said, absent-mindedly demolishing a scone. 'It's just . . . I wanted to tell you something.'

'Why didn't you tell me last week,' said Max, 'when Edgar and I came to visit?' Was it only last week? It seemed years ago.

Bill took a gulp of tea and choked. His face was redder than ever and his eyes bulged alarmingly. Max wondered whether he should pat him on the back or just wait until the paroxysm had passed. He settled for waiting.

'It's difficult,' said Bill, when he could speak. 'Didn't want to talk in front of Jean.'

'Ah.' Now that, Max could understand.

'She gets . . . well, *difficult* sometimes. Women often get like that when they've had a baby.'

'Do they?'

Bill nodded solemnly. 'You wouldn't know . . . well, at least I . . . that is. . . .' He seemed about to choke again.

Max took pity on him. 'No, I wouldn't know. So what was it that you didn't want to say in front of Jean?'

In answer, Bill took a sheet of notepaper from his pocket and spread it out on the table in front of them.

The letter was written in a bold sloping hand.

Dear Bill,

A voice from the grave, eh? Bet you're surprised to hear from me. Got your address from old Gormley. I hear you've got yourself pretty well set up—wife, baby, all that. Well, old fruit, if you want to keep it that way, you need to come and see me in Brighton. Saturday 12th August, 1.15 p.m. at the address above. I've got something to show you. Trust me, this is important. You can't afford to ignore me. Not this time anyway.

I'll expect you on Friday.

Pip pip!

Tony

PS Not a word to Edgar or any of his pals.

Max looked across the table at Bill. *A voice from the grave.* It was as if he could hear Tony's voice—those mocking Londoner's tones—echoing around the conservatory. He had always known that Tony was vaguely malign, but now it was as if his old comrade had thrown a grenade into their midst, shattering the glass walls, impaling them with tiny, vicious shards. *Bet you're surprised to hear from me . . . if you want to keep it that way . . . You can't afford to ignore me.*

'August the twelfth,' said Max, 'that was the day he died.' The glorious twelfth, he thought. A big day in his father's calendar. Lots of marching over dreary fields slaughtering innocent birds.

'I thought it must be,' said Bill. The date obviously meant nothing to him. He was looking warily at the letter as if he expected it to rise up and attack him. 'Edgar said Saturday. I got the letter on the Thursday. You came to see us the next Tuesday.'

And Edgar was also due to meet Tony that Saturday at one-fifteen, thought Max. He remembered Edgar wondering about the strangely precise time. What the hell had Tony been playing at? *Got your address from old Gormley.* Diablo said that Tony had been in touch with Major Gormley and that they'd quarrelled. What about?

He saw that Bill was still frowning down at the letter. What had Tony got on Bill? Something

209

pretty explosive by the sounds of it. He was struck with a sudden desire to know exactly what Bill had been doing that Saturday afternoon.

'You weren't tempted to go, then?' he asked.

'No.' Bill's voice was suddenly loud. The china rattled on the table and, in the background, the piano stopped momentarily.

Max looked at the letter again. He too felt curiously reluctant to touch it. 'What was that about: "You can't afford to ignore me. Not this time anyway"?'

'I've no idea.'

Max sighed. You didn't need to be an expert on body language to know that Bill was lying. But why? And about what?

'Why did you show me this,' he asked, 'if you'd already decided to ignore it?'

'Well, he's dead. He died that same day. It can't be a coincidence, can it?'

'Why didn't you go to Ed? He's the policeman.'

Bill pointed at the letter. 'He said not to tell Edgar.'

Or any of his pals, thought Max. Did Tony mean Edgar's fellow policemen or the Magic Men?

'But Tony's dead,' he said aloud, 'he can't do anything about it now.'

Bill laughed hollowly. 'Is that what you think?'

Max looked at Bill. There was no doubt about it: the big man was genuinely scared. But why?

What did Bill think had been waiting for him in Brighton?

'Bill,' he said, 'why are you showing me this? What can I do about it?'

Bill rubbed his eyes. His hands were large and efficient, thick fingers, square-cut nails. Workman's hands. Those hands couldn't shuffle a deck, cutting and cutting again, dazzling the audience with false passes so that they failed to notice the mystery card appearing at the top of the pack, but, Max couldn't help thinking, they could do someone a whole lot of damage.

'I thought . . .' said Bill, 'I thought you might have had a similar letter.'

Now it was Max's turn to speak too loudly. 'You thought *I* might have . . .'

'Well, yes.' Bill reddened again but, at the same time, he looked Max in the face for the first time that afternoon. 'He must have written to someone else, mustn't he?'

'Why?'

'Because that person killed him.'

CHAPTER 21

'I'll just have a quick cat nap,' said Diablo. With that, he collapsed onto Edgar's bed (the only bed) and was snoring within seconds. Edgar placed the cardboard suitcase on the bedside table and resigned himself to sleeping on the sofa for the duration of Diablo's stay. He wandered into the kitchen to make himself a cup of tea, discovered that there was no milk and wandered out again. It was nearly five o'clock. He could sit down and try to read a book, listening to the reverberations that now seemed to be shaking the whole house. He could go for a walk, up and down the endless hills. He could stroll down to the Old Ship to see Max, but he had a feeling that Max wanted to be left alone for a while. Maybe he should go down to the station and catch up with some work. He might even be able to have a drink with Bob afterwards. Edgar picked up his hat.

Bob, who was clearly just about to slope off early, did not look overjoyed to see his boss. Edgar didn't detain him.

'I'll just have a look at that photograph you mentioned and then I'll join you in the pub. Are you going to the Bath Arms?'

Bob looked at his feet. 'We might be going somewhere else. Haven't decided yet.'

From this, Edgar deduced that his company wasn't welcome.

Edgar heard Bob clattering up the stairs, his shouted goodbyes to the night sergeant, then the door banging behind him. One by one, he heard the other officers leaving. Edgar sat in his subterranean office listening to the old building talking to itself, the water hissing in the tank, the floorboards sighing as they expanded and contracted. He thought of Bill and Jean in their little house, of Major Gormley tending his roses, of Diablo currently snoring on Edgar's bed. Could Tony have known a secret about any of them? Tony, the expert on mind-games, Tony who took the greatest pleasure in bad news. What had been his last explosive truth?

Maybe it would help to look at the pictures in the Incident Room. Edgar walked quickly along the clammy corridors. The cells were in this part of the basement too. They were empty at the moment, but the little airless rooms always made his flesh creep. Really, it was true what Max said; he was temperamentally unsuited to being a policeman.

The Incident Room was deserted. One wall was a gruesome collage of photographs: the black boxes containing Ethel's body, the cabinet with swords protruding, Ethel herself, in glamorous film-star mode, Tony doing the gimlet-eyed stare Edgar remembered from his stage act. 'I can see into your soul,' Tony used to say. Edgar had laughed at the time, but now, turning his back to go through the incident log, he had the uncomfortable feeling that Tony was still staring at him. Why had Tony wanted to see him that day at one-fifteen? What news could he have about the Magic Men, that disparate group of individuals who singularly failed to make any mark on the progress of the war? But, whatever information

Tony had, someone had killed to keep it a secret.

Edgar looked at the pictures again. Ethel, the beautiful showgirl, was pouting across at Tony. Had they known each other? It was certainly possible. Maybe there was a link there that they had overlooked. Maybe he should talk to Ethel's husband again. He should certainly see Major Gormley again. The Major had lied about seeing Tony, even if only by omission. Why?

The ringing of the phone made him jump. Feeling ridiculous, he picked up the receiver. It was the night sergeant.

'Call for you, Detective Inspector Stephens.'

It was Max.

'Max. Hallo.' He was ashamed how glad he was to hear another human voice.

'Ed. I thought you'd be at work.'

'It was the only way I could get away from Diablo.'

Max gave a short laugh. 'Look, Ed. I have to be quick. I'm here with Bill.'

'Bill?'

'Yes. Bit of a surprise visitor. Anyway, he has some news. Apparently Tony had written to him.'

'Tony wrote to Bill? When?'

'A few days before he was killed. He asked Bill to meet him on Saturday at one-fifteen.'

'*What?*'

'Yes. Looks as if it was going to be rather a crowded little meeting.'

'Did Tony say why he wanted to meet Bill?'

'Said he had something to show him. Said it was important.'

Edgar digested this. Tony's face glared down at him from the wall. Was there something mocking in that gaze? *I know something you don't.*

'Why didn't Bill come to me?' he asked.

'The letter said not to. You know Bill, always one for obeying orders.'

'Do you think Tony wrote to anyone else?'

'Bill thinks so. And we know there was someone in his room before he died.'

Edgar thought of the chair by the bed. Tony hadn't been frightened of his visitor. Probably even when he was drinking the tea laced with atropa belladonna or deadly nightshade (traces had been found in one of the cups on the bedside table), he hadn't been afraid. When had he started to guess? When his assailant had loomed over him, forced him to his feet, dragged him into the wardrobe? When the sword had shattered the flimsy wood, its blade shining like poison?

'Who else could Tony have contacted?' he asked.

'I've no idea.'

'You didn't get a letter then?' Edgar hated himself for asking the question.

Max's voice was icy. 'You don't think I would have mentioned it to you?'

'Of course you would have. I'm sorry.'

There was a silence. In the room above,

something—probably a mouse—scuttled across the floor.

'I think I'll go back to see the Major,' said Edgar. 'It's a bit suspicious that he didn't mention meeting Tony.'

'You might try Bill again too,' said Max. 'He's obviously holding something back, but I don't know what.' He didn't offer to accompany Edgar on the visit.

'Did you mention the photograph to Bill?' asked Edgar. 'The one with the face crossed out.'

'No. I didn't want to make him even more nervous.'

'All the same,' said Edgar slowly, 'we ought to warn him. I haven't seen the picture yet, but the implication was that we were being picked off one by one. Diablo should be safe, staying with me. What about you?'

'Don't worry about me. I can take care of myself.'

So could Tony, thought Edgar, but he knew better than to argue. Instead he said, 'We need to find Ruby. I think she ought to be on her guard. After all, it's possible that Ethel was killed because of the link to you.'

Another silence and then Max said, 'I told you I don't have an address. She said her parents lived in Hove, but I never met them. She shared a flat with a girlfriend.'

'And you had no idea where that was?'

'No.'

'I'll get Bob to search the electoral roll.'

'She's not old enough to vote,' said Max. 'She's only twenty.' Then, 'Christ, I hope she's not in danger.'

'I'm sure she'll be fine,' said Edgar, in the soothing tone that he used to the relatives of victims. It didn't seem to work on Max, though. He rang off with the briefest of goodbyes.

Putting down the phone, Edgar turned back to the case file. There, filed neatly, was the letter that had arrived two days ago. The envelope was typed. Edgar made a note to check it against the address label on the box and against the letter from Hugh D. Nee requesting a Post Office box. He drew out the photograph. Even though he was prepared, it was still a shock to see their faces laughing up at him. Max, dark and handsome, cigarette in hand. Diablo in that ridiculous hat. The Major, parade-ground straight. Himself— God, Bob was right, he did look young, callow and innocent, one hand raised in a half-salute. Tony, his face almost completely erased by the heavily scored lines. And, at the edge of the picture . . . Edgar looked again, holding the image up to the light. The girl described by Bob as 'quite pretty' smiled back at him.

It wasn't Charis. It was Jean.

CHAPTER 22

Elsie was having a bad day, said the Major, ushering Edgar to the now familiar rustic seat in the garden in Worthing. It was a humid day, hot without being sunny, and the sea was a pale band in the distance. The Major was sprucely dressed in shirt and tie, but, as he stretched out his legs, Edgar saw that he still had his slippers on.

'I'm sorry to just drop in like this,' he said.

The Major grunted. 'Don't worry. I expected you to come back.'

'You did?'

'Yes. Expected you to come back without Massingham. He's a smart fellow, but he's not one of us.'

'One of us?'

The Major pointed to his regimental tie. 'Services. King and country, that sort of thing. Massingham's clever enough, but he's a foreigner when you come down to it.'

'He's half-Italian,' said Edgar. He wondered why it disturbed him so much to be classed in the same category as the Major.

'Half's enough. And the fellow's a magician. The things he can do with a pack of cards. It's indecent.'

Edgar remembered a trick of Max's where he

had substituted a picture of a naked girl for the Queen of Hearts and the Major's apoplectic face when the offending image had been found in his breast pocket.

'I really came to see you about Tony,' he said.

'Tony Mulholland?' Was it Edgar's imagination or did the Major stiffen slightly?

'Yes. I spoke to Diablo . . .'

'Oh, you tracked him down, did you? What's the old rascal doing now?'

'He's staying with me at the moment.'

The Major gave a short bark of laughter. 'Good luck getting shot of him is all I can say. Man's a born scrounger.'

Edgar thought of Diablo, who had so far commandeered not just Edgar's bed but his best dressing gown and exclusive use of the wireless. Any suggestion that Diablo might leave the house, even if only for exercise, had been countered by an airy wave of the hand. 'Resting, dear boy. Just resting.'

'Diablo thought you might have seen Tony quite recently,' said Edgar. 'I wondered why you didn't mention it before.'

Major Gormley turned to stare at him. Despite the carpet slippers, he suddenly looked formidable, even intimidating.

'What are you implying?'

'Nothing.' Edgar tried the soothing tone again. 'When Max and I came to see you last week, you said that you hadn't seen Tony in years. Diablo got the impression that you'd met him fairly recently. Given the manner of Tony's death, I'm interested in any information about him. That's all.'

The Major seemed to relax slightly, but his tone was still disgruntled. 'I can't remember every damn silly young toerag I meet. I might have bumped into Tony last year some time.'

'Can you remember exactly when?'

'Think it was about Christmas time. We had the tree up. Elsie likes it up early.'

'Did he come here? To the house?' asked Edgar, thinking that this was hardly 'bumping into' someone.

'I think so.'

'Why? Did you invite him or did he just drop in?'

'Think he was just passing. Just wanted to wish us a happy Christmas.'

There was a brief silence whilst Edgar considered this unlikely possibility.

'Diablo said you quarrelled,' he said at last.

'And you believe that drunken old fool?'

I'd sooner believe him than you, thought Edgar. Aloud, he said, 'And you can't remember what you talked about?'

'Oh, this and that. You know how it is.'

'Why didn't you mention this before?'

That glare again. 'I told you. I forgot. That's not a crime, is it?'

Edgar said nothing. The bees buzzed in the

hollyhocks. A neighbour's lawnmower droned and whined.

Major Gormley broke the silence. 'You married, Stephens?'

'No,' said Edgar, rather surprised at this conversational turn.

'You were cut up about Captain Parsons, I know.' The Major's voice was surprisingly kind. 'She was a beautiful girl.'

'Yes,' said Edgar, 'she was.'

'But take my advice and forget her. After all, Cosgrove did. Find a nice girl and get married. Chap needs a wife.'

Edgar looked across at the shuttered windows of the bungalow. Was the Major, a tired old man caring for his sick wife, really such a good advertisement for marriage? Well, maybe he was. A few years of nursing in return for a lifetime's companionship. To his horror, he thought that he might be about to cry.

Luckily, the Major's voice was harsh again. 'Take Massingham, now. He's a wolf, a womaniser. He'll never settle down.'

Edgar thought of Ruby. Did Max really have no idea where she was? Had she really vanished, as a good magician's assistant should?

'Max has changed a lot,' he said.

The Major stood up. 'Men like him never change. Fancy a walk by the sea? We could even have a snifter at the golf club.'

Edgar could think of nothing he'd like less, but he reflected that the Major probably didn't get out much these days. He got up and followed the still-military figure towards the house. He'd have to think of some tactful way of mentioning the slippers.

Max was at the Theatre Royal. He was trying to talk to Roy Coulter about Ruby, but it was proving extremely difficult because Coulter was preoccupied by the next week's bookings.

'We're doing an Agatha Christie,' he said. 'Pre–West End run. It's a strange play. Called *The Mousetrap*. Ever heard of a name like that?'

'Isn't it from *Hamlet*?'

'I wouldn't know,' said Coulter. 'I didn't have the benefit of a classical education.'

Max wondered what sort of education Coulter was imagining. His boarding school—cold baths, endless team games, general sneering at anyone thought 'clever' or 'foreign'—could hardly be less like the Platonic ideal. But he said nothing and Coulter continued to discuss the play.

'My bet is that it'll only run a few weeks, never make it to the West End. Mind you, it's an easy set, just a few bookcases and suchlike. But it's not my sort of thing, people sitting round chatting, bang bang someone's dead, who did it more chat, oh it's the butler. It's not like Variety, is it?'

'Variety's dying,' said Max, getting out his cigarette case.

'Don't you believe it,' said Coulter. 'People will always love a good variety show. Dancing girls, a bit of juggling, a few magic tricks. That's what people come to the theatre for.'

'If you say so.'

Coulter looked up sharply. 'You're still all right though, aren't you, Max? Still getting the bookings?'

'I'm in Hastings next week.' His two weeks' holiday was almost over and they'd come no closer to catching Ethel's murderer.

'On the pier?'

'Yes.'

'Top of the bill?'

Max raised an eyebrow. 'Yes.'

'That's all right then. There'll always be a future for acts like yours.'

'Tony Mulholland thought that television was the future.'

'Don't like to speak ill of the dead,' said Coulter, 'but Tony was an idiot. That act he was doing here. No jokes, no excitement, no *glamour*. That's what the theatre's about. Glamour.'

Max looked round the cluttered little room. Coulter's desk fought for space between towering piles of packing cases and laundry skips. The only window was high on the wall and almost obscured by grime and seagull shit. He opened his mouth to speak, but shut it again when he realised that Coulter wasn't being ironical. Poor sod. He really believed in the glamour of showbusiness.

Coulter reached for a ledger on a shelf behind him. 'Ruby French,' he said, suddenly business-like. 'Here she is. Age twenty. We don't have an address for her.'

'Why the hell not?'

Coulter bristled. 'She was paid by you, if you remember. As your personal assistant. She wasn't on the books.'

'Don't you have a ration book? Passbook? Anything?'

'She was meant to give us an address,' Coulter admitted, 'but she never did. Lovely girl though. Now she had glamour, if you like.'

'She's hardly more than a child,' said Max. He didn't like the way Coulter referred to Ruby in the past tense.

'Not from where I was sitting,' said Coulter.

It was late afternoon when Edgar left Worthing. The Major's snifter turned into lunch at the club plus two or three for the road.

'Won't your wife need you back?' asked Edgar weakly.

'Oh no. Our daily woman will make her lunch and Elsie always sleeps in the afternoon.'

Edgar had surreptitiously substituted tomato juice for Bloody Mary, but even so he felt rather dazed as he headed back along the coast road. It wasn't an unpleasant feeling at all, rather it was a dreamy, dislocated state, as if he were off on holiday rather than pursuing a murder investigation. The police-issue Wolsey wasn't the Bentley, but it was still a pleasure to drive, bowling along with the sea on one side and the solid villas and hotels on the other. He contemplated not going back to Brighton, just carrying on up to London to question Bill, but he knew he should check in at the station. Maybe Bob or Max had managed to find Ruby.

Bob had left for the evening but a note, written in his clear schoolboy handwriting, explained that he'd had no luck in tracing 'the lady in question'. He'd had more success with the landlady's daughter though. On Edgar's instructions, he'd gone back to question her again and clearly his fresh-faced charm had done the trick. This time the girl recalled that Tony had been visited by a man a few days before his death. This man was described as 'quite old, at least thirty'. Edgar winced. Who could this ancient visitor have been? Bill? Someone from the theatre? Max, who could easily look thirty? But Max would have mentioned it if he'd been to see Tony. Wouldn't he?

Edgar put the note in his pocket and set off for the Old Ship. It was still only six o'clock. Surely Max wouldn't yet have set out to do whatever Max did at night.

He was right. From the lobby, he could see Max at the bar, cigarette and whisky in hand.

'Hallo, Max.'

'Evening, Ed. Want a drink?'

'Just some soda water, thanks.'

'Some whisky in it?'

'Oh, all right then.'

Edgar sat down next to his friend. Outside he could see the lights going on along the promenade, the two piers shining like paths to nowhere. It was almost September. Soon the evenings would be getting dark and the killer was still not found. He took a gulp of his drink and saw Max looking at him sardonically.

'Have you fallen off the wagon?'

'I saw the Major today. He forced me to have drinks at the golf club.'

'I sympathise. How was the old fool?'

'He admitted that he'd seen Tony. Said Tony had popped in around Christmas-time.'

'Did he say why?'

'No. Some rubbish about Tony wanting to wish them a happy Christmas.'

Max grunted. 'I can't quite see Tony as Tiny Tim.'

'No, nor can I. The Major was holding something back, I'm sure of it. I'm just not sure what.'

'Clearly Tony thought he knew something about the Magic Men. Maybe he was blackmailing him.'

'About what?'

'Didn't the Major say that someone was a spy? Maybe Tony knew who that was? Maybe it was Gormley himself?'

'I can't see it. He's got king and country stamped through him like a stick of Brighton rock.'

'Classic misdirection,' said Max. He waved his hand in a magician's gesture. Suddenly he looked very foreign, and Edgar remembered what the Major had said to Max, the first time they visited him. *If anyone knows, it's you.*

'Why would he mention it,' said Edgar, 'if he was the spy?'

'Misdirection,' said Max again. He seemed to be tired of the subject.

'Any luck with finding Ruby?' asked Edgar.

Max sighed. 'No, nothing. They didn't have an address for her at the theatre. I remembered her saying once that her flat was in a crescent. I've been to every bloody crescent in Brighton. Do you know how many there are?'

'Have you asked your friend, the one she used to work for?'

'I wrote to him today. But he's touring, I had to write care of his management. God knows when he'll get the letter.'

'Did Ruby have a manager? An agent?'

'No. I offered to introduce her to an agent, but she said that she wanted to be independent.'

'She's that all right.'

'Yes she is.' Max stared into his glass. Then he

asked, in a tone that Edgar had never heard him use before, 'She will be all right, won't she?'

In his turn, Edgar tried to make his own voice authoritative and reassuring. 'I'm sure she will. After all, she wasn't in the photograph. It looks as if the killer is only after people in the picture.'

Max didn't remind him that Ethel hadn't been in the photograph either. Instead he said, 'Did you tell the Major? About the photograph?'

Edgar sighed. 'Yes. I tried to warn him, said he might be in danger and that I'd order police protection and all the rest of it. All he said was, "I'm not afraid. I'm an Englishman."'

'Idiot.'

'I'm going up to London tomorrow to talk to Bill.'

'Will you tell him that I told you about Tony's letter?'

'No. I'm going to wait to see if he tells me first.'

'Better get him on his own then. He'll never talk if Jean's in the room.'

Edgar drained the rest of his whisky. 'I need to see Jean. After all, she was in the picture too.'

It was nearly nine, but still warm when Edgar walked up the hill to his lodgings. He had to stop several times to get his breath back. He wasn't fighting fit anymore. All that riding around in Bentleys and drinking in hotel lounges had made him soft. His legs ached and his right foot (the one with the missing toe) felt as if it were on fire. He inhaled deeply, expanding his lungs as his army PT instructor had taught him. 'Breathe it in, lads, breathe it in. Fresh air won't kill you.' But this air felt soft and smoggy, as if it were filling his chest with cotton wool. Edgar continued on his way, trying to make his pace more military. He never thought he'd feel nostalgic for PT drill.

He wondered if Diablo would be in the flat. He even thought he might have left altogether, disappearing into the showbusiness half-life that had claimed him in Yarmouth, But, as he entered the front room, there he was, sitting on the sofa in Edgar's dressing gown, eating potted-meat sandwiches washed down with beer. At least the beer meant that he had been out of the house that day. There were three empty bottles on the floor, one filled with cigarette ends.

'Edgar, dear boy! Where have you been? I was worried about you.'

'No you weren't.' Edgar sat in the chair opposite. 'Is there any beer left?'

'Sorry, I only bought four. You're welcome to share this one.'

'No thank you.'

Diablo leant back on the cushions, apparently completely relaxed. The wireless was playing swoopy versions of old love songs. Diablo sang along in a reedy tenor. 'If you were the only girl in the world . . .'

'I went to see Major Gormley today.'

'Did you? How is the old monster?'

'Not so good. Lonely, bored, looking after his sick wife.'

'He must be getting on a bit now.'

By Edgar's calculations, the Major was at least ten years younger than Diablo, but he didn't want to spoil the old boy's good mood. 'Major Gormley said that Tony had dropped in last Christmas, just to wish him the compliments of the season.'

Like Max, Diablo seemed to find this amusing. 'Tony paying a social call? Can't quite see it, old boy. No, if Tony called on Gormley, it was because he wanted something.'

'Yes,' said Edgar. 'But what?'

Diablo shrugged his shoulders. After a few moments, he started to sing along to the wireless again. 'A garden of Eden, just made for two. With nothing to mar our joy.'

'Did you go out today?' asked Edgar, indicating the beers. 'You have to be a bit careful, you know, with a lunatic on the loose.'

'Oh, I'm used to lunatics,' said Diablo. 'After all, I've been on the circuit for almost fifty years.'

'All the same,' said Edgar, 'I wouldn't want anything to happen to you.'

'You are sweet, dear boy.' To Edgar's surprise, and consternation, Diablo's eyes filled with tears. 'We are good friends—aren't we—you, me and Max? I often think about those two years in Scotland. Happiest time of my life.'

This struck Edgar as profoundly sad, if true. He said nothing.

'I often think about them,' said Diablo. 'And about her, Charis. Such a lovely face. Sometimes, you know, I think I see her. Just out of the corner of my eye. And then she's gone.'

Edgar was startled. He too had often had this sensation. A flash of red hair, a way of walking, a tilt of the head. Once he had followed a woman the length of Western Road, only to have her turn and accuse him of stalking her.

But this confidence seemed to have exhausted Diablo. He shut his eyes and the wireless segued into 'The Blue Danube'.

Edgar went into the kitchen in search of food.

CHAPTER 23

Edgar set off early the next morning. He had commandeered the Wolsey again and had steeled himself to call in on his mother on the way to Bill's. He knew he had to do it like this: a quick visit with a limited time frame, otherwise he'd find himself sucked into Esher Time, an endless Sunday afternoon with no hope of redemption. It wasn't that he didn't love his mother, he told himself defensively as he passed the Brighton gates, it was just that, however much she complained that he didn't visit enough, she never seemed to get much pleasure from his actual presence. Even Jonathan, always her favourite child, had been the cause of endless worry—his sickness, his sore throats, his woeful lack of road-sense. When she got the telegram about Jonathan, she had looked up at Edgar and Lucy and said, 'I always knew this would happen.' Had she really always thought all through Jonathan's child-hood that her youngest child would end his days as part of a doomed expeditionary force, be shot and killed, his body lost under the sea? It was profoundly depressing if so.

He hadn't warned her that he was coming. That way she might be out and it wouldn't be his fault. But, as he drew near to the house, he could see his mother at the kitchen window, washing up. Why was she washing up? There was only one person in the house. He used the same plate every day, rinsing it immediately after use. He resented cleaning up after Diablo, who seemed determined to use every utensil in the house.

Edgar walked slowly up the path. The garden was the same, paved (less trouble), with a neat border of annuals around the edge. His father used to enjoy gardening, he remembered, but to his mother Outside was an accident waiting to happen. He wasn't surprised to see that the hanging baskets had been taken down. Those things were a death-trap.

The doorbell played the same tinkling theme. And there was Rose, still wearing her rubber gloves.

'Edgar!' she exclaimed. 'What's happened? Is it Lucy?'

Max was making his way round the Royal Crescent. He knew that this was far too expensive an address for a twenty-year-old secretary, but it was the only crescent in Brighton that he hadn't tried. This was hardly a crescent anyway, just a shallow curve of tall houses built of shiny black brick. Nevertheless, Max knocked on every door and was met by flat denial, blank incredulity and (once) a brazen invitation upstairs. Refusing politely, Max raised his hat and backed away. At the end of the row, he stood for a minute looking at the houses. The closed doors and shuttered windows stared smugly back at him. Where was Ruby? Was she hiding behind a similar door or was she somewhere more unexpected entirely? She wanted to be a magician and it seemed that she had successfully performed her first disappearing act. He remembered the clues, the half clues, the misdirections—the parents in Hove, the flatmate, the recommendation from Raymondo. Was it an illusion after all?

Max crossed the road and stood looking out over

the sea. It was another cloudy hot day, the sky the same colour as the water. It was Friday and he was due to leave Brighton on Sunday. How could he leave without having found Ruby? How could he perform on stage in Hastings, knowing that she might be in danger? But he couldn't cry off. Unreliability was the greatest sin in the showbusiness world. If word got round that Max Mephisto had missed a gig, he would be finished.

At least he was only in Hastings. He could be in Brighton in a couple of hours if Edgar needed him. But would Edgar need him? He sensed that over the last few days Edgar had been edging away from him. When they had driven back from Yarmouth with Diablo, there had been a sense of reunion, of recreating those days in Scotland when the Magic Men had seemed a closed circle, isolated from a world at war. But, ever since Bill's visit, he thought that Edgar had been distancing himself, making it clear that he was the policeman and Max was a civilian. There was no more Dick Barton stuff; him and Ed on the road together, fighting crime and righting wrongs. Max had been furious when Edgar had asked him if he too had received a letter from Tony. For a moment it had seemed that he was actually a *suspect*. He lit a cigarette, forcing himself to think rationally. Of course he should be a suspect. Clearly the killer was someone who knew about the Magic Men. Tony was dead, that left him,

Edgar, Diablo, the Major and Bill. There were other people as well—a number of WAAFs, Colonel Cartwright, the staff at the Cally. Could one of them be a murderer?

He was leaning on the railings looking down on Madeira Drive, the broad promenade next to the sea. As he watched, a figure in a white suit passed below him, walking briskly. He noticed the suit at first. Men didn't wear white suits these days, it was something you associated with gangsters and old theatricals. Co-respondent shoes too. He saw them flash as the man hurried by. He looked again. The white-suited man was walking faster, almost running, and his face was stern and purposeful. Not an expression he would associate with a befuddled old magician. But there was no doubt that the man was Stan Parks, alias Diablo.

'You should have told me you were coming. It was a shock, seeing you standing there.'

'It's just a quick call. I'm on my way to London.'

'A quick call.' Her face fell. 'How long?'

Cursing himself, Edgar said breezily, 'I've got at least an hour. I'm not in any real hurry.'

'I have to go out at eleven,' said Rose. 'It's my day for helping at the hospital.'

That was typical of his mother, reflected Edgar, as he waited in the sitting room while she made tea. First she made him feel guilty, as if he were depriving her of time with her only surviving son, and then she made him feel unwelcome, as if he were intruding on her busy schedule. He looked around the room. On the mantelpiece over the electric fire there were three photographs: one of Lucy on her wedding day, a large one of Jon in uniform and one of himself on a bicycle with a fatuous expression on his face. Why on earth had she chosen that picture? Here's my happily married daughter, my hero son and the village idiot. Why not one of him in uniform? He'd had a respectable army career, if you ignored the Magic Men years. Or one of him in police uniform? But he knew that, however much she denied it, his mother was ashamed of his job. This wasn't why she had made him stay inside and do his homework, so he could mix with low-life and criminals. He wondered what she'd say if he told her about his present case.

'Is that your car outside?' asked his mother, returning with a laden tray.

'No. It's a police car. I've got a friend with a Bentley,' he offered, wondering if the possession of a successful friend would make up for his failure to acquire a car of his own.

But Rose pursed her lips. 'A bit flash.'

'He is a bit flash. It's Max Mephisto. You remember, my friend from the army.'

'The magician?' Rose looked shocked. 'Why are you in touch with him again?'

'He's appearing at the theatre in Brighton.'

'I expect they like that sort of thing in Brighton.' Rose disapproved of Edgar's adopted town.

'Uncle Charlie took Jon and me to see Max when we were children,' said Edgar, accepting a cup of beige tea. 'At least, I think it was Uncle Charlie.'

Rose nodded, pursing her lips again. 'On Hastings pier,' she said. 'Johnny was sick afterwards.'

'He was always being sick.' Sometimes Edgar thought that it would be better if they could talk about Jonathan normally.

But his mother's eyes filled with tears. 'He was very sensitive. Not like you,' she added.

Edgar accepted the rebuke. 'Have you seen Lucy recently?' he asked.

'She came last weekend with the boys. They're getting so big.' This was said not admiringly, but rather as if Lucy's sons were growing bigger for the specific purpose of inconveniencing their grandmother.

'I haven't seen them for ages. I must go up to Hertfordshire. Or invite them down to Brighton.' He thought of Lucy and her family sharing the flat with Diablo and suppressed a grin.

'No,' said his mother, on a falling note which immediately quenched any desire to smile. Ever again. 'She said she hadn't seen you.'

'What about you? Are you keeping busy? What are you doing at the hospital?'

'It's the incurables,' said Rose. 'They keep very cheerful, considering.'

Edgar looked at the clock over the mantelpiece. Only half an hour to go.

Max watched the white figure until it disappeared into the crowd by the Palace Pier. What was Diablo doing, dressed up to the nines and clearly on a serious mission? According to Edgar, he hardly left the house, rotting gently in a miasma of alcohol and nostalgic dance tunes. But, on the day that his host was out of town, here was Diablo, positively running to some assignation. Max stood for a moment, undecided, then he too headed back towards the centre of town. He didn't know where Diablo was going, but there was one cast-iron rule where pros were concerned. In any given town, they would always head straight for the theatre.

By eleven o'clock, Edgar was ready to leave. Or kill himself. Whichever was the quickest. Rose had moved on from the incurables to her neighbour's heart problems and the butcher's obstinacy in refusing to stock pie veal. Edgar drank his tea and wondered what would happen if he burst into this recital with the news that he was tracking a man capable of sawing a woman into three. He imagined his mother's mouth pursing as it used to do when he mentioned something that wasn't very *nice*. 'Not our sort of person,' he could hear her saying, as she did when he brought the rag-and-bone man's son home.

The cuckoo clock in the hall chirped the hour. Edgar reached for his hat. 'I'd better be off, Mum.'

Rose's face fell. 'So soon?'

'You said you had to go out at eleven.'

'I could always cancel it,' said Rose, fiddling with the tea things. 'I never really know what to say to the incurables.'

'You go, Mum,' said Edgar, edging towards the door. 'They'd miss you if you didn't go.'

'They wouldn't,' said Rose. 'They prefer Millie White. She plays poker with them.'

'Next time I'll make it a proper visit,' said Edgar. He kissed his mother's cheek. She smelt of Penhaligon's Bluebell.

Rose sniffed, but she kissed him back and told him to look after himself. She took the tray into the kitchen and gathered up her handbag and hat, clearly resigned to the hospital visit. At the door, Edgar asked, 'Why have you got that awful picture of me on the mantelpiece? The one with the bike?'

Rose reached out to pat his cheek in a way that was almost spontaneously affectionate. 'It's the only picture I've got where you look happy,' she said.

Max reached the theatre just as Roy Coulter was going out for lunch. 'Join me if you like. I've only got half an hour.'

They went to the same cafe in the Pavilion Gardens where Max had drunk coffee with Edgar. Max ordered coffee again, but the theatre manager worked his way through tomato soup followed by a cheese roll.

Max tried not to watch Coulter burying his face in his soup. English food, he thought with a shudder.

'I'm looking for Stan Parks,' he said. 'You know, The Great Diablo. I'd heard he was in town.'

'Diablo!' Coulter gave a snort. 'Had him on the bill once and ended up having to bail him out. Drunk and disorderly in a public place.'

'But have you seen him today?'

Maddeningly slow, Coulter wiped the soup stains from his moustache.

'Funny you should ask that . . .'

'Well, have you?'

'Yes, he came in this morning. All dolled up in a white suit. For one horrible moment I thought he was going to ask me for work.'

'What did he want?'

Coulter looked at him impassively. 'Same thing as you. He was looking for the girl.'

'Which girl?'

'Your assistant. Ruby Whats'ername. Seemed very keen to speak to her.'

Edgar reached Wembley at one o'clock. An innocuous time of day, he thought. Lunchtime.

240

Mothers making sandwiches, children picnicking in gardens, grandparents snoozing in the shade. He remembered his father coming home for lunch every day of his working life and wondered whether Bill would do the same. Well, if not, it would be a chance to talk to Jean on her own. He shivered slightly at the thought of what this might entail. Could Diablo really be right about Jean having a crush on him? Apart from that one memory on the towpath, he had no recollection at all of Jean in Inverness. Those days were all illuminated by Charis—her sleepy smile, her creamy skin, her blazing crown of hair. Sometimes even looking at a map of Scotland could make him blush, remembering. There was no room for Jean, or anyone else really. He remembered playing cards with Max in the Caledonian bar, the stags' heads looking down as if they wanted to offer advice (despite offering generous handicaps, Max always won). He remembered walking with Charis by the Ness. He remembered floating in the open boat with Max and Diablo. He remembered—even though he wasn't there—the *Ptolemy* burning in the darkness. This last was almost the strongest image, despite being second-hand. He thought that he could smell the flames, hear the desperate cries of the onlookers, even, beneath the shouting and the confusion, hear Charis's voice calling piteously for him. But, try as he would, he couldn't remember exchanging a single word with Jean.

The house with the wishing well was silent. Edgar knocked on the door. The sound echoed dully, but no smiling housewife appeared at the door, ready to welcome him in for a chat about the good old days. A bird was singing manically in the apple tree and, a few doors away, children were laughing as they played in the garden. Had Jean taken Barney to play with them? Was she shopping or visiting her own version of the incurables? He doubted it somehow. On impulse, he tried the door handle. The door opened.

Afterwards, he wondered why he had been so sure that something was wrong. After all, it wasn't unknown to leave front doors open in safe suburban streets. But Edgar's skin crackled with fear and he felt at his waist for his police-issue truncheon (he had forgotten to bring it, as ever).

Edgar entered the sitting room. The sun streamed in through the windows illuminating the beflowered furniture, the neatly arranged ornaments and the giant playpen in which Jean lay, gagged, bound and, unmistakeably, dead.

PART 3

Raising the Stakes

CHAPTER 24

Edgar reached through the bars. Jean's body was cold. She must have been dead a few hours. Even so, it seemed wrong to leave her like that. The trouble was that the playpen was built for lifting out a baby, not a full-grown woman. Edgar could not get enough grip on the body to lift it out of the cage. Eventually he seized the ornamental poker that lay by the (electric) fire and broke through the bars. He was aware that he was destroying evidence, but he couldn't leave Jean there, her arms and legs tied together, that terrible expression on her face. He laid her on the hearth-rug and, mechanically, listened for a heartbeat. Nothing. He went into the hall and found a telephone. He dialled 999 and explained the situation in terse policeman's language. Then he went back into the sitting room to wait.

It wasn't until he looked at the broken playpen that he remembered the baby. If Jean had been in the pen, what had happened to Barney, the massive baby that Bill had introduced so proudly? As he thought this, he heard a sound upstairs. A muted, shuffling sound as if something was moving from side to side. He grabbed the poker and climbed the stairs. Three identical doors faced him and from one came the sound, now accompanied by tiny whimpering noises. Edgar pushed open the door. A terrible smell almost pushed him back and, for a second, he thought that he'd find a decomposing corpse behind the door. But then he saw that he was in a bathroom —pink and black bath, pink tiles—and that the smell was coming from the baby who lay, scarlet-faced with distress, rolling in a bath that was smeared with his excrement.

When the local police arrived, ten minutes later, they found Edgar in the kitchen, holding the smelly baby wrapped in a towel. It hadn't seemed right to expose Barney to his mother's dead body and Edgar certainly didn't feel up to changing a nappy.

'Bloody hell,' said the sergeant. 'Where did that come from?'

'It's the dead woman's child,' said Edgar stiffly. He resented the London police for their uniforms and their tactless boots trampling down the path by the wishing well. He resented the flashing blue light on their car and their air of callous competence. He was also extremely relieved to see them.

The sergeant swaggered into the sitting room accompanied by two constables. Two minutes later, he was back, even his boots sounding subdued.

'What's going on?' he said, looking suspiciously from Edgar to the baby. 'Who the hell are you?'

'Detective Inspector Edgar Stephens of the Brighton police,' said Edgar. 'Who the hell are you?'

'That's all very well,' said the sergeant, but he sounded respectful all the same. 'How do I know that's true?'

'My warrant card's in my pocket,' said Edgar. 'I didn't want to wake the baby.' Incredibly enough, Barney had fallen deeply, odorously asleep.

'O'Shea!' the sergeant shouted at one of the constables. 'Come and take hold of this baby.'

'It's all right.' For some reason Edgar felt reluctant to relinquish his hold on the sleeping Barney. 'I can manage.' He eased his card out of his pocket and passed it across the table.

The sergeant examined the card with narrowed eyes and then straightened up to the salute. 'Sergeant Alan Deacon.'

'Sergeant.' Edgar nodded at him, feeling ridiculous. Barney snored slightly and Edgar shifted his weight against his shoulder. He was incredibly heavy.

Sergeant Deacon looked towards the sitting room, almost fearfully. He was a large, red-faced man and Edgar couldn't imagine that he looked fearful very often.

'What's going on?' he asked.

'The dead woman is called Jean Cosgrove,' said Edgar. 'I arrived about an hour ago and found her lying inside the playpen. I broke down the bars to get her out, but I think she'd been dead some time. The baby was in the bath. He was very distressed, but I don't think he's been hurt.'

Edgar watched Deacon absorb these facts and was impressed that he was not distracted by babies, baths or playpens.

'Why are you here?' asked the sergeant. 'Social call, was it?'

'Not exactly,' said Edgar.

Deacon waited. The two uniformed policemen flanked him in the doorway, waiting for instructions.

'I'm investigating another case,' said Edgar at last. 'I wanted to see Jean's husband, Bill Cosgrove.'

'Is he a suspect?'

'Not necessarily.'

'Where is he now?'

'At work, I suppose.'

Sergeant Deacon looked at Edgar almost pityingly. 'You'd better telephone him. Give the little fella to me.'

Bill arrived as the ambulance was taking Jean away. He saw Edgar in the doorway and ran up to him, grasping his arms painfully.

'What is it? You said bad news.'

'Bill, I'm sorry. Jean's dead.'

Bill let go of Edgar's arms. His big, handsome face looked completely blank.

'Dead?'

'I called in at lunchtime and she was dead. I'm so sorry.'

'But how . . .' For the first time, Bill seemed to register the ambulance in the driveway. He ran up to it and started to bang on the sides. 'Jean! Jean!'

Edgar caught hold of his arm. 'They're taking her to the hospital. You can see her later. I'll take you there.'

Bill looked at Edgar as if seeing him for the first time.

'Ed. What are you doing here?'

'Come into the house. We can talk there.'

'Barney!' Bill looked around him wildly. 'What's happened to Barney?'

'He's fine. A policewoman's looking after him.'

Sergeant Deacon had summoned a WPC from the local station. She had given Barney a bath and changed his nappy and was now playing with him on the sitting room floor. Bill surveyed the scene with a kind of dumb horror.

'What happened to the playpen?'

'Mr Cosgrove.' Deacon stepped forward. 'I have to ask you some questions. Janice,' to the policewoman, 'make us some tea, there's a good girl.'

Janice got up obediently, hoisted Barney onto her hip and went out of the room. Bill watched them go. He made no attempt to take his son.

'Mr Cosgrove. I'm Sergeant Deacon from the

Wembley Police. I believe you know Detective Inspector Stephens?'

'Ed? Yes, I . . .'

'We need to ask you about your movements today.'

'Why?'

'You'd better sit down.' Deacon gently pushed Bill into one of the floral armchairs. 'Mr Cosgrove, your wife was murdered. We need to find out who did it.'

Bill looked at Edgar. 'Murdered?'

Edgar nodded. 'Strangled, we think.'

'Oh God.' Bill covered his face with his hands. Edgar wondered what he had done when Diablo told him about Charis. What did Bill feel, now that both the women he had loved were dead?

'So,' persisted Deacon. 'Where were you this morning, at about ten o'clock?'

Bill looked up. 'At work. Surely you don't think . . .'

'Where do you work, Mr Cosgrove?'

'At GEC. I'm a general manager there.'

'So people can vouch for you?'

'Of course.' Bill was getting angry now, his big hands clenched on the arms of his chair. 'I went to work at eight. I stayed there all morning until I got the telephone call from Edgar. And I come home to find my wife's been murdered. My wife . . .'

'What did you do for lunch?' asked Deacon.

'I normally come home.' (Bingo, thought Edgar.)

250

'But there was a rush on, so I stayed at work. One of the secretaries got me a sandwich.'

If Bill had come home for lunch, he would have been the one to find his wife. Would he then also have been a suspect? Did the killer—the thought was so dizzying that Edgar had to hold on to the back of the chair—know that he, Edgar, was on his way? Was Jean's body meant for him to find?

Janice came back into the room. She placed a cup of tea in front of Bill and then, with matter-of-fact kindness, put Barney in his lap. 'Here's your little boy for you.'

Bill sobbed into his son's hair.

It was past midnight when Edgar got home to Brighton. He had taken Bill to the hospital and waited in the 'visitors' room' of the mortuary while Bill said goodbye to his wife. Then he had driven Bill back home where his sister was waiting for him. She was a large, capable woman and Edgar felt relieved to be leaving Bill—and Barney—in her charge. His clothes still smelt of the baby.

Then Edgar had driven to Wembley police station where he had put Deacon and his boss, an Inspector Jarvis, in the picture about the Brighton murders.

'So you think the same bloke may have killed Mrs Cosgrove?' said Jarvis, a sharp-looking Londoner with a nice line in understated irony.

'I think it's possible,' said Edgar. He explained about the photograph. 'Two people in the picture are dead now.'

'For my next trick, The Wolf Trap,' said Deacon. 'What did that mean?'

'I don't know,' said Edgar, 'but Jean was in a kind of cage. A friend of mine, an old magician, said that The Wolf Trap could be a kind of escapology act where someone escapes from a cage.'

'Mrs Cosgrove wasn't doing much escaping,' said Jarvis dryly. 'You'd better watch yourself, hadn't you, Inspector Stephens?'

Would things have been different if he had warned Jean about the photograph? wondered Edgar as he took the Brighton Road, that straight thoroughfare once famous for highwaymen and footpads. Would Bill have stayed with her? Would he have prevented her from opening the door to a murderer? Because that was what had happened, Edgar was sure of it. Deacon's men had found two teacups in the sitting room and Edgar would bet his life on one containing traces of belladonna. None of the neighbours had seen anyone approaching the house, everyone in the respectable suburb was respectably minding their own business that Friday lunchtime. Edgar thought of his mother setting out to visit the incurables. Jean must have been killed while he sat drinking tea with Rose and trying not to look at the family photographs. Could anyone have known that he was on his way to see Bill? Had the body been placed behind bars for him to find?

The roads were quiet at night. The journey took barely two hours. There were still a few drunks staggering out of the Brighton pubs, but the town was mostly silent and the moon was silver on the sea. Edgar drove up the hill to his house thanking God that he wasn't on foot. He was so tired that he could barely think. He just wanted to lie down on the sofa and sleep for a week. He let himself quietly into the flat. The last thing he wanted was to wake Diablo and have to tell the whole awful story. There'd be time enough for that tomorrow. He stood in the hallway listening for the old magician's distinctive snores. Silence. An owl called from the garden. Gently Edgar pushed open the bedroom door. The bed was as smooth and empty as the sea.

CHAPTER 25

'So the old boy's done a moonlight flit?'

'Well, there's no sign of him. And his suitcase has gone. You know, that terrible cardboard affair.'

Max smiled, but he was looking rather troubled. It was Saturday morning and they were in Edgar's office at the police station. Usually the station was quiet at the weekend, but today, with another possible murder by the Conjuror Killer, the place was buzzing. Frank Hodges had already called in to tell Edgar that the force was becoming a laughing stock and he would hold Edgar personally responsible if the killer struck again. 'He might kill me,' muttered Edgar, 'then we'd all be happy.'

Max's appearance had caused rather a stir. Word got round that Max Mephisto was in DI Stephens' office and at least three WPCs knocked on the door and offered to make tea. Edgar found out later that there was another rumour that Max had come to confess to the murders and, in his dark suit and startlingly white shirt, Max did look appropriately Mephistophelean. When Edgar told him about Jean, he put his hand over his eyes, but when he raised his head, his eyes were tearless and rather hard.

'What about Bill? Could it be him?'

'He was at work. He had an alibi for the whole morning.'

'When he came to see me at the Old Ship, it struck me that he could be an ugly customer if roused.'

Edgar remembered looking at Bill's hands, clenched into fists on the flowery armchair. 'I had the same thought,' he admitted, 'but I can't really see Bill as a murderer. Why would he kill Jean? He seemed really happy with her.'

'He had a motive for killing Tony,' said Max. 'If only we knew what Tony had on him . . .'

'And now we've got Diablo on the loose.'

'Yes.' Max was silent for a moment. He got out his cigarette case, glanced up at Edgar's 'No Smoking' sign and grimaced. 'You know,' he said, 'I was on the bill with Nosmo King.'

'I'm still not going to let you smoke in here.'

'I saw Diablo yesterday,' said Max. 'He was all dressed up in a white suit. He didn't see me, but apparently he'd been at the theatre asking about Ruby.'

'About Ruby? But he doesn't know Ruby.'

'As far as we know he doesn't.'

'I've been thinking,' said Edgar, 'what if it's all an act, the forgetfulness, the drinking? What if Diablo's sharper than we think?'

'It can't be an act,' said Max. 'You saw him in that nightclub in Yarmouth. The man's a mess.'

'I don't know,' said Edgar. 'I keep remembering that Diablo used to be a serious actor. Remember he kept going on about playing Hamlet? What if he's been acting all this time?'

'Seventy-odd years is rather a long time to play a part. Diablo's been the same as long as I've known him. He's got a hell of a reputation in the business.'

'Well,' said Edgar, 'if he's not the killer then

he's in danger. And we don't know where he is.'

Max frowned. 'Do you really think the killer—whoever he is—is picking us off one by one?'

'Think about the photograph. Tony's dead, Jean's dead. There's only you, me and Diablo left.'

'And the Major.'

'Yes, and the Major. I'll have to tell him about Jean. Try to get him to be careful. He can't just dismiss it now.'

'You know the Major. He can dismiss anything.'

'Maybe. But I've got to try.'

Max gave an odd, one-sided smile. 'What about you, Ed? Are you going to be careful?'

'I'll be all right. I'm a policeman. It's you who ought to watch out. You really shouldn't go to Hastings. Everyone knows you'll be there. The bills are up everywhere.'

Max sighed. 'Believe me, I'd rather not go. I don't exactly feel in the mood for performing magic tricks on Hastings pier. But, if I don't appear, I'm finished.'

'When are you leaving?'

'Tomorrow. Sunday's changeover day, remember?'

'Well, at least let me know your address. I'll have the Hastings police keep an eye on you.'

Max smiled. A proper smile this time. 'Now why doesn't that make me feel any safer?'

• • •

When Max had left, causing the WPCs to flutter like hens who have caught sight of a fox, Edgar got out his notes.

To do (he had written)
Ring Bill
Visit Ethel's lodgings
Ring Major Gormley
Find Ruby

Edgar looked at the list for a few minutes before adding, in capitals, FIND DIABLO. He didn't like the way that people involved in the case kept disappearing. Ethel had left her home on the Isle of Wight and had been found a year later, cut into pieces. Why? There had to be some link between Ethel and the Magic Men that went beyond her connection with Max. Ruby had twirled her way into Max's life and then vanished. Who was Ruby? Was she just a pretty girl (here Edgar stamped firmly on his own feelings) who wanted a career in showbusiness, or was there more to her appearance and disappearance than that? And Diablo, who had sunk below the waves for so many years, had resurfaced and was now lost again. Or rather, he wasn't lost, he was wandering around Brighton asking after Ruby. Why?

The questions formed and re-formed themselves, growing like the heads of the Hydra.

Edgar, sitting in his office in the bowels of the old building with the ghosts of the police station around him, felt as if he were just on the verge of understanding everything. If only he could put together the final pieces . . .

The phone rang. Edgar was informed that a Sergeant Alan Deacon was on the line for him. For a moment, the name meant nothing, but then he remembered a suburban kitchen and a baby lying heavily in his arms.

'Deacon! Good to hear from you.'

'Got some information for you, Inspector Stephens.'

Well, actual information would make a nice change.

'We've had a sighting of a man seen at the Cosgroves' house at midday yesterday.'

'That's great.'

Deacon laughed sardonically. 'You won't think so when you hear. It's the usual witness rubbish.' He put on a high-pitched voice. ' "A young man, quite slim and slight, wearing a coat and peaked cap." Nothing useful, no distinguishing features or anything like that.'

Nevertheless, it was interesting. The man who bought the flowers and the sword-purchaser had also been described as small. The clothes were the same too, coat and peaked cap. Could it be the same person?

'What was this man doing?' he asked.

'Hurrying away from the house apparently. Woman couldn't see his face properly because of the cap.'

'Odd to be wearing a coat and hat in summer.'

'Yes, that's what we thought. Worth following up anyway.'

Putting the phone down, Edgar thought he would follow it up immediately. He'd go back to the flower-seller and the antiques shop, see if they had remembered anything else about the man they described. Was the small man the killer? That adjective couldn't really be applied to anyone involved with the case. Max and Bill were both tall. The Major was short ('Napoleon complex,' Diablo used to say), but he could hardly be described as slight. Diablo was also above average height and, in any case, it was hard to think of his shambling gait being taken for a young man's walk.

The flower-seller at the station was doing a brisk trade.

'It's Saturday, you see,' she said. 'People come to visit their loved ones in their old people's homes by the sea and they want to bring them some flowers. Make up for neglecting them the rest of the time.' She tied some asters with a flourish. 'No, thank *you,* madam.'

'Do you remember me?' asked Edgar. 'You came to see me a few weeks ago. About the body parts found in Left Luggage.'

'Hardly something you'd forget, is it?' said the woman. 'Lovely roses. Five for half a crown.'

'I was wondering if you had remembered anything else? Sometimes things do occur to people quite a long time after the event.' He attempted an engaging smile.

The woman tied a bow absent-mindedly. 'He had small hands,' she said at last. 'I always notice hands. I thought he was young at first. He had a young voice. But then I saw his hands. They were old hands.'

'What do you mean "old hands"?'

The woman shrugged impatiently. 'Oh, you know. Old. Wrinkled.'

'But his face wasn't old?'

'I don't think so, but I couldn't see his face very well. He was wearing a cap. I told you that before.' She glared at Edgar as if he were trying to catch her out.

'Yes, you did.' The man leaving the Cosgroves' house had been wearing a peaked cap. He had been described as young, but the witness hadn't been able to see his face, let alone his hands. Who was this strange being with a child's voice and an old person's hands? For some reason Edgar thought of a woman he had once seen in a variety show. She had been quite old, but dressed up as a schoolboy. Watching her sing 'Don't tell Mamma' had been a genuinely disturbing experience. What was her name? Max would know.

'Thank you,' he said to the flower-seller. 'You will let me know if you remember anything else?'

'You'll be top of my list,' said the woman rather enigmatically. But she did present him with a carnation for his buttonhole. 'Nothing sets off a suit like a nice carnation.'

Ethel's lodgings were in Trafalgar Street, one of the steep roads leading up from the station. The pub at the top of the hill was called the Belle Vue, but it was hard to see what was belle about the view over the railway tracks and the gasworks and the rows of houses that stretched as far as the downs. Edgar stood for a moment, leaning on the wall, trying to get his breath back. Why on earth did old people retire to Brighton? The hills alone were enough to kill them.

The lodging house was number 159, a neat end-of-terrace with window boxes and a discreet sign advertising rooms to let. Edgar remembered the landlady from his previous visit. Mrs Steptoe her name was, though he was pretty sure that she wasn't a Mrs and that her rigid respectability hid a pretty racy past. She greeted him now with extreme civility.

'Inspector Stephens. How nice to see you. No, it isn't an imposition at all. Would you care to take tea?'

Edgar accepted the tea because experience told him that this was always a good move. Mrs

Steptoe presented the drinks on a silver tray that would have impressed Edgar's mother. There were also two small biscuits on a plate. Edgar felt his stomach rumble. It was two o'clock and he hadn't eaten since breakfast.

'If it doesn't distress you too much, Mrs Steptoe,' he said, trying for the boyish grin again. 'I'd like to ask you some more questions about Mrs Williams.'

'You still haven't caught the killer then,' said Mrs Steptoe, with an exaggerated shudder. 'Poor soul. What a terrible way to die.'

'We've got several new leads,' said Edgar, trying to sound as if this were true. What he really had was two more bodies. Jean's murder hadn't hit the newspapers yet and, in any case, he was hoping that no one would make the connection with the Conjuror Killer. He took a photograph from his pocket.

'I know you said that Mrs Williams didn't have any callers,' he said. 'But I wondered if you had seen this man.' The photograph was a publicity still showing Tony in full mesmerist mode, arms crossed, eyes staring. Mrs Steptoe recoiled slightly.

'He might have said that he was a relative,' said Edgar, just to give her an escape route. He had sent the same photograph to Michael Williams and had received a curt note back: 'I've never seen this man in my life. If Ethel knew him, she didn't mention him to me.'

'I don't think so,' said Mrs Steptoe. 'Like I say, Mrs Williams didn't have any gentlemen visitors.'

'What did she do all day?' asked Edgar. 'And what about the evenings? Did she go out in the evenings?'

'She was out most of the day,' said Mrs Steptoe. 'I assumed she had a job. She stayed in most evenings. She went to the pub sometimes. Now that I can't like in a woman.'

'Which pub?' asked Edgar. 'The Belle Vue?'

'No. There's a more respectable place around the corner. The Battle of Trafalgar.'

'Thank you. I'll call in there on my way back. Can I give you my card? Do telephone me if anything does occur to you. Anything, however trivial it might seem.'

Mrs Steptoe assured him that she would. As he gathered up the picture of Tony, she gestured towards it and said, almost in a whisper, 'Is that the killer? I can always tell. It's in the eyes, you know.'

CHAPTER 26

Max was also thinking about lunch. Usually on a Saturday there was the last show, a party after the second house, addresses exchanged, promises to keep in touch (promises destined to be broken in Max's case). But he was still officially on holiday; he had a day off before travelling to Hastings tomorrow. There was nothing to stop him having a really good lunch in the Grand or in one of the Italian restaurants in the Lanes. Nothing, that is, except the knowledge that a killer was on the loose and that he might be the next victim. Actually, he was surprised how little that thought scared him. As he had told Edgar, he had an unshakable belief in his own indestructibility. He had never once thought that he might die in the war though, during the early years, he had certainly been in some pretty tight spots. Even drifting out to sea in that boat with Edgar and Diablo, he had thought only about how to pass the time, not about the possibility that time might run out for him. Anyway, whatever he felt life had in store for him, it was not death at the hands of some murderous magician. But Jean's death had disturbed him more than he had admitted to Edgar. The thought of her—poor silly girl—being strangled and then placed within her own baby's playpen, filled him with a murderous rage of his own. What had she done to deserve that, for God's sake? Jean was a simple girl who had probably only aspired to marriage to a nice man and a house and baby of her own. She had achieved all this, only to be struck down by someone who thought it was funny to recreate old magic tricks with human beings as props. It just didn't bear thinking about. Max strode on, thinking about it.

He was irritated to find that his footsteps had

taken him almost to the door of the Theatre Royal. Why couldn't he keep away from the place? The posters outside advertised the Agatha Christie play. *The Mousetrap.* Who on earth would go to see a play like that? People want escapism on a Saturday night, not sordid crime. As he stood, frowning up at the billboards, a voice hailed him.

'Max!' It was Roy Coulter.

'Hallo, Roy. Just admiring your playbills.'

'Yes,' said Roy, puffing out his chest. 'It was a sell-out. Smartest decision I ever made.' Clearly Roy had forgotten his earlier misgivings about straight drama.

'Congratulations.' Maybe Max should reinvent himself as a character actor. He could just see himself twirling a villain's moustache.

'Glad I ran into you,' Roy went on. 'I wanted to tell you, your friend was here.'

'My friend?' For a crazy moment, Max thought he meant Tony. Had Tony 'The Mind' Mulholland come back to haunt him?

'Stan Parks. The Great Disaster or whatever he calls himself.'

'Diablo was here? When?'

'This morning. He turned up in some ghastly old white suit with stains all down the front. He was asking after you.'

'He was?' This meant that Diablo was still in Brighton. What the hell was the old fool playing at?

'What did he want to know?' asked Max.

'He wanted to know where you were appearing next. I told him Hastings. I hope that was all right. After all, I know he's a friend of yours.'

'Yes,' said Max, staring up at a poster of a bug-eyed actor clutching wildly at the air. 'He's an old friend.'

The Battle of Trafalgar provided Edgar with an excellent lunch, but not much in the way of information. The barman didn't recognise Ethel's picture and had remarked sourly that he'd only been working in the place a month 'and that's a month too long'.

Edgar retired to a corner table to eat his steak and kidney pie. The surly barman aside, it was a pleasant pub with mullioned windows and red velvet seats. Even though it was summer, a fire was burning in the grate and he could see that it would be a cosy place to come on a winter's night. Two elderly men were playing chess by the fire. Is that why Ethel had come here, to indulge in a board games habit?

'Excuse me.' Edgar looked up to see a woman with a tray of glasses. 'I'm Marnie,' she said. 'I've been working here for a while. Jack said you were asking after a lady?'

Feeling as if he had misjudged Jack, Edgar showed Marnie the photograph.

She nodded, hitching the tray higher on her hip.

She was about fifty, with a tired, attractive face. It was a face that looked as if it deserved more from life than collecting dirty glasses in a pub.

'I remember her,' she said. 'She came here once or twice. Nice lady. Polite.'

'Was she on her own? Do you ever remember her meeting someone? A man?' He got out the picture of Tony.

'No,' said Marnie decisively. 'I would definitely have remembered him. I do remember her talking with another woman once or twice. They sat in the snug, it's quieter in there.'

'Another woman? Can you describe her?'

Marnie looked over towards the snug, as if imagining the woman there. This, in Edgar's opinion, was the sign of a good witness.

'Youngish but she dressed old,' she said at last. 'She had one of those hats with a veil. They haven't been fashionable since the twenties.'

A hat with a veil reminded Edgar of Tony's mother at his funeral. He hadn't been in touch with the family since. Maybe he should send them a card or something.

'Anything else?' he asked.

'She had a nice voice. Educated. Thought she might have been a teacher or something. Don't know why.'

'Do you know what they talked about? Not that I'd suggest you were listening,' he added hurriedly.

Marnie laughed. 'Don't worry. You can't help listening in this job. No, I didn't hear what they were saying, but I'm betting it was something about the theatre. It was all she talked about.' She gestured to Ethel's picture. 'How she'd once been the assistant to a famous magician.' She looked at Edgar. 'Was that true?'

'Yes,' said Edgar, putting away the photographs. 'That was true.'

The antiques shop in the Lanes was easy to find because it had a large stuffed bear outside. 'Brings in the custom,' said the owner, a small man attached to a large moustache. 'I call him Henry. I dress him in a Santa suit for Christmas.'

Briefly, Edgar thought about Christmas. He supposed he'd have to go to Esher. Lucy would be with her family, it would just be him and Rose and a chicken small enough for two.

'I wanted to ask you some more questions about the man who bought the sword,' he said when the owner had bustled him into a small room behind the scenes. It reminded him of being backstage at the theatre. There was even the same smell of damp.

'I don't know what more I can tell you,' said the shopkeeper rather fretfully. 'I gave you a full description at the time.'

Edgar read from his notes. ' "I think it was a man, a smallish man. I think he had a moustache."

Think back. Can you remember anything else?'

'I don't think so,' the antiques dealer picked up a cloth and starting polishing a tray of stones. 'We get a lot of customers.'

As the shop was empty on a Saturday afternoon, despite the attractions of Henry, Edgar rather doubted that.

'You say he was small,' he prompted. 'Smaller than me?'

'Well yes,' said the owner, drawing himself up. 'You're quite a tall man.'

'About your height?'

'Possibly.' Slightly offended tone.

'Can you remember what he was wearing? Coat? Hat?'

'He might have had a hat. Men don't take their hats off anymore. There's no respect.'

'You said he might have had a moustache?'

'I think so.' Unconsciously, the man stroked his luxuriant whiskers. Was he so proud of his moustache that he imagined one attached to everyone he saw?

'What about colouring? Was he fair or dark?'

'Dark, I think. I can remember a black moustache.'

I bet you can, thought Edgar. Aloud, he said, 'What about age? My sort of age?'

'Younger, I think. I had an impression of someone young.'

'Did you notice his hands?'

'His hands? No, I don't remember his hands. As I say, we get a lot of customers.'

'What about the sword? Was it expensive?'

The man shrugged, his moustache moving on its own. 'Not particularly. It was a replica of a cavalry sword. Looked fairly impressive, but not a real antique.'

But the sword was a prop, thought Edgar, all that mattered was what it looked like.

'Thank you,' he said. 'You've been very helpful.'

He imagined Henry staring at him as he walked away.

His last call was to Tony's digs. The landlady's daughter had described a man visiting Tony a few days before he died. Would this visitor too be described as small and hat-wearing? Would there be a phantom moustache or ancient hands?

At first, the landlady took him for a potential lodger. Then her smile faltered as recognition dawned. It faded away altogether when Edgar explained that he wanted to ask a few more questions about the murder of Tony Mulholland. She looked quickly up and down the street, clearly terrified that people might overhear the 'm' word.

'It's about the gentleman who called on Mr Mulholland a few days before he died,' said Edgar.

The landlady was ushering him inside. 'I don't

know about any gentleman,' she said, putting suspicious quotation marks around the word.

'You daughter mentioned it to my sergeant.'

'Oh, did she?' The landlady seemed to swell slightly with nerves.

'Desdemona!' she shouted. 'Get down here.'
Edgar hoped that he hadn't got the girl into trouble.

The daughter appeared, half-hidden behind lank, greasy hair. Who on earth had the idea of naming her after Shakespeare's tragic heroine? And why Desdemona? Why not Juliet or Ophelia? Did the landlady (prosaically named Lil) think that her daughter was about to be spirited away by a dashing black general?

'Er, Desdemona,' Edgar began. 'I hope this isn't too upsetting for you, but I wanted to talk to you about the man who visited Mr Mulholland the week before he died.'

'Des still has nightmares about that,' put in the mother. 'She's very sensitive.'

So do I, Edgar wanted to say, I'm sensitive too. Instead he said, 'I'm so sorry, Desdemona. I could probably arrange for you to see a doctor if that would help.'

'A trick cyclist?' said Lil. 'No thanks. We've never had anything like that in our family.'

'I wanted to ask you about the man who called on Mr Mulholland a few days before he died,' said Edgar. 'Do you feel up to telling me a bit about him?'

'I told the other policeman,' said Desdemona. 'The young one.'

'Sergeant Willis,' said Edgar, remembering that Desdemona had described Tony's visitor as 'quite old, at least thirty.' He wondered how old he seemed to her.

'I just wondered if you had anything to add to your description,' said Edgar. 'Could you describe this man? Was he tall or short? Young or old?'

'Tall,' said Desdemona.

'Really?' Edgar leant forward in surprise. 'As tall as me?'

'No,' said Desdemona. 'Smaller. I just meant, taller than me.'

As Desdemona was approximately five foot nothing, this didn't seem to get them very far. 'How was he dressed?' Edgar asked. 'Was he wearing a coat and hat?'

'He had a hat,' volunteered Desdemona. 'Like the ones sailors wear.'

'A peaked cap?'

'Yes.'

'Did you talk to him? What was his voice like?'

For the first time, a genuine look of fear crossed the girl's face. 'He had a horrible voice,' she said. 'Sort of whispery.'

'Whispery?'

'Yes. He asked me if Mr Mulholland was staying here. I said yes. He asked me where his

272

room was. I told him. Mr Mulholland was out so I told him he could wait.'

'Well you shouldn't have done,' said Lil. 'I don't know what you were thinking, Des. We don't just let strangers into the guests' rooms. What will the inspector think of us?'

She glared at Edgar as if it were his fault.

'Did the man threaten you in some way?' asked Edgar.

'No,' said the girl uncertainly, 'it was just his voice.'

'What about his voice?'

'It kind of made you do what he wanted.'

That was Tony's trick, thought Edgar. Persuade the audience to give you the answer you wanted in the first place. In this case, the visitor had wanted entry into Tony's room and he had got it.

'What happened when Mr Mulholland came in?' he asked.

'I told him that he had a visitor and he went upstairs.'

'Did you happen to hear what he said when he saw the visitor?'

Edgar had expected to make his usual disclaimer: 'I'm not suggesting that you were listening', but Desdemona seemed quite happy to share the fruits of her eavesdropping.

'Yes. I heard Mr Mulholland say, "I thought I'd be seeing you sooner or later".'

At the door, Edgar thought to ask about the

girl's unusual name. 'That was my husband,' said Lil. 'He was an actor. Nuts about Shakespeare. He had a big success in *Othello*.'

'As Othello?' Though, judging by Desdemona, there can't have been much Moorish blood in her father.

'No,' said Lil with a laugh. 'Iago. He always played the villains.'

CHAPTER 27

Max found that he didn't have the heart for lunch after all. He had a drink at the Pavilion Tavern and walked back to his hotel. There, he forced himself to call Bill and offer his condolences.

'It's a bit much,' said Bill, with rather touching understatement, 'to come home and find that your wife's been murdered. It's a bit much for a chap to take.' He sounded tearful and slightly drunk.

'It is,' said Max. 'It must have been terrible.'

'Terrible,' said Bill, stretching the word out. 'Yes, it was terrible. You wouldn't know, you've never been married, but you get used to someone being there and when they're not . . .'

'Is there someone with you now?' asked Max. He didn't think that Bill should be on his own, especially if he was in charge of the baby.

'No,' said Bill, sounding truculent. 'My sister's looking after Barney. I'm alone here.'

'Why don't you go and stay with your sister?' said Max. 'I'm not sure you should stay in the house on your own.'

'I've got to stay,' said Bill. 'The bastard might come back, mightn't he?'

Would the bastard come back, thought Max, as he began to pack his case. He didn't think so somehow. So far, the killer had relied on surprise. He was hardly likely to go back to a house where there was a large ex-sergeant waiting for him. He thought about what Bill had said to him. 'You wouldn't know, you've never been married.' Max had often congratulated himself on reaching the age of forty and remaining unmarried. But, over the past few weeks, he had found himself wondering if a bachelor's life was really all it was cracked up to be. Being fancy-free was all very well, but there was nothing particularly glamorous about packing for another week in a grim seaside town. The same old audiences, the same old tricks, the same girls (if you're lucky, he supposed that the standard of girl went downhill too as you got older). He thought of Diablo attempting to perform the bottle trick in front of a hard-faced audience who were only there for the striptease. Would there come a time when he too would be unable to perform the simplest trick? He palmed a bow-tie just to reassure himself that he could still do it. Open your hand and the tie is gone. Big bloody deal. He continued to pack his

275

shirts, pressing each one between tissue paper. He always had his linen professionally laundered. You had to keep up appearances.

But why? Max looked around the hotel room. It was luxurious enough, he supposed. Nice double bed, ensuite bathroom, view over the promenade. He was still successful, the top of the bill. But who would care if his shirts weren't snow white? What was the point of being the great Max Mephisto—smart car, hand-made shoes, the best dinner jacket in the business? Who the hell was he trying to impress? He took out his cigarette case, irritated with himself. He couldn't afford to crack up, not now. He had a week in Hastings to get through first. As he leant out of the window, blowing smoke towards the sea, he thought that he would even welcome the appearance of the man Edgar had (with a grimace) called The Conjuror Killer. At least that would shake things up a bit.

I thought I'd be seeing you sooner or later. Those words kept echoing in Edgar's head as he returned to Bartholomew Square, completed his paperwork and wished Bob a good Saturday night. Who was it that Tony had expected to see? He had obviously known his visitor. They had sat down and drunk tea together. What's more, the visitor had been someone Tony had *expected* to see. Who could it have been?

It was only five o'clock, but the station was

almost empty. Just the desk sergeant upstairs and a constable guarding the cells. Everyone else had departed to enjoy the rest of their weekend. Edgar imagined them in the Bath Arms, downing pints and laughing at how Inspector Stephens couldn't catch a killer even if the killer took the trouble to write to him personally. Maybe they thought that he was the Conjuror Killer? After all, he had been the first person to find the bodies of Tony and Jean. Maybe he should just arrest himself and have done with it.

The police station was quiet but, as usual, not silent. Water gurgled in the pipes and the floorboards creaked and sighed. Edgar thought of Henry Solomon, the upright lawman who had made the mistake of turning his back on a suspect. He thought of Solomon's ghost watching him sorrowfully, wondering what sort of policeman had succeeded him. The feeling of being watched became so strong that Edgar went to the door and looked up and down the corridor. A single bulb swung to and fro. What was making it move? There was no air here in the cellars. Edgar walked to the stairs that led to the cells.

'Dawson!' he called.

'Yes, sir?' came the constable's voice.

'Is there anyone down there?'

'Just the drunk in cell two, sir.'

Edgar walked back along the corridor. This time he thought he saw a flash of white, like a long skirt whisking up the stairs. Was it the ghost of one of the monks, on his way to the kitchen gardens? Don't be ridiculous, he told himself. You don't believe in ghosts. 'What are ghosts?' Max had once said. 'Only illusions. It's one of the first rules of magic, people see what they want to see.' They used to tell ghost stories in the bar at the Cally on winter nights. Charis had specialised in haunting Welsh tales of enchanted harps, voices singing in the hills and water spirits whose evil little hands would pull you under the waves. When Charis had died, Edgar had longed to see her ghost. He couldn't believe that she could have gone like that, without a word. But he had been outraged when one of the WAAFs claimed to have seen her 'walking in the grounds, wailing like a banshee'. Charis would never have wailed and banshees were Irish not Welsh. And, above all, if she had appeared to anyone, it would have been to Edgar.

If he was thinking about Charis, it was time to leave. Edgar gathered up his papers, climbed the dark stairs and said a cheerful goodbye to the desk sergeant. The town was just waking up for the night. People were queuing for the cinema and drunks were already staggering out of the pubs. Saturday nights in Brighton were starting to have a real edge of violence. Young lads would come down from London intent on trouble; on Sunday mornings the cells would be full of them. When

278

did young people start to move in packs? There were the racecourse gangs too, organised criminals who ran betting rackets and indulged in a little knife crime on the side. They needed another war, Frank Hodges said: that would give them something to think about. Well, if the rumblings from Korea got any louder, Hodges might have his wish and there would be another war hundreds of miles away where British soldiers could go and die without ever really knowing what they were fighting for.

Tonight though, apart from the drunks, the mood seemed to be mellow, almost melancholy. It felt like the end of something, the end of summer perhaps. A hurdygurdy was playing outside the Pavilion and a couple started dancing, quick-stepping their way along the pavement, accompanied by ironical cheers. Edgar walked through the crowds feeling like a ghost himself. He didn't want to join the party, but equally, he realised as he began the long walk, he didn't want to go home.

All the way up the hill, he had wondered what he would do if he opened the door to his flat to find Diablo lying on the sofa, glass in hand. But the house was silent. No wireless, no hacking cough, no whisky-soaked voice calling, 'Dear boy, where have you been?' Edgar stood in the hallway, strangely reluctant to go any further. Letters were scattered on the floor. He had left before the post that morning. He bent down and picked them up. A statement from the bank, a postcard from Lucy, a handyman seeking work and a flyer for the variety show due to start next week on Hastings pier. Edgar smoothed this last one out and stared at it. The headline act filled half the page, the M's of Max and Mephisto standing on top of each other. That was all he could read, however, because the rest of the name was scored out in thick black lines.

CHAPTER 28

Max reached Hastings at three o'clock on Sunday afternoon and a more depressing time of day, he thought, would be hard be imagine. It was even raining, a thin grey drizzle that you didn't notice until it had soaked through to your skin. August had given way to September and there was a dour back-to-school feel about the whole town. Max was staying at digs recommended by a friend but, when he looked up at the stucco seafront building, he felt his heart sink a little lower. He was an expert at assessing lodgings, and he knew that this building would possess high ceilings and elaborate cornices, but also peeling paint-work and ill-fitting floorboards. He was sure the bathrooms would be freezing at night.

The door was opened by a pleasant-looking woman in her early fifties. 'Mr Mephisto? This is an honour. We're so glad Ray suggested us. I've given you the best room. It's got a lovely view.'

Slightly mollified by this welcome, Max followed the woman ('Call me Queenie, everyone does') up the stairs. He wasn't excited at the thought of a view. In his opinion, all rooms were improved by having the curtains drawn.

The room was as he expected. Handsome proportions, bay window, damp in the corners, as cold as a harlot's heart.

'You can see the pier from here,' said Queenie, drawing back the net curtains.

Max agreed that you could.

'We've got tickets for Monday first house. I can't wait to see you in action. Are you going to do the trick with the levitating table?'

Max smiled. 'That would be telling.'

Queenie lingered in the doorway. 'If you want anything, just shout.'

'I will.'

'Bye for now then. Supper's at six.'

'I think I might eat out if it's all the same to you.'

'But it's steak and kidney pie. My theatricals always like a steak and kidney pie.'

Max sighed and agreed to eat the pie. Queenie departed, only to reappear again.

'I'll forget my head next. I've got a letter for you.'

'You have?'

'It's from Ray. The Great Raymondo. He knew you'd be coming here, see.'

'Thank you very much.'

Max waited until he could hear the landlady's feet descending the stairs and then he opened the letter.

Dear Max,

Sorry it has taken me so long to reply to yours. Idiot agent sent it on to Blackpool but I'd already left. Anyway, I know you're at Queenie's in September so I'll send this to her. She's a good sort Queenie and a big fan of yours (if you know what I mean).

Anyway, to answer your question, I don't have an address for Ruby. I put an advertisement in *Variety* asking for a girl and she answered. She was good though, the best I've worked with. Frankly I'm amazed that Ruby would lose touch with you. All she ever did was ask about you. She seemed to know all about you—your career, your act. She begged me to recommend her to you which I did because—as I say—she was damn good. She's a deep one, though. My guess is—if you can't find her, it's because she wants to stay hidden.

All the best, old boy. Keep 'em laughing.
Ray

Max went to the window and looked out at the grey, rainswept promenade. So his meeting with Ruby hadn't been chance, providence, whatever you like to call it. Ruby had wanted to meet him. She had known all about him. She had engineered their encounter. Why? He thought of Ruby on stage, how she seemed to know instinctively where he'd be and how she was always ready with a twirl and a smile up to the gallery. Was she still one step ahead of him? He thought of what Ray had said in his letter. *If you can't find her, it's because she wants to stay hidden.*

'Where are you, Ruby?' he said aloud. And his voice echoed against the high, dusty walls.

Edgar was woken by a banging on the door. He sat up, disorientated for a moment. On Friday he had been somehow reluctant to sleep in the bed vacated by Diablo, so had spent the night on the sofa. But last night, after trying and failing to ring Max and warn him about the poster with the name crossed out, he had changed the sheets, drunk half a bottle of scotch and passed out. Now he wasn't quite sure where he was. The wardrobe seemed to be looming nastily and the empty whisky bottle winked from the bedside table. The knocking grew louder.

'Coming.'

Edgar rolled off the bed, registered that he had slept in his clothes and staggered towards the front door. A small square shape was visible through the glass. Who the hell could it be on a Sunday morning?

It was raining outside, but the light still hurt his eyes. The shape solidified into an angry man in a tweed hat.

'What time do you call this? It's nearly midday.'

'Major Gormley. What are you doing here?'

'Came to see you,' said the Major, unanswerably. 'Can I come in?'

Edgar led the Major into the sitting room and deposited him on the sofa. Then he went into the kitchen and took three aspirins with a pint of water. Then he made coffee and took it back into the room where the Major was standing, looking out of the window.

'Strordinary view. You can see the sea.'

'Yes, well, it's a steep hill.'

'I know,' said the Major with some asperity. 'I just walked up it.'

'How did you get here?'

'Took the train. Walked from the station.'

That was the wrong question. Edgar took a gulp of coffee and tried to think of the right one.

'*Why* are you here?'

The Major sat down and took a wallet from his inside pocket. Then, with hands that shook a little, he extracted a piece of paper and spread it on the table. It was an article, somewhat crumpled, cut from a newspaper. Edgar thought of the cutting that had been found in Ethel's room after her death. *Max Mephisto Mesmerises in Manchester.*

This article, too, concerned Max. It was a review of the show at the Theatre Royal, not the one from the *Argus* that Edgar had read after the show, but one that was fairly similar in tone; ambivalent about Tony, cutting about the dancers and positively gushing about Max. 'Max Mephisto is the greatest variety star of our age. His act never fails to enthral and surprise in equal measure . . .'

Edgar looked up. Why would Major Gormley leave his sick wife and get the train to Brighton just to show him an article saying that Max was a good magician? They all knew that. The world knew that. Heavens, even Hitler had known that.

'Why are you showing me this?' he said at last.

The Major jabbed an arthritic finger at the photograph accompanying the article. It was an action photograph showing Max on stage brandishing a sword. The cabinet was beside him and next to it was Ruby, smiling straight into the camera.

'That girl,' said the Major. 'She's the girl that came to see me asking questions about Massingham. The girl who said she was a journalist. I don't take the local paper normally,' he went on, 'but our daily uses it to wrap up the good china. Elsie took a fancy to have the willow-pattern cups yesterday. I took them out and there it was.'

'Are you sure it's the same girl?'

'Yes. Pretty little thing. I'd know her anywhere. She had a pretty name too, some kind of jewel.'

'Ruby?'

'That's it.'

'And she came to see you in July asking questions about Max?'

'Yes. Said she was writing a piece about Max Mephisto's contribution to the war. Well, I said to her, it'll be a fairly short piece in that case.'

Edgar felt an urge to defend Max's war record: the camouflaged tanks in Egypt, the deal with the imam, the *Ptolemy*. He forced himself to return to the topic in hand.

'Even if it is her,' he said slowly. 'Why's it so important? I mean, why did you feel that you had to come to see me?'

The Major looked at him in astonishment, shocked that anyone could be that stupid. The expression brought back the days at Inverness so clearly that Edgar almost felt the chafe of his battle tunic against his neck.

'When you came to see me last time,' said the Major, speaking slowly and clearly as if to an idiot (or junior officer), 'you said that we were all in danger. I remember it plainly. Well, what if it's her?' He pointed at the picture. 'That girl. What if she's the one who's tracking you all down?'

'But why?'

'I don't know why,' said the Major impatiently,

'that's your job. But it seems pretty damn suspicious to me.'

'Jean's dead,' said Edgar. 'Bill's wife Jean. She was murdered in her home. I think it was the same person who killed Tony.'

The Major looked at him. He didn't seem scared or even surprised. If Edgar had to name an emotion reflected in the little grey eyes, he would have said that it was pity.

'So there's just the four of you left. You, Massingham, Cosgrove and Parks.'

'And you,' said Edgar, wondering why everyone seemed to forget that the Major had actually been in charge of the Magic Men.

'I wasn't really one of you though, was I?'

Edgar looked down at the picture. Ruby smiled back up at him. Who are you? Edgar wanted to say. What do you want with us all?

'What do you mean?' he asked.

'I'm not a *magician*.' A wealth of contempt went into the last word.

'Nor am I.'

'No,' said the Major. 'That's why he's the one in danger.'

He didn't have to say who he meant.

The steak and kidney pie was everything he imagined it would be. Queenie presided regally over the supper table and introduced Max to his fellow pros: Big and Small, the double act (who, disconcertingly, were exactly the same size), Professor Van Blum, who played the organ, the four Fantinis, acrobats, and Madame Mitzi who did an act with a performing poodle. The dog made a particular impression as it was sitting on its owner's lap throughout the meal.

'Sadie's partial to steak and kidney,' explained Madame Mitzi, whose accent hailed from the exotic climes of Blackburn.

'Does she always eat with you?' asked Max.

'Bless you, yes. She's that clever, this dog, you couldn't give her dog biscuits. I bet she's even cleverer than you, Mr Mephisto.'

'I'm sure she is,' said Max politely.

The Fantinis remarked to each other, in Italian, that this sort of thing would never happen in Naples. Max was inclined to agree with them.

'Ah, you're wrong there, Mitzi,' said Queenie, carving out second helpings, 'no one's cleverer than Mr Mephisto.'

Max smiled uncomfortably. Throughout the meal, Queenie had shown signs of singling him out for special favours. He had had the biggest slice of pie and the plate showing scenes from Shakespeare plays. He was also occupying the chair at the head of the table. 'My husband's place,' said Queenie, lowering her eyelids. 'God rest his soul.' Max wondered uneasily what Ray had meant by writing, with sly parenthesis, *She's . . . a big fan of yours (if you know what I mean)*.

'More pie, Mr Mephisto?'

'No thank you, Queenie, I couldn't. And do call me Max.'

'Oh!' Queenie showed signs of being overcome. Signor Fantini remarked to his eldest son that the magician was in with a chance there. 'He's welcome to it,' replied Pietro Fantini.

The appearance of the maid brought an end to this comedy of manners. The girl stood in the doorway as if she had something momentous to announce. Max had to admire her stage presence.

'Please, ma'am, there's a policeman at the door.'

Big and Small looked at each other, Sadie barked and the Fantinis agreed that there had always been something suspicious about the magician.

'What does he want?' asked Queenie.

'Please'm, he wants to talk to Mr Mephisto.'

Max discouraged Queenie from following him out of the room. A uniformed constable was standing nervously in the hall, holding his helmet in front of him like a shield.

'Mr Max Mephisto?'

'That's me.'

'I'm PC Ian Granger. I've been sent to guard you.'

'What?'

PC Granger held his ground. 'We've had a message from Detective Inspector Stephens of the

Brighton police. He has reason to believe that you're in danger.'

For a moment the name meant nothing to Max. Military ranks had always struck him as absurd —he'd never once used that ridiculous Acting Major handle—and police titles didn't seem much better. Then he remembered. Stephens. Edgar Stephens. He sighed inwardly. This was Edgar's promised police protection. Really, it was rather insulting.

'I'm not in danger,' said Max. 'And you can tell Inspector Stephens that with my love.'

PC Granger winced at the last word. 'I've been told to guard you,' he said.

'Well, you can guard me from a distance,' said Max. 'I'm going back to my dinner. Good night.'

When he got back to the table, Sadie was finishing the last of the pie.

CHAPTER 29

When the Major had left, trundling back down the hill like an angry steam train, Edgar sat on the sofa and thought about Ruby and Max. He had thought that Ruby might be in danger, the Major was convinced that she *was* the danger. Either way, the girl had vanished without trace and Edgar was still no closer to finding the person who had killed Ethel, Tony and Jean. Was Max marked out as the next victim?

He wished that he could telephone Max, but he had no idea where he was staying in Hastings. Eventually he rang the local police station. After a long explanation ('You're saying a *magician* is in danger?'), the officer in charge promised to find out where Max was staying and send someone round. 'He'll say that he's not in danger,' said Edgar. 'I just want you to keep a discreet eye on him.' 'Don't worry, Inspector Stephens,' said the officer reassuringly. 'We'll be very subtle.'

Edgar went out for a walk, hoping that it would clear his head, but it was a dull rainy evening which only seemed to make him feel more befuddled. He bought some chips from the shop at the corner and walked home eating them out of the newspaper. Even in his current state of worry, it still gave him a small feeling of satisfaction to think how shocked his mother would be if she could see him.

Back home, Edgar poured himself a whisky (hair of the dog and all that), sat back down on the sofa and thought about the Magic Men. What had happened up there at Inverness that had led to this—this gruesome game of cat and mouse? A ship had burnt and a girl had died. That was it. After Charis's death, the unit had been disbanded with what felt like unseemly haste. Edgar was sent to a desk job at the Ministry of Information where he waited out the last months of the war in a welter of misery and frustration. To everyone's surprise, Max volunteered for active service and was sent back to Egypt. Diablo was invalided out and Tony, too, claimed to be suffering from stress. Bill joined the RAF base at Watnall. Come to think of it, that was probably where he had got to know Jean. A lot of the WAAFs had ended up at Watnall, a place that had the distinction of having a mixed mess and, in consequence, a decidedly racy reputation.

Edgar remembered Bill coming to see him early in 1945. The doodlebugs were still coming over, silent and purposeful, but otherwise London was getting back to normal. Children were playing in the parks and the words, 'Second Front Now', chalked on the wall opposite Edgar's digs, were looking faded and apologetic. They had sat in a pub near Gordon Square and talked about the prospect of peace.

'I just want a house and a job,' Bill had said. 'I'm not ambitious. I don't want my name in lights like Tony used to say.'

'I don't know what I want,' Edgar had said. 'To make a difference, I suppose.' He thought now that, while Bill had at least achieved his ambition, his was still as remote as ever.

They had stayed in the pub quite late, he remembered. Edgar and Bill had never been close and, while Charis was alive, they were rivals. But, now that she was dead, they found an odd comfort in each other's company. Not that they spoke about

Charis. Or about Jean. Edgar did remember one thing that Bill had said. 'Do you think we'll ever see Max and Tony again,' he had asked, over his fourth pint. 'Or will they be too grand for us, being stars and all that?' Even at the time, this had seemed curiously bitter. Edgar was sure that his friendship with Max would survive the war. He didn't care whether or not he saw Tony again. But Bill obviously thought that he would be snubbed by his old army comrades. Was this why he had invited them all to his wedding? To show them that he was on his way to success in civilian life? Or was it just for a reunion? Either way, they had all refused the invitation. Why? He knew that, in his case, it had simply been because seeing Bill again would remind him of Charis. Had it been snobbishness on Max's part, indifference on Tony's? Had Bill been angry? Angry enough to kill?

Edgar thought of Tony greeting his visitor. *I thought I'd be seeing you sooner or later*. Why had Tony wanted to see Edgar and Bill that day at one-fifteen? Tony liked power, Edgar knew, that was why he favoured mind-games and hypnosis over other kinds of magic. He had obviously looked forward to making his former comrades sweat. But someone had called on him before the fun could start. Who was it? Who had sat beside Tony in that squalid little bedroom, drugged him and then stabbed him, leaving the sword stuck into the cupboard like a bloody exclamation mark?

Edgar remembered something Max had once told him about card tricks. 'You cut the cards and then you ask the punter to tap the deck twice. Why? Because then he feels that he has some control over the trick. He's making it happen.' Was Tony's message the equivalent of an audience member tapping a pack of cards? The trick was already in motion, the die was cast, but Tony still wanted to make it seem as if he were in control.

Max had told him in Eastbourne, 'The thing about The Zig Zag Girl is that it's a trick that depends on the girl.' Some of Max's illusions depended on having a stooge in the audience, they looked like solos but they were really duets. What if there were two murderers designed to look like one? Bill, for example, may have had an alibi for Jean's murder, but he could easily have killed Ethel and Tony. Maybe the flower-buyer and the sword-purchaser were really two different people? There was still the problem of motive though. Try as he might, Edgar couldn't unearth one reason why anyone should want to kill a retired showgirl, a comedian and a housewife. They were linked, albeit tenuously, by the Magic Men.

The whisky was making him feel worse. It was almost dark outside now. Edgar had a bath and got ready for bed. If only he could sleep really deeply tonight, wipe out everything that had happened over the last few days and wake feeling properly refreshed. But, as he lay in bed, thoughts and images insisted on whirling around in his head.

I thought I'd be seeing you sooner or later.

You thought it might be a lunatic magician.

Love 'em and leave 'em, eh, Max?

I used to be his girl.

This guy's a showman and I know about showmen.

There was a spy, you know. In the Magic Men.

And, as he was falling into an uneasy sleep, he thought of Diablo's warning, that first day in Inverness.

If you're playing cards with Max, never take your eyes off his hands.

Max's room proved every bit as uncomfortable as he'd feared. The eiderdown escaped in the night and the windows rattled every time a bus drove past. The bathroom was, of course, freezing. In the morning he didn't wait for Queenie's special breakfast, but headed straight for the theatre, stopping at a cafe on the way for a black coffee and a cigarette.

As soon as he stepped through the pass door, he felt better. Here at least he was at home. The smell of Calor gas and greasepaint was as soothing as an anaesthetic. He stood for a few minutes, drinking it in. Even if he did manage to give up the stage, would he ever really be happy anywhere else?

'Mr Mephisto?' A trilling female voice brought him back to the present.

A woman with shingled hair like a twenties model was standing at the back of the auditorium. As she came closer, Max saw that she was younger than she first seemed. Her clothes (she was squeezed into a skirt suit, very tight around the hips) and hair made her seem almost middle-aged, but she was little more than a schoolgirl.

'I'm Beryl,' said the vision. 'Uncle Terry suggested me for your assistant.'

Uncle Terry must be Terry Urquhart, the stage manager. Max remembered asking him for a girl to perform the disappearing act. This girl looked far too solid to vanish. Max wished that he had signed up Queenie's housemaid. She, at least, had some sense of dramatic timing.

'Have you done anything like this before?' he asked.

'Oh yes,' said Beryl, she had an over-genteel voice, the vowels squeezed very thin. 'I was in lots of plays at school.'

'Do you want to be an actress then?'

'More than anything,' she simpered.

'Well, this is about acting the part of an ordinary member of the audience. Think you can do that?'

'I'll try.' Beryl laughed, showing too many teeth.

The theatre on the pier had been destroyed by fire during the First World War and completely rebuilt in the 1930s. It was now an art deco gem floating on the sea. The outside was vaguely Egyptian in design and this had given Max the idea of adding a kind of Tutankhamen twist to the act. He had designed a folding pyramid which would cover the girl. It was semi-transparent, which would give the audience the idea that they were seeing everything, but, as all magicians know, audiences never really see anything.

Max took Beryl backstage and showed her the props.

'So you lie on the table,' he said, 'and I cover you with the robe.' The robe, covered in hiero-glyphs and jackal-headed gods, was deliberately eye-catching. There was a headdress too. 'Then I'll put the screen round you. The robe is stiff so it'll stay in place and with any luck the audience will be watching it rather than you. Then, when the drum rolls start, you slip off the table and into the trapdoor.'

At first, she couldn't even get on the table without help. In the end she managed a sort of laborious hop, a far cry from the elegant glide that Max had envisaged. The trapdoor was greeted by a squeal and a warning that she was afraid of dark places.

'It's not dark,' said Max, 'and there'll be a stage-hand waiting at the bottom.' He thought of Ruby and how neatly she would have performed this trick; how effortlessly she would have garnered the audience's affections, rising slightly awkwardly from her seat and dipping her head in embarrassment, how ruthlessly she would have held their attention, still and dignified in the pharaoh's robe and how quickly and easily she would have slipped out of sight, leaving just a slither of material behind.

'Let's try it again,' he said. 'You can wear the headdress this time.'

'I feel like Cleopatra,' said Beryl.

I feel like a cigarette, thought Max.

It had rained in the night, but Monday morning was fresh and hopeful, the blue sky reflected in the puddles as Edgar walked to work. He was feeling, if not completely refreshed, at least a little more human. It was the start of a new week. He had a slightly better description of the main suspect, he could commission a police artist and circulate the picture. He had alerted the Hastings police and, with any luck, he would be able to talk to Max. He could redouble his efforts to trace Ruby and Diablo. After all, finding the old magician would surely only be a matter of scouring the dodgiest pubs in Brighton.

In the Incident Room, he pinned up the playbill that had been posted through his letterbox. It seemed that the killer knew not only his army rank but also his address. It was hard to shake the feeling that someone was watching him all the time, a shadowy figure moving backstage, just out of view of the lights. He remembered the footsteps in the corridor last night, the flash of white on the stairs. Was there a spy, here, in the police station? It was possible, he supposed. He stared up at the poster advertising the Flying Fantinis and an act with a talking dog. The words 'Max Mephisto' had been crossed out with a thick-nibbed ink pen. Was this the same pen that had deleted Tony's face in the earlier photograph? Edgar looked closer, as if the ink itself held the clue. The names on the board swirled and danced in front of him. Ethel Williams, Tony Mulholland, Jean Cosgrove. What did they have in common? There were lines from Ethel and Tony to Max Mephisto and from Jean to Bill Cosgrove. With a slight jolt, Edgar realised that his name should be on the board too, somewhere between Max and Bill, the third man, the stooge in the audience. A little to the side was the name 'Stan Parks, alias The Great Diablo.' Where the hell was The Great Diablo?

Bob appeared in the doorway wearing the trilby hat which he hoped made him look older.

'Is that the latest from the Conjuror Killer?' he asked, gesturing towards the playbill.

'Don't call him that,' said Edgar.

'No, seriously, sir. Who do you think it is?'

Edgar looked round. The 'sir' sounded suspicious, but Bob's expression was one of earnest enquiry.

'If I knew,' said Edgar wearily, 'don't you think I would have done something about it?'

'People are saying it's Max Mephisto.'

'Are they?'

'Do you think it's him?'

Edgar had long given up counting to ten with Bob. 'Max is my closest friend,' he said. 'We served in the army together. So no, Bob, I don't think he's a sadistic killer.'

'Just asking,' said Bob.

When Bob had left, expressing disappointment with his boss in every fibre of his being, Edgar went back to his office and telephoned the Hastings police. Yes, the chief inspector replied, they had traced Mr Mephisto's lodgings and had sent an officer round last night. Mr Mephisto had denied that he was in any danger. 'Quite forthright he was, apparently. Said that we could tell you so with his love.'

Edgar smiled, but he asked if someone could be sent to the theatre that evening. 'A threat has been made against Max Mephisto,' he said, 'and we're taking it very seriously.'

'I'll send my very best officer,' promised the chief inspector. 'I expect he'll be grateful for a night out.'

Edgar dispatched Bob to search the pubs and dosshouses for The Great Diablo. He commissioned a picture from the police artist knowing, as he did so, that the result would not look like any human being, alive or dead. He then telephoned Sergeant Deacon in Wembley.

'We've had some results back from the lab,' said Deacon. 'Wonderful what they can do these days, isn't it? Seems that one of the cups held traces of atropha belladonna. That's . . .'

'I know what it is,' said Edgar. 'It's our man's modus operandi.'

'Think it's definitely the same man then?'

'Yes I do. The descriptions tally too, vague as they are. How's Mr Cosgrove? Have you interviewed him again?'

'Dropped in to see him yesterday. Seemed in a pretty bad way, but that's only to be expected. Babbling on about some people called the Magic Men. Course he was half drunk. Can't say I blame him.'

Edgar didn't feel up to explaining the Magic Men to Deacon. He rang off, promising to keep in touch.

Edgar had his lunch sitting at his desk. Bob returned to say that he hadn't been able to find any trace of Diablo.

'For God's sake,' said Edgar, 'Someone must have seen him. He's not exactly hard to miss, a fat old man in a white suit.'

'I tried my best,' Bob put on his offended voice.

'Well, keep trying. Go to the Theatre Royal and the Hippodrome. Those theatrical types always hang round theatres.'

By five o'clock, Bob still hadn't returned. Edgar wondered if his research had led him into the orbit of the Bath Arms. Edgar worked on at his desk, going through transcripts and witness statements. *I thought I'd be seeing you sooner or later.* Who was the person Tony had expected to see? But, then again, hadn't Tony said that the trick was never to seem surprised at anything the audience might throw at you? Maybe it was all an elaborate bluff. Maybe he hadn't been expecting his visitor after all? Edgar's head swum. Perhaps he should give it a rest and join the others in the pub. A drink or two might sharpen his wits and it would mend some fences with the team too. He was just standing up when the internal phone rang.

'Lady to see you, Inspector Stephens,' said the desk sergeant.

For one mad moment, Edgar was sure that it was Ruby. It suddenly seemed natural that she would have come to him, rather than Max, for help. And he would help her, he would protect her . . . He ran along the corridor and up the stone steps to the lobby. But the woman sitting meekly by the door wasn't Ruby with her shiny hair and bold brown eyes. It was someone altogether younger and less captivating.

'She says her name's Desdemona,' said the sergeant with a kind of aural shrug.

Edgar approached the girl, who seemed to be trying to shrink back against the wall.

'Hallo,' he said, trying to make his voice sound reassuring. 'Why did you want to see me?'

The landlady's daughter looked up at him with watery blue eyes. 'It wasn't my fault,' she said. 'He told me to do it.'

Edgar felt as if the supernatural cold of the police station had seeped into his heart.

'Who told you to do what?'

In answer, Desdemona held out a letter. Edgar recognised the typewriter, the slightly raised 'a' which had been seen in all the correspondence from Hugh D. Nee.

'He told me that I had to give you the letter at six o'clock on Monday. Not a moment before or after. He said that if I didn't do it, he'd come back for me and kill me like he killed Mr Mulholland.'

'When did you see him?'

'This morning. He turned up at the door as soon as Mum left for the market.'

So the killer had been in Brighton that morning. He had been watching the lodging house, just as he had watched Edgar and Tony and Jean. He had marked out Desdemona as his stooge, knowing that she'd be too frightened to do anything other than obey him.

Edgar opened the letter.

Dear Edgar,
   You'll be pleased to know that I've moved on to the main event. At seven-thirty I'll be in Hastings.
   Your comrade-in-arms,
   Hugh D. Nee

Underneath the signature was a crossword clue. 'Death by a thousand cuts', three letters. Edgar worked it out almost without thinking. A thousand was always M. Cuts must mean an implement of some kind. Three letters. M-ax. Max.

He looked at the clock on the wall. The hands were in a straight vertical line. He thought of the playbill in the Incident Room downstairs. The show on Hastings pier started at seven-thirty. He thought of the Major, standing in his sunny garden.

Take Massingham now. He's a wolf, a womaniser. He'll never settle down.

And how do you catch a wolf? With a wolf trap.

CHAPTER 30

Max stood in the wings watching the Fantinis flying past the gilded thirties chandelier. They were good. Ernesto Fantini had told him that, before the war, he and his brother had performed for all the crowned heads of Europe. Ernesto had fought in Egypt and ended up as a prisoner of war; his brother had been killed on the Russian front. Now he had built up the act again with his sons, but the crowned heads didn't entertain like they used to (and some, like the Italian royal family, had disappeared altogether). But the Fantinis continued to leap and somersault because that was all they knew how to do. Max, watching them, felt a surge of fellow feeling. A good tumbling act was once a passport to the world; now it was just something to entertain the burghers of Hastings on a Monday night.

And the burghers were a sticky audience tonight. Of course, it was Monday so the royal circle was full of landladies with giant handbags perched on their laps and expressions of stoic indifference. Max had already spotted Queenie, wearing a rather moth-eaten fox fur. He hoped that she wouldn't come backstage after the show. At least there was no second house.

The Fantinis were reaching a crescendo: four bodies spinning in a whirr of spangles. Max listened to the applause, thinking that the acrobats had done well to produce such a sound from a Monday audience. Ernesto Fantini bowed jointlessly, like a marionette. His sons stepped forward in perfect unison. The clapping died away (the landladies weren't prepared to exert themselves for long) and Max readied himself to go on. He could see the orchestra were about to start the 'Danse Macabre'.

'Mr Mephisto.'

Max turned in surprise. It was an unwritten law that you didn't talk to someone waiting in the wings. He half-expected to see Beryl there, having second thoughts about her appearance. But he'd already checked that Beryl was in her seat and, besides, he knew that nothing short of a direct hit would stop her going on stage.

'Mr Mephisto.' The whisper was urgent now. In the auditorium the orchestra was playing his tune. Max peered into the darkness. He saw a tall, uniformed figure accompanied by diminutive Archie, the stagehand.

'Mr Mephisto.' It was PC Granger, the policeman from last night. 'We've got reason to believe that a threat's been made against your life.'

'Bugger off,' said Max. 'I'm on in a minute.'

'A letter came for you,' piped up Archie.

With one eye on the stage, Max opened the letter. It was typewritten and brief.

I've got Ruby. If you value her life come to 1 Fisherman's Walk immediately.

Max looked about him almost wildly, but his entry music was playing and, obedient as a performing poodle, he threw down the note and walked onto the stage.

Edgar pressed his foot to the floor. The Wolsey surged forward, causing two elderly ladies to jump away from the kerb, hands on hearts. But, even as he shot the lights at the Steine, Edgar knew he'd be too late. There was no chance that he could get to Hastings before seven-thirty. Hugh D. Nee had done his work well. Six o'clock was too late to save Max, but, agonisingly, there was just enough time to make Edgar feel that he had to try. Black Rock, Roedean, Rottingdean, Saltdean, they all blurred into one as the police car streaked along the coast road. Maybe a miracle would happen. Maybe the theatre wouldn't open. Maybe Max would be taken ill. But he knew that these were both remote possibilities. The theatres had kept open all through the Blitz. There was no way a lone madman would prevent the curtain from going up. As for Max, he'd never had a day's sickness (apart from hangovers) in all the time that Edgar had known him.

Before he left the station, Edgar had rung Hastings police and told them to warn Max. But, as he took the bridge at Newhaven, he knew that Max wouldn't listen to warnings. He would go on stage, unless the killer had already struck. According to Desdemona, the man had visited her at midday. 'He had a hat over his eyes, I couldn't see his face.' 'How did you know it was him?' A shiver. 'I knew all right. I recognised his voice.'

Edgar remembered how Desdemona had described the man's voice as 'whispery'. If the whispering man had left Brighton after depositing his letter with Desdemona, he could easily have reached Hastings before the start of the show. Maybe Max was . . . but Edgar couldn't let himself think that far ahead. He drove on through Seaford, hardly noticing that it had started raining again.

At first, adrenalin carried him through. In fact he was in the audience taking pearls out a stout lady's handbag before he realised quite what was happening. Then he stood there, the spotlight on him, thinking that perhaps Ruby was dead, or dying horribly, and he was in a theatre making jewellery appear from the sleeve of his dinner jacket.

'Are these yours, madam?'

'No!' A delighted titter.

'Quite right. Pearls mean tears. But every lady likes flowers.'

He passed the pearls through his left hand and opened his palm to show that it was empty. Then, reaching into the evening bag once more, he pulled out a bouquet of roses. Applause. One step in front of the other. Max was back on stage and the Egyptian music was starting, the pyramids projected onto a screen at the back of the stage.

'Egypt, land of mystery . . . This is a trick that I

learnt from my mummy.' A shrug at the hackneyed joke. He turned to the audience to check that Beryl was in her seat. She was, eyes bright, leaning forward, making it too obvious. Then Max looked again. The music swelled behind him and he took a step back, almost colliding with the trestle table draped with the Egyptian robe. For the first time in his life, Max stood on stage, utterly at a loss. Because there, in Row E of the stalls, was a face that shouldn't be there. Couldn't be there.

He saw the orchestra looking up at him, knowing that he was going wrong. He had once done a trick where the stage tilted, very slightly, but enough to make objects move in answer to his summoning hands. Now he felt as if the same thing were happening again, that the walls were closing in and the floor was disappearing beneath his feet. 'Egypt, land of mystery,' he said again. He scanned the audience. The face had vanished.

Edgar reached Hastings at eight-thirty. He drove the car almost onto the pier itself, parked it under the nose of a scandalised deckchair attendant and ran for the theatre. As he entered the lobby, he could hear applause. Was it for Max? At least the show was still going on. Surely if Max had been murdered there would be cancellation boards up?

'You can't go in there,' said the front of house manager. 'You haven't got a ticket.'

'Police,' Edgar flashed his card.

The auditorium was dark. On the stage, Edgar could just make out two men flinging custard pies at each other. He backed out hastily.

'Has Max Mephisto been on?' he asked the manager.

'Yes,' the man was still eyeing Edgar nervously. 'He closes the first half.'

'Where is he now?'

'In his dressing room, I expect.'

'He's not.' An urchin-like figure had appeared out of the shadows.

'What are you doing out here, Archie?' asked the manager. 'You're meant to be doing the props for Big and Small.'

'Tom's doing them.'

Edgar cut through this cross-talk act. 'Where's Max?'

'He left,' said Archie. 'Straight after his act. That policeman went with him.'

'A policeman went with him?' For the first time in two hours, Edgar found himself breathing a little more easily.

'Yes, the copper that talked to him before he went on.'

'Have you any idea where he went when he left the theatre?'

'I dunno. It could have had something to do with the note.'

'What note?'

'I gave him a note before he went on. He seemed shocked like.'

'Where's the note now?'

'Dunno. Could be in his dressing room.'

'Can you show me where that is?'

Fisherman's Walk was a row of cottages facing directly onto the beach. Max and PC Granger approached it from the back, stumbling over pebbles and clumps of coarse grass. The air was salty. There were no lights and the rain was coming down heavily now. Max couldn't see the sea but he knew it was there. He could hear it whispering in the dark. Number one looked just the same as the others in the row, a child's drawing of a house: door, window, two windows above.

'I'm going in,' said Max. 'You go round the front.'

'What shall I do there?' said PC Granger, who was evidently not a leader of men.

'Wait until I call you. Don't let anyone in.'

Max pushed open the back door.

Max's dressing room was just like his dressing room in Eastbourne and, Edgar supposed, dressing rooms everywhere. The mirror with lights around it, the make-up carelessly strewn on the table, the sink with a bottle cooling in the water. An Egyptian headdress lay on the floor and beside it was a string of pearls. The room smelt of cigarettes and Max's cologne.

Edgar sent Archie to search in the wings. He knew that it was a vain hope that Max would have left the note lying about, but he had to try. He scrabbled on the floor, disturbing years of dust and several spiders. Behind him, he heard the door open.

'Did you find it?' he asked, not turning round.

Then, with a sound like a curtain falling, darkness.

The back door opened immediately. Max was in a small kitchen: cooker, yellow-painted cupboards, Formica table. The whole place had a forlorn look, as if it had been empty a long time. The only signs of occupation were two cups on the table. Max thought of the cups on Tony's bedside table, of Ethel being forced to drink belladonna. Beautiful woman. Ruby was a beautiful woman and now she might be dead. There was a hatch through to a sitting room with a stained chintz sofa and chairs. The dust was thick and undisturbed on the floor. Max stood in the tiny hallway, he could see PC Granger's shadow through bubbled glass in the front door. Where was Ruby? Was she here at all? Was this just another false pass, more misdirection? He ran up the short flight of stairs and searched the two small bedrooms. Both were completely empty. In the bathroom a tap was dripping, leaving a green stain on the chipped pink bath. Max stood still for a moment, listening to muffled plunk of the water, eerily amplified by the complete silence. Ruby, where are you? Had the killer taken her somewhere else entirely, leaving Max trapped in this empty house, this stage set? Perhaps he should telephone Edgar, but by the time that he'd driven from Brighton, it would be too late.

Then he heard it. A slight sound, like a chair moving. He leapt down the stairs in one bound and stood, listening, in the hallway. The policeman still stood with his back to the door, oblivious to everything. There it was again and another noise too, a sort of dry slither. It wasn't coming from the kitchen but seemingly from somewhere below his feet. Then he noticed the door at the foot of the stairs. Treading lightly, as if he were on stage, he crossed the hall and opened the door.

Stone steps led into a cellar which was lit by a single bulb. The room was windowless and damp. It was empty apart from a few packing cases and a single bed on which lay Ruby, bound hand and foot. In an instant, Max was at her side.

'Ruby!'

She opened her eyes. 'Max.' She didn't even sound surprised. Her pupils were huge. He didn't know whether that was the belladonna or fear.

'Are you hurt?' He fumbled with the ropes. He, who could—in the dark—undo a different knot with each hand.

Ruby shook her head, but she was looking past him, her eyes wide.

'Is he here?' asked Max. 'Is he in the house?'

Ruby had her hands free and she used them, not to cling to him but to point towards the door.

Max turned, clenching his fists, expecting to face Hugh D. Nee, the man who had killed three times and surely planned to do so again.

Instead he saw a vast, moving coil, a creature moving towards them across the dusty floor, primeval and deadly.

'The snake,' whispered Ruby.

CHAPTER 31

Edgar was floating out to sea. He was being rocked to and fro and a voice was singing from the depths. He saw Jonathan, his hair long and wet like seaweed. These were the pearls that were his eyes. He saw Diablo and Max, side by side in a beautiful pea-green boat:

Willows whiten, aspens quiver
Little breezes dusk and shiver.
Thro' the wave that runs forever
Flowing down to Camelot.

He saw the Major standing in his garden. He saw a ship blazing on the sea. He saw Max leaning over a girl on a table. He saw the empty cabinet, the swords thrust through its sides. He saw Ruby twirling in her sequinned costume. The Zig Zag Girl. The Zig Zag Girl.

He opened his eyes. He was still in the dressing room, but somehow it seemed to be underwater. The air was wavery and uncertain, edges blurred into each other and, in the foreground, a vast mirror loomed, surrounded by glittering lights.

'Don't worry,' said a voice, 'it's the belladonna. It makes your eyes go funny.'

> And moving thro' a mirror clear
> That hangs before her all the year
> Shadows of the world appear.

'Am I dead?' he asked.

The voice was amused. 'Not yet.'

He saw Tony staring at him from the incident wall. A line of cabaret girls were high-kicking their way across the stage, their lips bared in manic grins. He saw the *Ptolemy*, blood-red in the sunset. He saw Jean snarling at him from inside a cage.

He saw Charis.

'Yes,' she said. 'It's me.'

He shut his eyes. The room rocked a little bit more and then was still. He opened his eyes again and the watery effect was gone. His head still hurt, though, and he couldn't move his arms or legs.

'You're tied up, that's why.' Again, the voice sounded amused.

'Charis?'

She was standing in front of him. She looked the same—flaming hair, creamy skin—but different, her features indistinct, as if she were wearing a veil.

'I thought you were dead.'

'Oh, a lot of people thought that,' said Charis, taking the chair opposite him. 'It was what you were meant to think, of course. I got off that stupid boat. Not entirely unscathed though.'

'But, how . . . ?'

'I was the spy. Typical of you not to suspect. The Major did, and I think Max did too. That's why I had to get out. They sent a plane for me and got me out of the wreck.'

'Who's "they"?'

'Oh, Ed, you really are too stupid. The Germans, of course. Our friend Jerry, as the Major used to call them. I was a double agent. A zig zag, they used to call us.'

'The Zig Zag Girl.'

'Yes, that's what gave me the idea. I practised on that stupid girl, the one who'd been Max's assistant. She lived near me in Brighton and she was always showing off about it in the pub. So I decided to start with her. I wanted to kill you all in really inventive ways, you see. They always thought they were so clever, the magicians. Sleight of hand, misdirection, all that. But they were no match for me, were they?'

'But why? Why did you want to kill us?'

She walked right up to him with all her old, sexy swagger. Then she thrust her face into his.

'Look at me!'

One side of her face was scarred. It wasn't so noticeable at first, but, close up, her lovely skin was criss-crossed with tiny lines. It was this that had given her the odd, veiled appearance. Edgar couldn't stop himself from turning away.

'Look at me!' She forced his head back and he thought about her strength. She had killed three people and had mutilated their bodies. He had no doubt that she was about to do the same to him.

'You used to think I was beautiful, didn't you? God, you were pathetic. You and Bill and all the rest. I knew you'd never suspect me because you were sooo in love with me.' Her voice soared mockingly, but, to Edgar's relief, she drew away from him.

'Did you kill Tony and Jean too?' He tried to see the clock on Max's dressing table. Surely the police would come soon? Charis must have locked them in, but Archie would raise the alarm, wouldn't he?

Charis saw the glance. 'Oh, everyone's gone home. The show's over and all that. I got the key from that idiot stagehand. Told him I was Max's girlfriend and, of course, he believed that. Everyone knows about Max's girlfriends.'

'What have you done with Max?'

'Oh, I took care of Max. The wolf trap. Did you get it? I just told him where Ruby was. When he gets there, he'll find a nice little surprise waiting for him. He won't be able to magic his way out of that one, the smug bastard.'

Edgar's head was still swimming, but he knew that, somehow, he had to keep her talking. 'Why?' he said, trying to sound friendly and innocent. 'I don't understand.'

She had sat down at the dressing table. He could see her face in mirror, the ruined side turned towards the light. Her hands reached up to her hair. They, too, were horribly scarred, much worse than her face. Old hands, the flower-seller had said. But they were small hands too. Women's hands.

'You always were stupid, Ed,' Charis said carelessly. 'Oh I know you were supposed to be brilliant at Oxford and all that, but you were always so stupid about real life. Even Tony was cleverer than you. He saw me at Brighton, you see, that's why I had to kill him.'

'He saw you? Where?'

She laughed. He remembered how he had once thought it the most beautiful sound in the world. 'I was in the chorus line. At the Theatre Royal. Oh,

I can cover this up with thick make-up.' She gestured at her face. 'It doesn't show from a distance and I made sure I was always at the end with my good side on the outside. He stood right next to me, the great Max Mephisto. "Magic is all about seeing."' She imitated Max's deep voice. 'Well, he stood next to me and he didn't see me at all. Of course, chorus girls are beneath his notice. He thinks he's God's gift. Always did.' Her voice changed again. 'But Tony did see me. He *was* one to look at the dancing girls, Tony. Well, he looked and he saw. He recognised me.'

That was why Tony had asked him and Bill to come to his digs that day, thought Edgar. Typical of Tony to want to tell the two of them together. They were the men who had loved Charis; they would receive the stunning news that she was alive.

'Is that why you killed Tony?' he asked.

'Yes,' said Charis. 'I might have killed him anyway. I was planning to kill all of you. But that's why he had to die first. I thought I'd make it look like the sword cabinet because that was Max's act that week. Not that he did it so brilliantly, in my opinion, and I thought his assistant was really common.'

'Ruby?'

'Yes, Ruby.' Her voice was sneering again. 'I've shared a dressing room with her and she's not everything she seems, believe me.'

'Is she all right?'

'No,' said Charis casually, peering at her face in the mirror. 'She's probably dead by now.'

For the first time Edgar felt himself near to despair. Ruby was dead; he was about to die. The girl he had loved had turned into this creature in the mirror. For a moment he felt that he would actually prefer to be dead. He closed his eyes and felt almost peaceful. Charis's voice jerked him awake again.

'No one guessed it was me. They all thought I was a man. All it takes is a cap and a bit of make-up.'

Charis was a tall woman, but a tall woman becomes a small man. Only little Desdemona had described her as tall. But it had been the voice that had scared the landlady's daughter. The 'whispery' voice of a woman trying to sound like a man.

'I sat just as close to Jean as I am to you and she still thought I was a man. Silly cow with her prissy house and her ugly baby. I almost killed him too, the way he kept screaming.'

'Why did you kill Jean? She hadn't done anything to you.' Edgar hadn't much liked Jean, but he suddenly felt a real pang for her, sitting down in her neat little sitting room to have tea with her deadly guest. He remembered the weight of Barney in his arms. He had seen his mother murdered. No wonder the poor kid had screamed.

'I was going to kill Bill,' said Charis. 'I expected him to come home for lunch. But, then, he wasn't there and Jean was. And I'd always hated her, the way she kept hanging around making eyes at you.'

Even after everything that had happened, Edgar was still amazed to think that Charis could be jealous of anyone. And jealous over *him* too.

'I never looked at her,' he said honestly. 'I never looked at anyone but you. I loved you.'

'No you didn't,' said Charis, taking a knife from her inside pocket. 'You've only ever loved one person. Max.'

'Max?'

'Yes, Max. You see, I knew Max would try to save Ruby and I knew you'd try to save Max. I know everything about all of you. And now, if Max escapes from his trap, he'll come back here and find you dead. It'll be my last little surprise for him. I hate him the most.'

'Why?' He wasn't even trying to keep her talking any more. He really wanted to know.

'Because he did this,' she held the knife blade to her cheek. 'He destroyed my face.' For a moment, she looked almost pleadingly at Edgar. 'I was beautiful, wasn't I?'

'You still are.'

'No.' Her voice was hard again. 'People look away from me. They cross the road to avoid me. It's like being one of the walking dead.'

'What are you going to do now?' Edgar stared at the knife. If she tried to stab him, he thought he had just enough strength to make the chair overbalance backwards. Then, if he could just get one hand free . . .

Charis saw where he was looking. She laughed. 'This? Oh, this is just for my own pleasure. I'm not going to cut you. I'm going to burn you. Remember Max's famous trick where he burns the table with the girl on it? Well, you and I are going to re-enact it.'

'As I remember it, the girl gets away.'

'Not in my version.'

Max edged towards the snake. He knew nothing about reptiles, but this looked like a particularly nasty one, earthy-coloured with a dark, wedge-shaped head.

'I suppose there's no chance this thing is harmless,' he said, almost to himself. But Ruby answered seriously, 'It's an African rock python, I think. They're very dangerous.'

'Oh good.'

The snake was between them and the door. Max must have almost stepped over it in his haste to get to Ruby. He held out his hand to her now. 'Come on, let's try to get past. No sudden movements.'

Ruby put her hand in his. For a moment, despite everything, he was only aware of the absolute rightness of it. It wasn't a sensual feeling at all, more like a great wave of protectiveness flowing over him. The snake watched them, its head waving slightly from side to side. Max moved in front of Ruby. That way it would get him first.

'It's all right, Ruby,' he said. 'I'll look after you.'

But, with a quick squeeze of his hand, she let go. Then she approached the snake.

'Ruby!'

Ruby crouched down and began to sing.

Charis took the bottle from the sink and doused him with the contents. Neat gin, by the smell of it. Then she kicked at his chair which collapsed, cracking his head on the floor. For a moment he saw black again, then he was sure he was going to be sick. In a haze of pain and nausea, he saw Charis looking down on him.

'Deckchair,' she said. 'Useful things, deck-chairs. Nice and flammable too.'

'You can't just set fire to me. The whole pier will go up in smoke.'

She shrugged. 'Well, it's not the first time, is it? Good thing too, in my opinion. I hate piers. I hate Hastings and Brighton too. Bloody English seaside.'

'I suppose you prefer Germany.' It felt ridiculous to be bandying words while he lay trussed up at her feet, but he was damned if he was just going to lie there and die. Surely someone would come to rescue him soon. What had happened to the bloody Hastings police force?

She considered the point seriously. 'I'm not a big fan of Germany. Anyway, it's pretty depressing there at the moment. No, it was more that— everyone was so *pleased* with themselves during the war. We'll fight them on the beaches, all that rot. You should have heard the rubbish they talked to us WAAFs: "Even women can do their bit." Well, I didn't want to be on the same side as idiots like Major Gormley, thank you very much.'

'The Major's not stupid.' He had known that it was a woman, even if he'd got the wrong woman. And, by Charis's own admission, he had suspected her, all that time ago in Inverness.

'He's an idiot. The Magic Men! Of all the ludicrous ideas. As if a bunch of has-been magicians could defeat the German army.'

'Well, they were defeated, weren't they?' muttered Edgar.

'Not by you,' spat Charis. 'All you lot ever did was set fire to a boat.'

'Max felt terrible about that.'

'Did he? Well, he's going to feel even worse when he finds your body, what's left of it. It's a horrible way to die, you know.'

He didn't know, but he could imagine. He almost hoped that she'd stab him first.

'Goodbye, Edgar,' said Charis, and her voice seemed to come from a long way away. 'It was fun while it lasted.'

He saw her turn away and heard the spark of a match. He tried, for one last time, to free his hands, but now they had the whole weight of his body on them. His legs too seemed to be bound by iron chains. If only he were Max, with all his escapology prowess. But Max was probably dead too. He thought briefly of his mother. He wished that he'd been nicer to her, he wished that he'd smiled in a few more photographs, he wished that he'd driven her to the incurables and sat with her while she tried to cheer them up. He wished he'd taken her out to lunch afterwards, somewhere genteel with lace tablecloths. He wished that he'd been a better son.

Charis threw down the match and, with a crack, the deckchair burst into flames.

Ruby continued to sing. The snake watched her, head swaying.

'What are you doing?' asked Max. But he was awestruck all the same.

Ruby raised her hand and the snake followed her, stretching, expanding vertically. Then she made a circular movement and, with sinuous ease, the snake began to coil up again. Her song changed and became slower. Max almost found his own eyes closing.

'Come on,' said Ruby. 'She's asleep. We should go.'

Max didn't ask how Ruby knew that the snake was female. He took her hand and they climbed the stairs together. PC Granger was still waiting outside. The rain was dripping from his helmet.

'Is this the young lady?' he asked.

'Yes,' said Max. 'Where are your reinforcements?'

PC Granger pointed towards the beach where torchlight was bobbing in the darkness like a will-o'-the-wisp.

'Over here,' he shouted.

'I'll leave you to it,' said Max. 'I need to get Ruby home.'

'But you can't just . . .'

'Goodbye, PC Granger. It's been a pleasure. Oh . . .' Max looked back over his shoulder. 'Tell your colleagues there's a bloody great snake in the cellar.'

And he and Ruby walked away over the pebbles and wet grass. In the car Max turned on the heating and asked, 'How the hell did you do that?'

Ruby smiled at him. 'My mother was a snake-charmer.'

Max stared. Somewhere in the distant past he saw a rush basket and a woman with long black hair plaited with gold. He heard the song so recently sung by Ruby.

'Her name was Emerald,' said Ruby.

'Emerald,' repeated Max.

'Do you mind,' said Ruby, massaging her wrists where the rope had cut into them, 'if I keep on calling you Max? I think Daddy's a bit much all at once, don't you?'

The heat was unbearable. Soon it would reach his face and then he too would be horribly burnt. But it wouldn't matter too much because he'd be dead in a few minutes. Edgar shut his eyes. He heard Charis laugh. 'Goodbye, Ed.'

Then many things seemed to happen at the same moment. The door burst open. A coat was thrown over the flames, covering Edgar's head. He heard Charis say, in a voice composed half of anger, half of amusement, 'You! What the hell are you doing here?'

'Drop the knife, Charis.'

'The hell I will. I'll kill you too, you old fool.'

Edgar somehow shook himself free of the coat. Through the choking smoke he saw Charis with the knife raised, ready to strike. And he saw Diablo, dressed in an extremely dirty white suit, holding a gun.

'Drop the knife.'

With a sound like a snarl, Charis launched herself at the old magician. The gun went off. Edgar just had time to see Charis's shocked expression as she fell to the floor. Then he shut his eyes.

When he opened them again, Diablo was untying the ropes with hands that seemed remarkably steady.

'It's all right, dear boy. It's all right.'

'Is she . . . ?'

'Yes, she's dead. It's better that way.'

Diablo helped Edgar to his feet. Charis lay sprawled by the door. The Egyptian headdress lay next to her.

'How did you know?' asked Edgar. He was shocked to find himself leaning heavily on Diablo.

'Remember I told you I thought I saw her in Brighton? Well, I saw her again. Knew she was up to no good. I've been following her.'

Edgar didn't ask how a large man in a white suit could tail someone without being noticed. He didn't ask how Diablo had got to Hastings; he didn't even ask where the old man had got the gun. All he said was, 'She had a lovely face.'

'God in his mercy lend her grace.' Diablo finished the quotation.

PART 4
The Reveal

CHAPTER 32

'I'm amazed the old boy was sober enough to shoot straight,' said Max.

'He was incredible,' said Edgar. 'Like the Lone Ranger. He even had the white suit.'

'And he'd suspected Charis all along?'

'Apparently he'd always had his doubts about her. Then, when he saw her in Brighton, he realised something was up. He tracked her down and trailed her for a while. He even guessed that she was dressing up as a man. Something about Burlington Bertie. I didn't follow it all.'

'Burlington Bertie was sung by a woman dressed as a man.'

'There you are then.'

'But why was Diablo asking questions about Ruby?'

'It seems that he knew that Charis was watching her. He was worried about Ruby. Then, when Charis turned her attention to Hastings, he was worried about you.'

'Well I'm very grateful,' said Max. 'But I must say that I thought my guardian angel would be prettier.'

Max and Edgar were on the Palace Pier. It was a beautiful September morning and the sky was a clear, pale blue. The pier was almost empty apart from a few fishermen at the very end. The holiday-makers were all back at work, the children back at school. Max and Edgar sat in deckchairs like pensioners on a day trip. A sea-gull watched them suspiciously from the roof of the penny arcade.

'I came here with Ruby,' said Max. 'She wanted to eat fish and chips on the pier.'

'I can't believe she's your daughter.'

'Nor can I.' Max stared out to sea where a sailing boat was tacking slowly across the horizon. 'It's a terrible thing, but I hardly remember Emerald. I was twenty, just starting out; she was a bit older. We were on the bill at Worthing. She had this incredible act with a python. It caused quite a stir that summer.'

'I bet it did.'

'That was the last I saw of her. I never even knew she was pregnant.'

'But she told Ruby about you.'

'Apparently that was only this summer. Ruby suddenly announced that she wanted to be a magician, so Emerald told her that it was in the blood, so to speak. Ruby had always thought that her stepfather was her father. He sounds a decent chap. Plasterer.'

'Are you going to tell *your* father?' Edgar was curious to know what Lord Massingham would think about a granddaughter who had been brought up by a snake-charmer and a plasterer. He remembered Ruby asking him, 'Is it true that his father is a lord?' Had she been pondering her own aristocratic heritage?

Max grimaced. 'I don't know. But he's always nagging me to get married and have children so . . .'

'Ruby's a granddaughter anyone would be proud of.'

'My thoughts exactly.'

'And who would have thought that snake-charming would come in so handy?'

'Yes. Charis couldn't have foreseen that, could she? Do you know where she got the snake, by the way?'

'From the aquarium. Apparently she got round one of the attendants. Said she needed it for her stage act.'

'She still had the old charm then?' Max had winced when Edgar had told him about Charis's face.

'It didn't really show,' Edgar said now. 'She was still beautiful.'

They were silent for a moment. Edgar thought about the fact that, if it hadn't been for Diablo, the beautiful girl whom he had once loved would have murdered him. He remembered something he'd once read: if you save someone's life, they belong to you. It was an uneasy thought, that he was now the property of an ageing magician called The Great Diablo.

'Are you going to see Emerald?' asked Edgar.

Max gave his one-sided smile. 'I'm having tea with them tomorrow. They live in Hove. Ruby was telling the truth about that.'

'Well, she didn't exactly lie about any of it. She just didn't tell you.'

'No. She's a true pro.'

Edgar thought that Max sounded rather sad. Maybe it made him feel old to have a twenty-year-old daughter. Maybe it was the thought of that summer in Worthing, so long ago, so easily forgotten. How many women had there been since then? He thinks he's God's gift, Charis had said. But Max was still on his own, moving from town to town, every Sunday a changeover day. For his own part he felt that his heart, once broken in two by Charis, was now smashed into a thousand pieces. But, in some ways, it was a curiously liberating thought. Nothing in the past was what it had seemed. Now he could get on with the future.

'I keep thinking,' said Max. 'When I got the note saying that Ruby was in danger, I still went on stage. I should have gone to look for her right away, but my music started and I went out there and did my act all the same. Nearly blew it when I saw Charis in the audience, but I carried on. What does that say about me?'

'That you're a good magician?'

'But a bloody awful human being.'

'We're all awful human beings. I was in love with a girl who murdered three people.'

'God. Charis. I never liked her much, but I never thought that she was capable of that.'

'I couldn't believe it. Even when she was about to kill me, I couldn't believe it.'

'Even when I saw her in the audience, I didn't work it out. When I got to the house, I kept asking Ruby, "Where is he?" I still thought it was a man. It's depressing to think that Diablo was quicker than we were.'

'He says it's because he always thinks the worst of people and he's usually right.'

'Cheerful bugger.'

'The funny thing is, he *is* a cheerful bugger. Considering everything.'

Diablo did seem to have recovered remarkably well from the events of that awful night. After the police had come and asked them a thousand questions, Edgar and Diablo had ended up back at Queenie's lodging house. Max and Ruby were already there and the five of them (because Queenie wasn't about to miss the excitement) sat up late into the night, talking and drinking Queenie's sloe gin. Diablo was still there. He had struck up an immediate friendship with the landlady and said that he preferred Hastings to Brighton. 'It's more peaceful,' he pronounced, without apparent irony. Edgar suspected that Max was now paying his rent.

'When are you back at work?' asked Max.

'Tomorrow.' Frank Hodges had given him a week off, but nothing, not even the apprehension of the Conjuror Killer, was worth longer than that. Besides, the case didn't exactly have the neat ending that the high-ups wanted. There was no killer to bring to trial, just a rather confused account of a fight and a gun going off and a girl lying dead. Well, that was Edgar's story and he was sticking to it. They had found Charis's male clothes in her room, together with the incriminating typewriter and enough deadly nightshade to wipe out an entire chorus line. There was even a false moustache. And there was also a photograph of a man and a woman standing on the banks of the Ness. The woman was laughing, her red hair blowing around her gorgeous face, the man looked young and stupid. Edgar had put the picture in his pocket.

'Did you tell Bill?' asked Max, leaning forward to light a cigarette.

'Yes. He seemed stunned. He did say that he'd always been a bit scared of Charis. You know, I always thought that Jean was second best to Charis, but she was the one he really loved.'

'Poor old Bill. Poor Jean.'

'Yes.' Edgar didn't tell Max that Bill had said, 'I always loved Jean but she had this thing for you. You didn't know, did you? It was always Charis for you.'

Now he said, 'Bill will be all right. They're staying with his sister for a bit, but I'm sure he'll marry again, find a mother for Barney.'

Rather to Edgar's surprise, Bill had asked him to be Barney's godfather, and he had accepted. Edgar was never going to have much in common with Bill, but the day when he had held the smelly child in his arms had formed a bond which couldn't easily be broken.

'Yes, Bill will be fine,' said Max. 'Women will always want to look after him.'

'Bully for Bill,' said Edgar. 'They just want to avoid me.'

As he said this, he thought of the only woman since Charis who had made his heart beat faster. He thought of the sudden fear when he thought she was in danger, the surging relief (despite everything else that had happened) when he knew she was safe. He looked at Max, who was engaged in lighting one cigarette from another. It would be hard telling Max that he wanted to go out with his daughter, but he'd have to do it some time.

They stood up and strolled back along the pier. The seagulls wheeled overhead and a woman called out for them to come and have their fortunes told.

'That's all I need,' said Max, raising his hat politely.

'You don't want to be told what's going to happen to you?'

'I know what's going to happen to me. On Sunday I'm going to London. I've got a nice stint at the Chiswick Empire.'

'A Number One.'

'That's right. Things are looking up.'

Max's voice was sardonic, but Edgar thought the spring was back in his step as they walked along the promenade towards the West Pier.

'Fancy getting some lunch?' said Edgar.

'Sorry,' said Max. 'I've got another appointment. Business.'

They said goodbye by the fishing boats and Edgar watched as Max disappeared into the distance, a tall figure in a well-cut suit, a magician walking through the world of men.

On the way to Worthing, Max thought about Emerald and that summer in 1930. It had been hot, he remembered, and they had swum in the sea one night. He remembered her body in the moonlight, but he couldn't recall them exchanging a single word. They must have talked, he supposed, but about what? Their acts? The python? The creature's name—it came back to him in a sudden flash of memory—was George. Did they talk about George or did they just make love on the beach, not thinking about anything very much? He suspected the latter. Why didn't Emerald tell him that she was pregnant? Maybe she had thought (quite rightly, as it turned out) that a twenty-year-old magician was hardly a suitable father for an infant. Even so, he wished he had known. It would have been something to think about during those long war years, something to live for. Thank God he had never tried to make a pass at Ruby. But, remembering the sensation of her hand in his, he realised that his feeling for Ruby had always been of a very different kind. He remembered his panic when he thought she might be in danger. So this is what it felt like to be a parent.

He parked on the seafront and walked through the suburban streets. The Major was waiting for him at the gate. Max didn't expect to be invited in, and he was right. They walked to the now familiar rustic seat with its distant view of the sea.

'How is your wife?' asked Max.

'Not too good,' replied the Major. 'It's only weeks now, they tell me.'

'I'm sorry.'

The Major shrugged, looking away. 'We've all got to go sometime.'

Max watched him for a minute and then he said, 'You bastard. You double-dealing bastard.'

The Major didn't seem surprised at being addressed in this way. In fact, he smiled slightly.

'So you've worked it out, have you?'

'The Magic Men never really existed, did they? A special unit to trick the enemy using stage magic. It was all a front, wasn't it? A trap to catch a spy.'

339

'Well, of course,' said the Major, unperturbed. 'You didn't really think we'd employ a lot of stage types to do important war work, did you?'

'So you knew all along that it was Charis.'

'We were pretty sure. Cartwright had been on her trail from way back. The idea was that we'd put her in charge of a special unit. We'd tell her it was all about illusion and stagecraft and what have you and she'd feed Jerry all this rubbish about dummy soldiers and invisible tanks. It would keep her away from the Operations Room and stop her from giving away any real secrets. In time, we thought she'd slip up and give herself away.'

'And you didn't think to take all of us into your confidence?'

'Be reasonable, man. The whole point was that you'd all believe in what you were doing. That was why it was so important to have you on board. There were all these stories about what you'd done in Egypt. Charis would have known about all that. You gave the whole thing some credibility.'

Max thought that it was the first time that this particular charge had been laid against him. 'What about Edgar?' he said.

'Oh, he was vital too. Decent chap, good war record. He was the perfect choice to front the whole show. Charis obviously bought the whole thing. That's why she seduced him, just in case she'd need him later.'

'Edgar was in love with her.'

'Yes.' The Major was silent for a moment, frowning down at the velvety grass. 'I felt bad about that. He's a good chap, Stephens, but, oh my Lord, such an innocent.'

'It's not the worst thing to be.'

'No,' said the Major, 'there's a strength in innocence, but there's also a strength in being devious. That's why you and I have always understood each other.'

Max didn't think there was any point in denying this. 'When you ordered Charis onto the boat,' he said, 'did you mean her to die?'

'I thought it was a distinct possibility,' said the Major calmly. 'Of course she outsmarted us there. I saw the German plane hovering over the wreckage, but I didn't think that there was any chance that she would get out alive.'

'Did Tony find out?' asked Max. 'Is that why he came to see you that time?'

'He suspected something,' said the Major. 'Remember he was there when the boat burnt. He saw the plane too.'

Max had turned away after a while, unable to look. He remembered the Major telling him, quite kindly, to go back to the Caledonian. But Tony had stayed watching almost until nightfall.

'I think he brooded about it over the years. Then, when he was down on his luck, he thought he'd try a spot of blackmail.'

'What did you say to him?'

'Oh I bluffed it out,' said the Major. 'He hadn't any proof after all.'

So Tony had always suspected that Charis wasn't really dead. That explained his taunting, that night in the restaurant. *You know I still can't believe that she's dead.* It also explained why he had recognised her in the chorus line. Because he had, in some sense, been looking for her.

'Three people are dead because of the Magic Men,' said Max. 'Don't you feel any responsibility?'

'No,' said the Major. 'I knew she was a spy. I didn't know she was a killer.'

'Bloody hell,' said Max. 'You make me sick.'

The Major looked at him curiously. 'Why? I always thought you'd be the one to suspect. That's why I said that you of all people should know. After all, it's all illusion, isn't it? Espionage, conjuring, whatever you like to call it. I thought that was what you were good at.'

'It's not that,' said Max. He stood up, feeling slightly ashamed for losing his temper with the Major who was, after all, an old man with a sick wife. 'It's just . . . my life hasn't been worth much. All I've ever done is stand on a stage and play tricks on people. But I'd always thought that the war, the Magic Men, that it was worth something. You know, if I ever had a child, I could say . . .' He stopped.

'That girl,' said the Major. 'Ruby. She's your daughter, isn't she?'

Max wheeled round. 'How did you know?'

'At first I didn't. I thought she was up to no good. That's why I went to see Edgar. But then I looked at the photograph again and I realised. She looks just like you.'

'She's a lot prettier than me.'

'Granted. But, when I met her that time, she reminded me of someone. I realised it was you.'

Max felt oddly proud to think that the Major had spotted some family resemblance between him and Ruby. He wondered if Ruby took after his mother, that far-off Italian beauty. Then he concluded that Ruby probably favoured her own mother, Emerald. He glanced at the Major, who was gazing out to sea. All things considered, it had been kind of the old boy to take his concerns about Ruby to Edgar.

'Well, it's all a long time ago now,' he said.

'Yes,' said the Major. 'You and I won't live to see the next war. More's the pity.'

CHAPTER 33

Edgar was waiting at Brighton station. The train wasn't late, but it felt as if it was. From where he stood, he could see the flower stall and the red-faced woman handing out carnations and long-stemmed roses. In a funny way the whole case started here, at the station, the ultimate in-between place where an ex-showgirl could pass shoulder to shoulder with a woman dressed as a man and not know it. High up in the vaulted glass ceiling, the pigeons were calling to each other. Despite everything, Edgar felt that a railway station was still a hopeful place, full of possibilities. The Brighton Belle was at platform one, blue paint gleaming. Maybe he should climb aboard and leave his old life behind him. But he stood where he was, watching people track to and fro across the concourse, intent and purposeful. Where were they all going on a Saturday lunchtime in October? He would never know, and it was strange, but the thought made him feel quite benevolent towards the world.

A month had passed since the events in Hastings, and already that night had acquired a distant, dreamlike quality. The case was closed and Max had enjoyed a triumphant week at the Chiswick Empire. Diablo was still living at Queenie's and no doubt entertaining her guests by performing the coin in the bottle trick. Barney had been christened and Edgar was the proud possessor of a framed photograph of himself with his godson, both of them looking rather the worse for wear. Even in the background of the photograph, Edgar could see several women looking speculatively at Bill. It wouldn't be long before young Barney had a stepmother. He just hoped she'd be kind to him.

The Major's wife was dead; Edgar had been informed of the event by a black-edged card. 'Peacefully in her sleep.' He had sent flowers, though he couldn't imagine what the Major would do with them. Well, at least he had his garden and the golf club. Edgar would drive out and visit him soon. He might even make Max go with him.

Alan Deacon had attended the christening, looking as solid as ever in his long policeman's trench coat. His parting words to Edgar were: 'Try to keep out of trouble, lad.' Well, he was trying. He had filled in endless reports and endured long interviews with Frank Hodges and his superiors. He had recommended Bob for a pay rise and taken a box of chocolates to Desdemona. And now he had a visitor for the weekend.

Rose always looked worried when she got off the train. Even though she must have seen Edgar waving at the barrier, she still clasped her handbag to her chest and looked around her as if fearful of abduction.

'Hallo, Mum.'

'Hallo, Edgar. You look smart, I must say.'

'Thanks, Mum.' He didn't tell her that this was because he had started going to Max's tailor. 'Shall we walk to the hotel? It's a lovely day.'

'I've got a suitcase.' She had too, pale-blue

leather. Edgar remembered his father buying a pair of them. Rose had a vanity case to match.

'I can carry it. It's downhill all the way.'

They passed the flower-seller and the Left Luggage office. As they headed out of the station, Edgar allowed himself one last look towards the Battle of Trafalgar. He imagined Ethel sitting there, nursing a port and lemon and boasting of her glory days with Max Mephisto. Rest in peace, Ethel.

They were part of a steady stream of day-trippers heading down towards the sea. Edgar enjoyed the feeling of being part of the crowd. He thought he'd had enough of centre stage for a lifetime.

'It's very busy, isn't it?' said Rose. 'So many foreign-looking people.'

'This is a quiet day, actually. You should see it in the summer.'

'I wouldn't like to. Millie White says the sea's quite unsanitary.'

'It looks good from a distance though,' said Edgar. 'Look, Mum. There it is, sparkling away.'

Rose agreed that the sea did look nice from a distance. She even conceded that it was a lovely day, 'for autumn.'

'I've booked you a nice hotel,' said Edgar. 'Very clean and quiet.' He had taken Max's advice and had asked Roy Coulter to recommend somewhere.

'You shouldn't go spending your money,' said Rose. 'I could have stayed with you.'

'My place is very small. I'm thinking of moving anyway.' Somehow Edgar's flat seemed too full of memories of the case, of Ethel, Diablo and the Major. He couldn't forget either that Charis must have seen the house, must have pushed the playbill through the letterbox. Had she been tempted to knock on the door?

'Moving away from Brighton?' Edgar heard the hopeful note in his mother's voice.

'No,' he said. 'I thought I might find a nicer flat, that's all. You know, if I ever meet a girl, I want to have somewhere presentable to take her.'

He thought that would mollify his mother, and it did.

'Oh, Ed, have you met a nice girl?'

Edgar had taken Ruby to the cinema once. They had talked only about the film and neither of them had mentioned Max. Edgar knew, though, that Max had offered to pay for Ruby to go to drama college and she had refused. 'I want to be a magician, not an actress,' she had said. 'Anyway, I don't want to go back to school. I want to go on the stage.' Edgar foresaw fireworks ahead. He was planning to take Ruby ice-skating next week. He realised he was smiling.

'I've met someone,' he said, 'but it's early days.'

He was quite proud of this cliché. He thought it

had a mature, considered feel. Certainly his mother seemed satisfied.

'If only you could find a nice girl and settle down, then I'd die happy.'

'Steady on, Mum. You've got quite a bit of living to do yet.'

Rose made a shushing gesture with her hand, but he could tell she was pleased. And there was quite a spring in her step as she walked down the hill at his side. In her good winter coat, with her hair freshly set, she looked spritely and attractive. She was only in her fifties, thought Edgar. She could get married again; she might even beat him to the altar.

'I thought we'd have tea at the Grand,' he said. 'They do a good tea there.'

'I'd like that,' said Rose.

They walked past the clock tower and the cinema and Sherry's nightclub. Outside Sherry's there was a poster for Max's old show at the Theatre Royal. 'Max Mephisto, the Master of Illusion.'

'Isn't that your friend?' said Rose.

'Yes,' said Edgar. 'That's my friend.'

'Master of Illusion. What does that mean?'

'It means that you never know when you'll see him next,' said Edgar.

ACKNOWLEDGEMENTS

After serving in the First World War, my grandfather, Frederick Goodwin, took the stage name Dennis Lawes and reinvented himself as a music hall comedian. I wish I'd asked him more about his life on the variety circuit, but such snippets as he did let fall I have included in the book. I'm also very grateful to my mother, Sheila de Rosa, for her memories of growing up in this world, living in different theatrical digs every week and having a succession of glamorous chorus girl 'aunties'.

Max Mephisto and the Magic Men are entirely imaginary. There was, however, a real group of camouflage experts working in Egypt in the Second World War called the Magic Gang. Amongst other illusions, they are credited with making the Suez Canal disappear. The Magic Gang was led by the famous magician Jasper Maskelyne and for details of his war years I am indebted to a fascinating book called *The War Magician* by David Fisher (Cassell).

Granddad was on the bill with Jasper Maskelyne, but, although he tried, he never managed to work out any of his tricks. I have tried too, but I'm not a magician so I apologise if any of my explanations are inadequate. I think

The Zig Zag Girl was actually first performed in the 1960s, but I have taken the liberty of taking it backwards in time and attributing it to Max. For an insight into the mind of a magician, I found Derren Brown's book, *Confessions of a Conjuror* (Transworld), absolutely invaluable. I have not, though, attempted to recreate any of Derren Brown's tricks.

It has been a joy to write about my home town of Brighton. I am very grateful to Mike Laslett for showing me the old police cells below Brighton Town Hall. If you'd like to visit the cells and the accompanying museum, contact: *info@oldpolice cellsmuseum.org.uk*. It's a wonderful tour and it's free!

I'd like to thank Quercus, and especially my amazing editor Jane Wood, for encouraging me in this new venture and embracing a whole new cast of characters. I'm also very grateful to my agent, Rebecca Carter, and all at Janklow & Nesbit.

Love and thanks always to my husband Andrew and our children, Alex and Juliet. This book is for my wonderful mum from whom I have inherited any writing talents that I possess.

Elly Griffiths, 2014

Center Point Large Print
600 Brooks Road / PO Box 1
Thorndike, ME 04986-0001 USA

(207) 568-3717

US & Canada:
1 800 929-9108
www.centerpointlargeprint.com